# Devil Inside

## Alicia Newton

Copyright © 2024 by Alicia Newton

All rights reserved.

No portion of this book may be reproduced in any form without written permission from the publisher or author, except as permitted by U.S. copyright law.

# Contents

1. Oh. My. God. — 1
2. A Little Bit Too Wet. — 8
3. Blood. — 15
4. Sleepless Nights. — 21
5. Fractured Reflection. — 27
6. Sad Eyes. — 32
7. Animal Instinct. — 39
8. A Father's Love. — 43
9. Sunlight? Crosses? Garlic? — 53
10. As Normal A Life As Possible. — 58
11. I Need Some Fresh Air. — 65
12. A Lot To Hide. — 74
13. Why Don't You Just Tell Me I Stink? — 79
14. Good Evening Ladies. — 85
15. Knock Back A Triple Whiskey. — 90

| | | |
|---|---|---|
| 16. | From The Roaring Flames Of Hell. | 96 |
| 17. | The Birds And The Bees. | 104 |
| 18. | You Like Bikes? | 112 |
| 19. | He's Fine Once You Get Him Talking. | 118 |
| 20. | Food And Entertainment. | 126 |
| 21. | Darkest Times. | 134 |
| 22. | Nope, Not Bears. | 138 |
| 23. | Merry Christmas. | 145 |
| 24. | Chapter 24 | 155 |
| 25. | The Altar of Sebastian. | 156 |
| 26. | Adrenaline Rush. | 164 |
| 27. | Sebastian. | 169 |
| 28. | Interspecies Relationships. | 177 |
| 29. | I Guess It Wasn't You We Needed To Be Worried About. | 187 |
| 30. | Isn't He Great? | 196 |
| 31. | Not All Right. | 206 |
| 32. | Monster. | 210 |
| 33. | Gone. | 218 |
| 34. | Angels Exist? | 225 |
| 35. | Tell Her Everything. | 233 |
| 36. | I'm Coming For You. | 241 |
| 37. | Go To Him. | 248 |
| 38. | That Level Of Violence. | 256 |

| | | |
|---|---|---|
| 39. | Piles Of Ash | 264 |
| 40. | Bodies. | 272 |
| 41. | Black Heart | 279 |
| 42. | Everything. | 285 |
| 43. | A Positive Initial Outcome. | 290 |
| 44. | Death Thou Shalt Die | 298 |
| 45. | Chapter 45 | 299 |

# Oh. My. God.

-------------------------------------------------

If he'd walked in to the opening riff of T-Rex's 20th century boy he could not have been more attractive. One minute Elsa had been staring a polystyrene cup of coffee, which frankly tasted like an ash tray and pretending to listen to her friends incessant chatter about her latest love interest, the next her senses were hit by the arrival of him. He walked into the college canteen alone, dark and brooding, tall and lean and with a definite air of 'stay away from me', which simply made Elsa want to get as close to him as possible. He moved steadily, like a prowling animal, towards the coffee machine. Elsa couldn't take her eyes off him.

"Hello?" Kate's voice snapped Elsa back to earth, she hadn't even realised Kate had stopped talking and was now simply staring at her and looking indignant. "Have you listened to a single word I've said?" Kate asked, with a hint of hurt to her tone, "What are you staring at anyw... Oh. My. God." As she spoke, Kate had turned and her gaze followed Elsa's. She turned back to her friend her eyes glowing, "Where did he come from?"

Elsa shuffled in her seat, embarrassed, "Who?" she asked innocently.

"Come off it Elsa," Kate grinned knowingly, "Cupid hasn't just shot you, he's clubbed you over the head!"

Elsa had to laugh, "Not everyone has a one track mind like you Kate," she said.

"So you're saying you don't fancy him?" Kate gave Elsa one of her patented looks, this particular one making her feel like a naughty child caught in a lie.

Elsa pulled a face, "No comment," she said.

"Leave it with me, I'll find out everything I can about him and have a report on your desk by the end of the day." Kate looked thrilled at the prospect of finally being able to organise her friend's love life, Elsa had always shown a disappointing lack of interest in anyone Kate had tried to set her up with and although they'd not known each other long she'd tried a LOT.

Elsa shook her head and couldn't help but smile at Kate's enthusiasm, "You are terrible," she said. For once though she didn't mind, she did want to know who he was and if anyone could find out Kate could. She glanced back in his direction and was surprised and disappointed to find he'd gone and she hadn't even noticed him leave. It was then that she realised everyone was leaving and she looked at her watch.

"Lunch can't be over already," Kate groaned theatrically, pretending to bang her head on the table, "Do you have any idea were the drama studios are?" It was their first day of college and Kate had already lost her timetable.

"History, Biology and Maths remember?" said Elsa, referring to her own chosen A-level subjects, a mix she thought perfectly reflected the fact that she had absolutely no idea what she wanted to do with her life, "I'm the last person that would know."

"Pants," Kate huffed and began searching her bag again for her lost timetable before catching sight of some fellow drama students and giving them a frantic wave, mouthing 'wait for me' across the emptying canteen. "See you later," she said to Elsa and tapped the side of her nose conspiratorially, "Full report on mystery hunk."

Elsa rolled her eyes and shook her head after her departing friend and began to gather her own things. She had never been one to surround herself with many friends, it wasn't that she was unsociable, she just didn't feel like she really fit in with most of the clichéd groups at school. However, when she'd started working at the local cafe over the summer to save up for the motorbike her father insisted he was never going to allow her to have, she'd met the exuberant and confident Kate who was new to town, and the two had fallen into an easy friendship. Kate got on with everyone and Elsa just sat back and went along for the ride.

Without really knowing how she got there, Elsa reached the door of her history classroom. As her hand reached to push the door open, she saw the young man that had taken her breath away in the canteen through the glass and stopped in her tracks. He was sitting alone and the class had already started. There was no hope of sneaking in unnoticed and Elsa realised with horror that the only seat left was next to him. She took a deep breath and tried to look confident and apologetic at the same time before opening the door.

"Sorry I'm late," she said, feeling her face redden as she sat down under the gaze of everyone in the class apart from the one person she wanted to notice her.

"That's fine," the tutor said, "I expect a few people to get lost on the first day, we've only just started so you haven't missed anything." she sat on the front of her desk, "Now I'm sure you've done this in all your classes today but I'm afraid I'm going to ask you to do it again because it's a good exercise and I'm sure you don't all know each other yet. For the next couple of minutes I want you to turn to the person to your right and find out a bit about them," The whole class groaned, their first day had consisted almost entirely of these awkward ice-breaking activities. The tutor held her hands up smiling, "I know, I know," she said, "We all hate it but it works people so, if you're sitting next to someone you already know, now is the time to move." There was a general shuffling of chairs as some people moved around and then a gentle hub-bub of conversation began to build.

Elsa bit her lip, took a deep breath and spoke; "Hi." There was no reaction apart from a noticeable tensing of muscles. "I'm Elsa," she said, her voice rising at the end of the statement and making it sound like a question.

There was a long pause before he looked sideways at her briefly and said simply, "Sebastian." His tone didn't seem to invite further conversation but Elsa ploughed bravely on. "You know she's going to ask us to feed back at least one fact we've learned about each other," she said, her words tumbling out just slightly too fast, "So er, why don't you ask me something first?"

Sebastian clenched his jaw, "You first," he said.

Elsa's brain was working furiously, she needed a question which didn't make her sound like an idiot and wasn't intrusive or nosey, something that wasn't embarrassing, something completely neutral. "What's you're favourite colour?" she asked, mentally smacking her hand to her forehead and shouting at herself, 'stupid, stupid, stupid!'

Sebastian looked at her then and she could have sworn she saw his mouth twitch before the moody, dark expression became fixed once more, "I don't have one." he said.

"Oh."

"What's yours?"

Elsa looked down at her black converse trainers, skinny black jeans and scruffy black Led Zeppelin t-shirt, "Er, black." It sounded like question again and she quite clearly sounded like an idiot because Sebastian simply nodded and made no further attempt to communicate with her.

What was probably only a minute felt like a lifetime until the tutor stopped them, "Ok then, let's hear what you've learned about one another," she said and she smiled at Elsa, "Last one in, first one up," she said to Elsa's dismay, "Tell us about the young man next to you."

Elsa felt herself going red again, she sank into her chair as if trying to blend in with it and disappear. "This is Sebastian," she said gesturing weakly to her right, "And, er, he doesn't have a favourite colour." The tutor looked at her expectantly, waiting for more and Elsa sighed, it was going to be a long hour.

By the end of the day Elsa was resigned to the fact that Sebastian found her repulsive and that he was rude, moody and arrogant. So why was she so ridiculously attracted to him? She walked out of the college grounds to find Kate waiting for her outside.

"His name.." Kate began

"Is Sebastian," said Elsa wearily, "He's in my History class and he hates me."

Kate looked a little deflated but rebounded quickly, "He's a loner," she said, "Maybe he just needs to develop his social skills. By all accounts he's a bit of a mystery man, no-one knows where he came from or where he lives but here's the bit you'll really love." She gave a dramatic pause, "He has a motorbike!" Elsa looked at Kate questioningly. "You love motorbikes!" Kate reasoned, "You've got something in common."

"That I'm a wanna-be biker who's over protective father will never actually let her own one?" Elsa said, "Forget it Kate, no match making, he's not interested and besides, he's just rude."

Kate shrugged, "He's new in town, he's got no friends, maybe he just needs time."

Elsa raised her eyebrows and shook her head, "No Kate."

"But if you just..."

"No Kate."

"But I.."

"Kate!"

Kate held her hands up in defense, "Okay, okay, have it your way." They walked in silence for a few seconds but Kate was not good at not speaking, "You know what you need?" she said.

"What?" Elsa asked sulkily.

"A girly night out." said Kate and Elsa could hear the 'won't take no for an answer' tone creeping into her friends voice. She sighed, this usually lead to a torturous night out with Kate's drama student friends who were all lipstick and heels - pretty much everything that Elsa was not.

"Kate, I don't know..."

Kate raised a finger to silence her protests, "No arguments, it'll do you good. Jacob Evans is having a house party on Friday night, everyone is going and that means you too. You can borrow anything out of my wardrobe, I'll do your hair and make-up, it'll be great."

Elsa was very sure it would be anything but 'great' but was getting to know when she had no choice but to go along with Kate's plans, somehow Kate would get her to that party, Elsa wouldn't put it past her to drug her and drag her there. She switched off from the sound of Kate's voice as the energetic girl filled her in on the who's who of the expected party crowd, and let her mind wander. Unfortunately it decided to wander back to Sebastian, no matter how much she tried to divert it elsewhere. With Kate's control of her time and Sebastian's domination of her thoughts, Elsa had the sudden disturbing sensation that her life was no longer her own.

# A Little Bit Too Wet.

To Elsa's surprise, the party wasn't that bad. In fact, if she was honest, she was quite enjoying herself. She had put her foot down as far wearing a dress was concerned and had managed find a sequined halter neck top in Kate's wardrobe which dressed up her torn skinny jeans just enough to be acceptable to Kate with the addition of some strappy black kitten heel sandals. The one-inch heel was about all Elsa could manage, anything higher and she was sure she would have completely lost the ability to walk. As it was she felt comfortable and had managed to limit her make-up to a touch of eyeliner and mascara. Kate had straightened her dark brown hair and all in all she was quite pleased with how she looked.

Kate was the life and soul of the party as usual and was currently enjoying being chatted up by the party's host. Elsa smiled and swapped the foul tasting bottle of blue chemical that Kate had given her to drink for a plastic tumbler of diet coke, before stepping out into the back garden for some fresh air. Jacob's parents were very wealthy and lived in a large house on the outskirts of the town which backed onto thick woodland. There was no back fence to their property, the garden just lead straight into the woods and away from the house it was quiet enough to hear the breeze blowing through the trees. Elsa liked the sound, it reminded her of the sound of waves meeting the shore and she found it calming.

"Elsa!" It was Kate following her on the arm of Jacob, with another boy walking slightly behind them. Elsa groaned inwardly, she could feel a match-making attempt coming on.

"Hi," she said, recognising the other boy as John Edwards, a friend of Jacob's. He was tall and a bit on the skinny side, with very short blonde hair. He had an easy smile and very bright blue eyes, Okay Kate, she thought, he's acceptable, I'll play along for now. Besides, she was determined to find a way to erase images of Sebastian from her mind. Sitting next to him in history all week had been like torture, somehow his mood and social skills seemed to get progressively worse as the week went on yet still she was undeniably drawn to him and she was getting very irritated with herself. Kate had been right about him having a motorbike too and Elsa loved bikes. She'd seen him leave on a Susuki Bandit 1200, her dream bike, something which also told her that despite being in the same year as her, Sebastian was obviously at least one year older. An attractive, sexy, older biker boy with a dark mysterious side - no wonder she was having trouble not thinking about him.

Kate, Jacob and John sat down on the grass next to here and she tried her best to focus on making conversation before Kate came up with an idea.

"Lets go for a walk in the woods!" she said excitedly, "It'll be romantic!"

"Kate, its dark," Elsa hated how sensible she sounded but it was a fair point, plus she was starting to get cold.

"I can get a couple of torches from the house," Jacob offered, immediately taken with the idea of getting Kate alone in the woods. He was back moments later with two torches and handed one to John.

"Come on Elsa, don't be boring," Kate encouraged her, "Grant is coming to pick us up in an hour, we're not going for a midnight trek, just a moonlit stroll."

Elsa stood up reluctantly and smiled nervously as John held out his hand to her, 'Oh what the hell,' she thought, 'I'm not getting any better offers.' she took John's hand which was cold and a little bit clammy and the two couples walked into the woods together. It wasn't long before Kate and Jacob took a different path and their torchlight and giggling disappeared, leaving Elsa alone with John.

"So..." he said.

"So what?" Elsa thought then admonished herself, he was perfectly nice and seemed just as nervous as she was.

"Let's go this way," she said, taking the torch, and they walked a little deeper into the woods. It was a bit eerie, as the trees got thicker there was less light from the moon and the torchlight created strange shadows which seemed to have a life of their own. John walked behind her sightly and suddenly he stopped and she felt a gentle pull on her hand. She stopped and turned around.

"I thought we weren't going for a trek." John said, grinning nervously.

"Sorry, was I marching?" Elsa said, aware that she had been, as if she was trying to escape the very situation she was now finding herself in.

"Just a bit," John said, moving in a little closer. "I'm glad we're away from the party though. I've been wanting to have you to myself all night."

"Oh?" Elsa asked innocently, feeling very awkward.

"Yeah, I, er," he was noticeably struggling and Elsa couldn't help feeling sorry for him, he really was nice and for some reason he seemed to like her,

"I think you're really cool," he blurted out, "Sorry, that sounds stupid, I mean, you're not the same as all the other girls, you're individual, I like that, I like you."

"We've never really spoke much before," Elsa said, "You might hate me when you get to know me." She mentally kicked herself, she was trying to put him off and she knew it.

"I don't think so," he said. He put one arm around her waist and drew her closer, his other hand came up to the side of her face and he leaned in. Elsa couldn't decide what to do with her hands and left them hanging by her sides, the torch in one hand now shining its light down at the floor and leaving them in darkness so niether could clearly see what the other was doing. By some miracle, their lips actually did meet. He tasted of beer and cigarettes and the kiss was awkward and just a little bit too wet. All in all a very disappointing experience, Elsa thought as John continued, obviously enjoying it far more than she was.

Suddenly a loud noise from above them made them jump apart. John swore, "What was that?"

"Shh, I don't know," Elsa whispered, shining the torch up into the trees. She thought she saw something move through the trees in the distance, not on the ground but up in the branches, something big, but as she blinked and tried to focus in the darkness amongst the shadows, she couldn't be sure.

"Did you see anything?" John asked her, his eyes wide, "That sounded like something really big."

"No, it was probably just an owl or a large bird," Elsa said, unsure. She gave a shiver, "Come on, lets go back, I'm cold."

"Do you want my jumper?" John asked, moving to put an arm round her.

Elsa neatly side stepped the move, hoping it wasn't too obvious because she didn't want to hurt his feelings, "No thanks," she said, "Once we're walking I'll be fine." She smiled at him though, "Thanks for the offer."

John smiled back and Elsa felt guilty, she hoped it was almost time for Kate's brother to pick them up so she could escape before she had to avoid any further romantic advances or, worse still, tell him she just wasn't interested.

Kate and Jacob were already back at the house and Kate smiled at Elsa knowingly, "Nice walk?" she asked.

John smiled and grabbed Elsa's hand as she gave Kate a 'I'm going to kill you as soon as we leave' look.

Kate ignored her, "It's a good job you're back, Grant texted me, he wants to pick us up early so he can go round his girlfriend's when she finishes work."

"You could stay here," Jacob offered, "Loads of people are staying, my parents aren't home for a few days yet."

Elsa looked at Kate just daring her to say yes, "We can't," she said, "My dad is expecting me home and so are Kate's parents."

Jacob shrugged.

"Besides," said Kate, "Grant wil be here any minute." She turned to kiss Jacob passionately, Elsa didn't know where to look. As Kate and Jacob parted, she disengaged her hand from John's grasp.

"Right, well we'd better go." she said, stepping away from John to stand next to Kate.

"So, I'll see you at college on Monday then?" John asked.

"I'll be there!" Elsa said with forced enthusiasm and without actually agreeing to meet him. She grabbed Kate's arm and virtually frog marched her to the front of the house where Grant's car was waiting. They both got in the back.

"Have you been smoking?" Grant asked his sister, "you stink."

"It wasn't me," she said.

"Well I'd get your clothes in the wash as soon as you get home because Dad will either think you've been smoking or spending time close to unsavoury boys who smoke and either way you'll be in trouble." He started the car and pulled out of the driveway, "Hi Elsa." he said. "Good party?"

"Hi, er, it had its moments," Elsa answered non commitally.

Grant grinned knowingly, "Ah ha, I know what you need, the perfect teenage party antidote" he threw a cd wallet onto the back seat, "Guns n Roses or Metallica?"

Elsa smiled and selected a CD from the wallet, Kate's brother seemed to know her better than Kate did. "How about Velvet Revolver?" she said, handing the cd through to the front of the car.

"Mmm cheeky," Grant said and put it in the player before cranking up the volume.

Kate stuck out her tongue, "You two have absolutely no taste in music," she said and then leaned in close to Elsa's ear, "How did it go with John?"

It was Elsa's turn to pull a face, "You have got to stop trying to set me up before you put me off men for life." she said.

Kate laughed and sat back. Suddenly she cried out, "Fox!"

Elsa saw a flash of movement and Grant pulled the steering wheel sharply to the right. For a moment everything seemed to go in slow motion as the back end of the car swung out and Grant struggled to regain control. They left the road and Elsa felt a sensation as if she was in an aeroplane during take off. She was pushed into her seat and closed her eyes, hearing Kate scream as the car flipped and everything went black.

# Blood.

-----------------------------------------------------

Elsa's eyes snapped open. She felt something warm and wet drip onto her cheek and trickle down to the corner of her mouth as she struggled to get her bearings. She was on her side and could see broken glass and twisted metal. Her left shoulder felt excruciatingly painful and she couldn't move. She felt the warm drip again, tasted salt in her mouth and looked up to her right. Kate was above her, head lolling down towards her, blonde hair matted with blood which dripped steadily onto Elsa's face. Suddenly everything flew into sharp focus and Elsa remembered exactly what had happened. She could smell petrol and knew they had to get out of the car.

"Kate?" there was no answer from her friend as Elsa struggled to release her seat belt, no longer aware of the pain in her shoulder. Grant was still in the drivers seat, silent and unmoving. The seat belt would not release and Elsa pulled it as hard as she could until it finally gave way and she slumped to the side of the car, the glass of the broken window crunching underneath her.

Kate gave a groan and Elsa struggled to her feet, "Kate, it's okay," she said, not at all believing her own words. Kate had a deep wound that was oozing thick, dark blood from her head. Elsa felt suddenly dizzy, the heavy, sickly smell of petrol was so strong and she knew they were in real danger as she felt heat and saw the orange glow of flame. Later, in the hospital, she would be unable to explain what happened next, she wasn't even sure she could remember. All she knew was that when the flashing blue lights arrived, she was lying exhausted at the side of the road with Kate and Grant lying unconscious beside her and the car was engulfed in flames.

"You," said the doctor, peering over his glasses at her with a warm smile, "Are a very lucky young lady." He turned to Elsa's father, "Other than bruising from the seat belt there's no damage, she'll be absolutely fine Mr Shaw, just keep a close eye on her for the next 24 hours."

Marcus Shaw put his arms round his daughter and pulled her close. "Thank god," he said, "And her friends?"

"Cuts and bruises, a couple of broken bones, nothing that won't heal given time."

"How did you all get out of the car?" Marcus asked his daughter.

"I don't know," she said, "I really can't remember."

"Well, let's just be glad you did." his voice cracked and Elsa hugged him tight, knowing what he was thinking. She looked to the doctor then, "Can I see my friends?"

"The young man is in surgery at the moment but your friend Kate is with her parents on ward 5, you can see her if you like but she's a bit groggy." Elsa nodded

"I'll come with you," her father said, "I'm not letting you out of my sight."

"Dad really, I'm okay," Elsa said smiling, "I'll just pop in for a few minutes, you wait in reception, get a drink or something. I don't think we should crowd Kate with visitors."

Marcus looked at his daughter and eventually smiled himself, "Ok," he said, "But if you're not there to meet me in 15 minutes, I'm coming back to find you."

"Deal." Elsa hopped off the hospital trolley and gave her father a quick kiss before walking out into the hallway.

Once out of Marcus' sight she took a deep breath and closed her eyes, leaning for a moment against the wall. There was a strange smell in the air of the casualty ward and it was making her feel nauseous but she dare not tell the doctors, she wanted to get out of here, away from the smell and back to her own bed and she wasn't going to give them any excuse to keep her in. She crinkled her nose and was trying to decide what the smell reminded her of when she thought she heard Kate's voice drifting up the hallway. Elsa shook her head to herself, it obviously wasn't Kate's voice, she was already on a ward. She set off in search of Ward 5, remembering her father's request that she wasn't gone long.

On the ward, Kate's parents were at her bedside and Kate appeared to be asleep.

"Elsa!" Kate's mother saw her approach and jumped up to give her a warm hug, "Thank goodness you're all right."

"I'm fine thank you Mrs Owen. How are they?" Elsa asked.

"Grant is having to have his leg pinned, Kate had a dislocated shoulder, a very deep cut to her head and a concussion. She's had a lot of painkillers so she's quite sleepy." Mrs Owen looked over to her daughter, "They will both be fine."

"It's a miracle you all got out of the car." Mr Owen spoke solemnly, "Thank goodness it landed upright."

Elsa blinked, she knew the car had been on its side when she'd come to but she didn't say anything, not wanting to discuss the accident any more than was necessary. Kate stirred and opened her eyes and Elsa moved to her bedside.

"Hey," she said, "You okay?"

"Mmm," Kate sounded groggy, her blonde hair was still matted with blood. Elsa leant in to give her friend a gentle hug but was suddenly overcome by dizziness. She sat back quickly.

"S'ok," said Kate quietly, "I won't break."

Elsa smiled nervously, not wanting anyone to notice the sweat she could feel herself breaking out in, "Can't be too careful." she said with forced brightness in her voice.

"Glad you're here," said Kate, her words coming out slowly and deliberately, as if it was an effort for her to speak. "Wanted to thank you."

"What for?"

"Getting us out."

Kate's parents both looked at Elsa, "You got them out?" Mr Owen said with surprise and disbelief.

Elsa frowned, "No," she said, confused, "I mean, I don't remember but I couldn't have could I?" she looked to her friend for confirmation but Kate's eyes were closed again.

"She's confused," Mrs Owen decided, "She's had a lot of medication."

Elsa was fast developing a headache, "I can't remember," she repeated, suddenly desperate to leave, "I have to go and find my dad, he doesn't want me out of his sight for long, please could you tell Kate I'll come back and see her tomorrow?"

"Of course," Mrs Owen hugged her again, "Take care."

Elsa nodded and hurried out of the ward, making her way to reception. Her father was waiting for her.

"Everything okay?" he asked, "You look very pale."

"I just need to go home, I hate hospitals,"

"Doesn't everyone?" Marcus smiled and put a protective arm around her shoulders, "Come on, we'll get you home."

Once out of the hospital and into the cool evening air, Elsa's head started to clear. By the time she got home she was feeling much better.

"Can I get you anything?" her father asked.

She shook her head, "No thanks, I'm just going to shower and go straight to bed." She gave her father a hug and he kissed the top of her head.

"There's arnica cream in the bathroom cabinet, it will help with the bruising to your shoulder."

Elsa paused on her way up the stairs; her shoulder wasn't even hurting anymore. "Okay," she said carefully, "Goodnight Dad."

"Goodnight sweetheart, love you."

"Love you too."

Elsa went into the bathroom and opened the cabinet, taking out the tube of arnica cream. She took off her jacket, which was caked in dried blood, none of it her own, as miraculously she didn't have a scratch on her. She put the jacket in the sink and turned on the taps to rinse it out. As the water ran through the material and dissolved the blood it became pink, then red as it flowed down the plughole and Elsa watched it, mesmerised. The strange smell from the casualty ward returned to her senses and she realised what it was. Blood. She placed her hand in the flow of water, watching the rivulets of pale red stained water run through her fingers. She could feel her own blood rushing in her head and she breathed in deeply. Suddenly perturbed her hand flew to the tap and she turned it off quickly before flinging her jacket into the washing basket. What was wrong with her? Maybe she had banged her head after all. She looked in the mirror intent on finding a bump that the doctors had missed but it was something else she spotted, something else that wasn't right. At the hospital, the doctors had spoken of bruising to her left shoulder caused by the seat belt and she'd seen for herself the band of angry red and purple that was developing. She raised her hand to feel across the left side of her chest and shoulder, there was no pain at all and absolutely, definitely no bruise to be seen.

Elsa undressed and stepped into the shower, checking herself all over. No cuts, no bruises, no marks at all. A strange feeling gripped her as she stood under the warm water and tried to wash it away. She closed her eyes and tried to remember what had happened in the car, how they had got out. But she couldn't.

Unable to shake the feeling of unease that had settled over her, she got out of the shower and dressed for bed. Just as she was about to leave the bathroom, she saw the tube of arnica cream on the side of the sink. She picked it up, slowly unscrewed the lid and squeezed a good quarter of the tube straight down the sink before rinsing it away and putting the tube back in the cabinet. This done, she switched off the bathroom light and went to bed.

*A/N - Thanks for reading, please comment and vote if you are enjoying it!*

# Sleepless Nights.

✱ A/N - For those following the soundtrack to this book try 'Sunburn' by Muse for this chapter :)*

The night of the accident was the first of many sleepless nights for Elsa. No matter what she did she just couldn't shut off and she spent hours just trying to remember how they had got out of the car, how it had righted itself when she knew it had been on its side and what exactly had happened after the fox ran out in front of them. She had managed to hide her miraculously disappearing bruising from her father and had been spending a lot of time alone in her room, quiet and withdrawn. Marcus had given her space and time to herself but he was worried about the effect of the accident on his daughter. He didn't know that Elsa was finding it increasingly difficult to be around him, around anyone. Despite her lack of sleep she felt wired, full of nervous energy, like she needed to do something. When she was near other people she felt hyper aware of them, as if she could sense what they were thinking and feeling, hear their hearts beating, see the tiny movements made by each and every muscle beneath their skin, feel the heat from their bodies. Her mind was on fire, her senses were reeling and she was overcome by waves of a terrible wanting feeling without having any idea what it was she yearned for.

"Elsa?" her father's voice came up the stairs. Elsa was lying on her bed, staring at the ceiling. She sat up, then stood and looked at herself in the full-length mirror on her bedroom wall.

"What?" she called back, studying herself. Three nights of pretty much no sleep didn't seem to have done her any harm. There were no bags under her eyes, her skin was smooth if a little pale, her hair looked better than it probably ever had and she felt – fine.

"Kate is on the phone, she's home." Elsa turned away from her reflection.

"I'll pick it up in my room," she shouted and reached for the phone on her bedside table. Her hand paused over the receiver for a moment. She felt terrible for not visiting Kate in the hospital but she couldn't bring herself to go back, the smell of the place, the smell of blood and of all the people in there, it was just too much for her. She'd made it as far as reception before turning away, aware that in reality she was feeling drawn in. It felt wrong though, to be drawn to those smells, to the sounds of people in pain. She picked up the receiver, "Got it," she said and heard the click of her father replacing the receiver downstairs, "Hi Kate."

""Hi Elsa," Kate sounded different, there was none of her usual humour or exuberance, "Where have you been stranger?"

Elsa felt another pang of guilt, "I'm sorry," she said, "I was going to come and see you but I just couldn't, I can't explain it, I'm really sorry."

There was a pause, then Kate spoke again, some of the guarded tone gone from her voice, "Elsa, it's okay. I suppose we've all been a bit shaken up, I can understand you not wanting to be around me and Grant. Would have been good to see you though."

"I know, I am sorry. How is Grant?"

"Good," said Kate, "Loving all the attention his girlfriend is giving him. He feels terrible about what happened though. When you didn't come to see us, he thought it was because you blamed him for what happened."

"What? No, not at all," Elsa said in surprise, "The thought hadn't even crossed my mind."

"I thought maybe you blamed me too," Kate said quietly, "It was me that shouted out about the fox and made Grant swerve."

"Don't be daft," Elsa forced lightness into her tone, "It was an accident and besides, I wasn't even hurt, there's nothing to blame either of you for."

She heard her friend release a breath on the other end of the line, "Do you want to come round and watch a DVD or something?" Kate asked, "I'm bored out of my brain already and Mum won't let me leave the house."

"Sure," said Elsa. It was actually the last thing she wanted to do but she couldn't avoid people forever, her father had tentatively suggested a return to college on Monday and she couldn't really argue. Physically she was fine, mentally she wasn't sure but she didn't feel able to talk to him about it when she didn't understand it herself.

"Great!" Kate sounded relieved, "See you in 10?"

"Give me 15," Elsa smiled a little; with Kate everything had to be immediate. She had missed her energy the last few days and blinking away a sudden image of Kate's head lolling towards her, glistening blood dripping through her blonde hair, Elsa replaced the receiver and went downstairs.

Her father looked up from his computer as she passed his study on her way to the kitchen.

"How's Kate?" he asked.

"She seems fine," Elsa called back from the kitchen. She opened the fridge with the intention of grabbing a quick snack but there was nothing in there that took her fancy, "I'm going over to watch a film with her if that's okay?"

"That's fine," said Marcus, feeling relieved. He was perplexed as to why Elsa seemed to be avoiding him but was glad she was finally leaving the house and seeing a friend. He heard the fridge door close and smiled to himself, so she was eating again too. Her strange behaviour must have been down to shock after the accident, "Will you be home for dinner?" he asked hopefully.

Elsa walked past the study again without stopping, "I don't know," she called as she left, "Don't make me anything just incase." And with that Marcus heard the front door slam behind her.

Approaching Kate's house, Elsa saw Grant coming in the opposite direction on crutches. He lifted his fingers in an attempt at a wave and she waved back.

"Just getting some fresh air," he said as she got closer, "Can't go far but Mum's smothering us with love at the moment so any break is welcome." He smiled awkwardly, "Good to see you Elsa."

"You too Grant," Elsa replied, "I'm really sorry I haven't been to see you both before, I've been feeling a bit, a bit weird." She couldn't think of another way to put it.

Grant squinted at her in the bright late September sunshine; Elsa could feel the heat of it on her back despite the cool day. "No worries," he said easily, "Hey, I got the new Muse album, do you want to borrow it?"

Elsa smiled back at him then, "That would be great, thanks!" She had been listening to a lot of music the last few days, jamming her headphones into her ears and trying to drown out the rushing sensation in her head.

Grant was struggling to get his front door key out of his pocket as the front door opened.

"Where have you been? You're supposed to be resting!" It was his mother and she looked horrified to see him outside, "Come inside now," she said, "It's freezing out there." She noticed Elsa then, "Oh, Elsa love, sorry you must be freezing, you haven't even got a coat on!" She waved Elsa inside and Elsa wrapped her arms around herself self-consciously. She wasn't cold at all; in fact, she was fast starting to feel like she was in a sauna. She had only ever been in one once and hated the sensation of breathing in thick, hot air. It made her feel as if someone was sitting on her chest, just as she was feeling right now. Mrs Owen gave her a quick hug and Elsa felt her head spin as she heard a now familiar rushing sound in her ears accompanied by a low, rhythmic throb.

"Kate's in the living room," Mrs Owen said, "Go on through. It's really lovely to see you Elsa." Grant was stood behind his mother and rolled his eyes putting a hand to his throat and mock choking himself silently. Elsa smiled weakly and made her way unsteadily to the living room.

"Hi!" Kate said brightly, any awkwardness over the phone seemingly forgotten. She held up two DVD's, "What do you fancy?" Kate had a large dressing on her head, just at her hairline and Elsa could see a small spot of blood seeping through it. Sensing her friend's eyes on it, Kate raised her hand to the dressing. "I cracked my head pretty good," she said.

"It's bleeding," Elsa said numbly, her throat felt suddenly dry and she swallowed hard, she could smell the blood.

"Is it? Oh pants, mum will have a mare," said Kate absently, "I bumped it on the cupboard door earlier, she'll be rushing me back to hospital." She frowned, "Elsa are you okay?"

Elsa was gripping the doorframe so hard that she could feel the wood splinter and pierce her skin, her eyes were fixed on Kate no matter how hard she tried to tear them away. She could see the carotid pulse in Kate's neck twitching rhythmically and the patch of blood on the dressing slowly expanding. Involuntarily she licked her lips, her throat suddenly feeling so dry it was as if she hadn't drunk for days and Kate was an oasis in the desert. Thoughts were rushing through her mind, thoughts she didn't understand and couldn't put her finger on but one thing was very clear to her, she had to get away from Kate right now or she knew something truly terrible would happen

"I'll get your mum," she managed through clenched teeth, "Your stitches…" it was all she could do to tear herself away as shaking she stumbled to the kitchen.

Mrs Owen looked up, "Elsa love, what's wrong?"

"Kate's bumped her head, it's bleeding," Elsa said, her words tumbling out as she tried to control herself. Everything in her being was telling her to go back to Kate but a small part of her was fighting it, she just knew she had to stay away.

Mrs Owen tutted, "I told her to be more careful," she said, "If she splits those stitches… Elsa, really, you don't look well."

"I need to go home," Elsa said, "Feel sick." She couldn't stay there any longer, she turned and ran straight out of the front door and kept on running.

# Fractured Reflection.

✱ A/N - For those following the soundtrack to this book, I chose 'Turn It Up' by Robots In Disguise for this chapter :)*

A good fifteen minutes later and not even out of breath, Elsa reached the park and stopped running. The sun was slowly setting but she still felt its warmth. Or maybe she was getting a temperature because the air around her and her skin felt cold. She had never been running in her life and she'd just run as fast as she could for over two miles and hadn't even broken a sweat. She sat on a bench shaded by a large oak tree and placed her head in her hands, closing her eyes. If only she could switch off. Maybe she had a head injury they'd missed and she was going slowly mad, right now she couldn't think of a better explanation.

Somebody sat down next to her silently and she caught her breath as the smell of them immediately sent her mind reeling more than any other person had until this point. She steeled herself and looked up.

"Sebastian!" she was genuinely shocked not only to see him, but that he had voluntarily sat next to her.

"You okay?" he said gruffly.

"Not really," she surprised herself by answering honestly, she swore she could actually hear his heart beating and tried not to watch his pulse in his neck. She had thought about him a lot this week, during the hours she lay awake each night. No matter how rude and ignorant he'd been, she was still ridiculously attracted to him and right now, the smell of him was sending her over the edge.

"I heard about your car accident." he said, "You weren't hurt?" she thought she heard an actual note of concern in his voice. Elsa looked at him again, trying not to focus on his scent. She could sense a definite danger about him but she didn't feel scared, there was something she felt much more deeply than danger. Despair and sadness poured from Sebastian in waves that crashed against her heart and made it feel as if it would shatter.

"Are you all right?" she asked, turning the question to him and searching his grey eyes, which were darkly ringed. She realised that since last week he had become gaunt, his cheekbones prominent with a shadow of stubble along his jaw line. He visibly tensed and suddenly his emotional tidal wave on her senses ceased, it was as if he had realised she was reading him and closed himself off from her.

"I was asking you," he said, no longer looking her in the eye, "It's cold and getting dark, you should go home."

Elsa stared at her hands, gritting her teeth and pressing her finger tips together hard, resisting a growing urge to pounce on Sebastian and ... well she wasn't sure what she wanted to do. "I'm fine here," she said, "I just need to be alone for a bit."

Sebastian sat in silence and she wondered if he could feel the electricity she could feel between them. She wanted him close to her so badly but also wished that he would just go away so she could find some peace in her mind and her body, just for a little while. She stole a sideways glance at him; he looked like he was having an internal mental struggle of his own.

...stay away...

Elsa head snapped up, "What did you say?" she asked.

Sebastian looked confused, "I didn't say anything." he said, "Look, it's really getting dark quickly now, you can't walk home on your own, can you get someone to come and pick you up?"

"I'll walk," Elsa said, "I didn't bring my phone out with me." She was sure she'd heard him speak but she could somehow tell he wasn't lying.

Sebastian sighed as if he was being forced to something he really didn't want to do, "I'll have to walk you back then." he said with resignation.

Elsa felt offended, for a moment she'd hoped he was warming to her but it was obvious he just felt some obligation to ensure she got home safely so he didn't have it on his conscience if he left her and something happened. She stood up and started walking, "Don't bother," she said, "I'll be fine on my own."

Sebastian jumped up and followed her, "I'll walk you back," he repeated but he stayed a couple of feet behind her.

Elsa stalked off in silence, now he was behind and down wind of her, his scent was not as over powering and she could concentrate her mind on being annoyed at him. Eventually she couldn't hold it in any longer. She stopped abruptly and turned to tell him exactly what she thought of him. He was watching his feet as he walked and didn't notice, walking straight into her. She gasped as he touched her and she felt as if she had been punched in the chest, as if he had given her some kind of electric shock.

"What are you doing?" he asked, suddenly looking angry. His eyes flashed and for just a moment, Elsa could see the real danger that lurked below his sullen exterior. She saw it and it scared her, but not enough to tear her away from him and certainly not enough to stop her confronting him once she had recovered her breath.

"What are you doing?" she asked back, "You obviously don't like me so why are you walking me home? You won't even walk with me, you're two metres behind me! I don't bite you know. What is your problem? No, I'll tell you. You're moody, ignorant and rude." She stood facing him, staring him defiantly in the face and as she did she saw the anger in his eyes peak then disappear, to be replaced with the sadness and despair she had felt from him before. She swallowed suddenly feeling terrible as Sebastian looked down to the floor.

"You're nearly home," he said, "You'll be fine from here." and with that he turned and walked away into the night.

Elsa's shoulders slumped, "Good one Elsa," she said out loud and turned to walk the last five minutes home. There was a note from her father in the hallway saying he'd popped to get milk for breakfast. She marched up the stairs to her room and slammed the door behind her. With a crash her mirror fell off the wall and smashed against her desk. Cursing her day once more, Elsa lifted the mirror and leant what was left of it back against the wall then knelt down to pick up the broken pieces. She hadn't felt it but she smelt blood and saw a cut on her finger which she immediately and instinctively brought to her mouth. As the taste of her own blood hit her tongue it was like she had been given a drug. In that split second she realised what she'd been craving for days. The sweet, metallic taste of blood was what she wanted, for that moment more than life itself, and the taste of it now made her feel euphoric.

Suddenly she caught sight of her fractured reflection in the broken mirror, her eyes glowing, a spot of blood on her lips. She pulled her hand away from her mouth in disgust with herself. What the hell was happening to her? She looked at her cut finger and froze. The cut oozed blood gently for a second then began to dry up. The cleanly sliced edges of skin drew back together and the cut became a silvery scar before finally disappearing all together. Holding her breath, Elsa grabbed another piece of glass and drew it painlessly across her palm. Once again she watched the cut dry up and disappear in just a few seconds. She clenched her fist then opened it again. Still no cut, her skin was completely smooth and unbroken.

Slowly and deliberately, Elsa cleared up the rest of the glass before picking up her MP3 player, putting the earphones in her ears and turning it up as loud as she could bare. She lay on the bed as she had every night since the accident, staring at the ceiling and trying to block out the screaming in her mind that told her she must be going mad.

# Sad Eyes.

✱ A/N - for those of you interested in the soundtrack to this book - Sad Eyes by Bat For Lashes goes with this chapter. Enjoy!*

"Are you sure you're all right to go back to college today?" Marcus asked his daughter as he watched her turning her cereal over and over with her spoon, she hadn't eaten a single mouthful.

"I'm fine," she said without looking up. She didn't want to go back to college, to be around people, but she didn't want to be at home either. Every time her father spoke to her, tried to give her a hug or make any kind of contact she just wanted to.. she wouldn't allow herself to even think of what she wanted to do

"I don't think you are. You haven't been yourself since the accident." Marcus reached out to place his hand on top of Elsa's but she moved hers away and got up from the table before he could touch her.

"I've just not been sleeping too well," she said, "I'll be fine, really Dad you don't need to worry about me." It was tearing her apart not being honest with him. She'd always had a close relationship with her father. She'd never known her mother as she had died during Elsa's birth, something that she tried not to dwell on too much. All she had was her dad and she'd always been able to tell him anything. But how do you tell someone that you can smell blood, that you crave the taste of it and that you imagine hurting the people you love to get at it?

"I've been thinking it might be a good idea for you to see someone," Marcus said, "To talk about how you're feeling."

"Like a counsellor?" Elsa asked frowning.

"There's nothing wrong with it Elsa, you've been through a trauma which is obviously affecting you. Maybe some professional help could help you understand the way you are feeling and get past it."

Elsa looked at her father and felt tears well up in her eyes. Before she knew it she was sobbing and her father rushed to put his arms around her. For a moment she let him, if only he knew how right he was. The thoughts she was having, the things she was seeing; none of it could be real, she must be going mad. All too soon the close proximity of her father, his scent and the sound of his heart beating was too much for her and she pushed him away.

"Elsa?" he looked so worried, so confused.

"You're right Dad," she said, wiping her eyes and picking up her bag, "I do need some help I think, will you sort it out for me – please?" She couldn't hide the desperate pleading from her voice, she wanted so much for her father to make everything all right again, to make these feelings she was having go away. She wanted to believe that a counsellor could help her, that all she needed to do was tell someone what was going on, someone who knew about diseases of the mind who could give her a reason for how she was feeling and a pill to make it stop. Maybe it could be that easy.

"Of course I can sweetheart," he said, "I've got some contacts at the hospital, I'll sort it out today but I really think you should stay home." Elsa's dad worked for a company selling medical equipment, he usually spent a lot of time travelling around the country but he'd been home much more since the accident.

"No!" she didn't mean it to come out so forcefully. She swallowed and tried again, "No, I need to get things back to normal." She attempted a smile; "I'll see you later."

"Okay," Marcus relented, "But promise me you'll come home if it's too much."

"I promise." Elsa said and she slung her bag over her shoulder and left the house.

Elsa had purposely left home as late as she possibly could to avoid any of her friends in the canteen before lessons. She had history first though and was not looking forward to seeing Sebastian. She made her way straight to her history classroom, head down, trying to ignore the overpowering scent of so many people.

"Hey Elsa wait!" She recognised John's voice and didn't stop but heard his pace quicken behind her. He came up behind her and grabbed her arm and she felt just one beat of his heart in his touch before she pulled her arm away, "Don't touch me!" she cried.

"Woah!" John held his hands up in surprise and stepped back, "It's just me!"

Elsa gathered herself, aware that her reaction had been ridiculous, "I'm sorry," she said, "You made me jump."

"I tried calling you," John said, he sounded hurt, "Why wouldn't you take my calls, I was worried about you."

Elsa couldn't look at him, "I've not really felt up to talking to anyone," she said, "Things have been a bit..." she wasn't sure how to finish the sentence.

John seemed to accept her pathetic attempt at an explanation, "You look great," he said, "Really great. Did you do something different to your hair?"

Elsa touched her hair self consciously, it had always been so untidy with a complete mind of its own but lately... when she looked at herself in the mirror she was noticing more and more that everything about her was becoming strangely flawless. Her hair was dark and glossy and every strand placed itself perfectly without any coaxing from her, her skin was ivory smooth and blemish free and her eyes shone, glittered in fact at times. She had taken to avoiding anyone's eyes in case they noticed. "Thanks," she said awkwardly.

"Now you're back," John said, "Do you want to go out sometime, maybe watch a film or something?" He was moving closer to her and she found herself with her back against the wall.

"Look John, you're really nice and everything but, I just can't go out with you, I'm sorry." Elsa was squirming and not just because she hated letting John down. He was staring at her mesmerised, a strange, slightly vacant expression on his face.

"You don't mean that," he said, his voice low and somehow desperate, "We had a connection, we have a connection Elsa."

Elsa's eyes darted down the corridor, everyone had gone to class, she was alone with John and she was finding his behaviour very unsettling.

"No John, we don't, you really need to go, I have to get to my lesson."

John placed one hand on the wall above her shoulder and with the other reached to gently touch her cheek. It was as if he was in a trance, "But I want you Elsa," he breathed as he leaned in.

Her head swam with thoughts of violence as she could feel the warmth of the blood flowing through his body and longed for the feel and the taste of it.

"Leave me ALONE!" she shouted, closing her eyes and forcing herself not to touch him as if she knew that making that physical connection with him would leave her unable to control herself.

"Leave her alone!" She opened her eyes just in time to see Sebastian grab John by the scruff of his neck and throw him to the floor. He stood over the smaller boy literally snarling as John scrambled to his feet looking dazed.

"Elsa I'm sorry," he said looking horrified, "I don't know what…"

"Go!" Sebastian growled, "Now, before I do something I regret."

John didn't need telling twice, he looked from Sebastian to Elsa in pure fear and confusion before turning and hurrying away.

Elsa breathed deeply not sure what had just happened. Sebastian looked at her, his eyes flashing, "Okay?" he asked. She nodded. He looked terrible, his skin was pallid, his eyes sunken. Looking into his eyes tore at her soul; she could see such pain in them, such sorrow.

"Your eyes," she said before she could control the words coming out of her mouth, "You have such sad eyes." She didn't know what made her say it, it was true but why did she say it out loud? Sebastian looked at her as if she had just invaded the deepest, darkest secrets of his soul. He opened his mouth as if to speak then he too simply turned and walked away.

Cursing herself for pushing him away yet again, Elsa waited until she was sure he was a good few minutes ahead of her before following his route to their history classroom. She heard voices coming towards her as Kate and another girl from her drama class came around the corner chatting animatedly to each other. Kate stopped when she saw Elsa. "Hi," she said guardedly.

"Hi," Elsa said weakly, once more Kate's presence seemed to have a worse effect on her than anyone else's, the images that flashed through her mind, the things she wanted to do. She clenched her arms tightly around her folders, clutching them to her chest, her whole body tense and on edge.

"What happened to you the other day?" Kate asked, clearly upset with Elsa, "I tried to call you, I even came round to your house."

"I was ill." Elsa said, her voice almost a whisper.

... liar ...

Elsa stared at Kate in horror, she heard her voice but she knew Kate hadn't spoken. She could feel that Kate didn't trust her, was wary of her. Elsa knew she should be, if she could see the things going through her mind right now she'd want to be as far away from Elsa as possible. She hated herself but in that moment she knew that the only way she could be a true friend to Kate was to push her away and keep her away.

"You're right," she forced herself to say, "I just didn't want to see you."

Kate looked like she'd slapped her in the face and the other girl shifted awkwardly from one foot to the other suddenly not sure where to put herself.

"Why?" Kate asked.

"I can't explain." Elsa said. Please, please go away.

"Try." Kate's voice was like steel.

"Fine, I do blame you for the accident." Elsa shouted, "I do, and I don't want to be around you so please just leave me alone."

The tears in Kate's eyes and the expression on her face told Elsa she'd just lost her best friend. Without another word Kate walked away. The other girl looked at Elsa in disgust and followed Kate, putting an arm round her shoulder and muttering words of comfort to her as they disappeared down the corridor.

Elsa clenched her jaw; in a matter of minutes she'd scared, angered and upset four people. In frustration she clenched a fist and without thinking punched the wall as hard as she could. Her hand drove deep into the wall and paint and plaster went flying. She felt and heard the bones in her hand snap and pulled her hand back out of the wall staring in shock at the hole she'd created and the large crack which stretched from it up to the ceiling. Looking then to her broken hand she watched the grazed knuckles quickly heal, felt the bones knit back together and flexed her fingers, she'd barely even felt any pain.

It was too much, she couldn't do this any more and before anyone could come and question what the noise was all about and how she'd managed to all but knock the wall down, she decided it was time to go home and tell her father that she needed help and she needed it now.

# Animal Instinct.

-----------------------------------------------

Once out of the college grounds she broke into a run. Faster and faster she ran but her breathing didn't change, it was no effort to her at all. She had the sensation that she could keep going forever, building her speed until people wouldn't even notice her pass, they would simply feel the disturbance of the air as she sped along. Within minutes she was home and as she opened the front door she smelt it straight away. Blood.

"Elsa, is that you?" her father's voice came from the kitchen.

"Yes," she replied, trying not to breath in. Why was the smell so strong? "Dad, I need to talk to you."

"Can you just give me a quick hand sweetheart?" Marcus called back, emerging from the kitchen with a towel wrapped round his hand, "I just had a little accident." He looked at her sheepishly.

Elsa stepped back and put her hand against the wall to steady herself. She stared at the blood on the towel and couldn't hide her hunger. Marcus looked at her questioningly, his expression turning to alarm as his eyes settled on hers.

"What's wrong?" he asked and then all of a sudden a look of horrified realisation crossed his face, "Oh Elsa no," he stepped forward towards her.

"Stay – away – from – me," Elsa spat the words through gritted teeth and, before her father could get any closer, she forced herself to turn and run as fast as she could.

She had no idea how long she ran for, or how far. When she stopped she didn't recognise her surroundings. She was in a town, not a nice area of the town either by the looks of it. She really didn't care anyway. She was disgusted with herself, terrified of what she wanted to do to the people she cared about. No one was safe around her since she was either completely insane or was fast developing into some kind of homicidal maniac. With no idea what to do or where to go, Elsa wandered the streets of the strange town into the night, keeping to dark alley ways and poorly lit streets, avoiding anywhere with people. She could sense danger lurking in the darkness; this is where I belong now.

For hours she walked. Finding somewhere to sleep wasn't an issue since she didn't seem to need sleep anymore but she suddenly felt so hungry. Not for food, no, this was a hunger that had been building inside her for days and one that she was losing the battle to control. She wanted blood, she needed it. The smell of it excited her, thinking of the feel of it passing her lips and flowing down her throat, imagining the taste of it on her tongue, all this made her head rush and her body throb shamefully.

She heard a noise behind her, someone was following her, trying to creep up on her but she heard them, she smelt them. Let them come.

When the person pounced she allowed them to pull her into a side alley-way. It was a man, small and wiry but bigger than her and, so he thought, stronger. She knew different. He smelt of alcohol but more than that he smelt of blood and of evil. Elsa was sure that this man was not a good person, she could sense the darkness in his soul, she knew what he wanted to do to her, what he had done to many other vulnerable women before this night. A calm came over her. She had a need and here was a person who deserved nothing more than to fulfill that need. He pushed her roughly against the cold, damp alleyway wall and leaned against her, a knife in his right hand held against her throat. She felt the tip of the blade break her skin and a small trickle of her own blood began to trail down her neck. She was not afraid of him.

"Get on the floor," he grunted in her ear, "I won't hurt you if you do as you're told."

She knew that wasn't true and in her mind, what she was about to do to him was justified because of what he was about to do to her. She looked him straight in his yellowed, bloodshot eyes. "No." she said simply.

He bought his face close to hers, his foul, hot breath on her face, "Get on the floor," he repeated with slow, dark menace.

He never knew what hit him. Elsa moved so fast that one moment he was standing over her, knife to her throat and the next he landed on the ground, fifteen feet away. All the air was knocked out of his body, his left leg lay at a strange angle and he howled in pain. Elsa appeared at his side, crouching over him, her hand on his throat. His eyes bulged as she picked him up by the neck with one hand and stood up, lifting him until his feet left the floor. He clawed at her hand choking as she turned and smacked him against the wall. A section of brickwork fell away and her would be attacker crumpled to the floor, blood flowing from a jagged head wound. Elsa dropped to her knees and placed her hands in the small pool of blood, reveling in its warmth, its life. Then she dragged the man's lifeless body into her lap and with pure animal instinct now her only guide she bared her teeth and lowered her head.

"Elsa don't!" She stopped abruptly, her mouth millimetres from the mans throat and the tiny bit of Elsa left inside her at that moment cried out for her father as her head snapped round and she saw him standing metres from her. Then she saw the glint of metal in his hand and her lips curled back in a snarl as she dropped her meal and flew towards him. In that same instant there was a crack, a flash and Elsa was stopped in her tracks. A strange sensation swept over her and the urge to feed melted away almost instantly. She sank to her knees and touched her hand to her chest where a small dart had pierced her skin. Her vision blurry, she slumped onto her side on the ground, barely able to focus as her father walked slowly towards her and lifted her into his arms. The last thing she felt was his wet tears on her cheek, "I am so sorry," he murmured, "So, so sorry."

# A Father's Love.

---

"She's coming out of it Marcus, it won't be long now." The woman's voice was low and silken smooth.

"What can I expect?" Marcus sounded weary and worried.

"It's hard to say, she must be very strong to have controlled herself as long as she did and she does seem to be responding well to treatment." The woman left the statement hanging without giving a definite answer.

Elsa was awake, she had been awake for a long time. She felt her father's hand touch hers, it was warm and comforting.

"She's so cold," he said quietly.

"That's normal." the woman's voice answered.

Elsa opened her eyes, "Dad?" she whispered.

Marcus had been looking down at her hand, stroking it gently. Now he looked at his daughter, his eyes full of pain. Why she thought what's wrong with me? "Hi sweetheart," was all her father seemed able to say.

Suddenly she remembered. The violence, the blood, what had she done? She pulled her hand away from her father's and sat up in bed abruptly, her eyes wide. Marcus jumped back as if afraid and Elsa suddenly noticed the woman she had heard speaking. She was at Elsa's side, an icy cold hand on her arm, her voice soothing.

"It's okay Elsa," she said, "You're safe, we won't let you hurt anyone."

Won't let me hurt anyone? She knows…

"Elsa, this is Hesper, she is a colleague and friend of mine, a doctor here. She has been taking care of you." Marcus stayed one pace away from her bed.

Elsa looked to the woman at her side. Despite the million and one questions racing through her mind she could not help but be distracted from her confusion by Hesper. She was breathtakingly beautiful and young, far too young to be a doctor. Her features and her skin were perfect in every way, her long, straight, white blonde hair was as smooth as silk and her ice blue eyes glittered behind impossibly long, dark eyelashes. Unsettled, Elsa, turned her gaze back to her father, taking in the unfamiliar, clinical surroundings at the same time. The room she was in was large and mainly white, with minimal furniture. It did not escape Elsa's notice that the room was by no means pristine, there were large chunks of plaster missing from the walls and her bedclothes were torn. Her eyes drifted to the side of the bed which thick metal manacles lay bent and broken.

"Where am I?" Her father avoided her eyes and looked as if he was trying to decide how best to answer. Elsa was impatient for answers and tried a different question.

"How long have I been here?" she asked. She remembered nothing but had a sense that time had passed.

"Two weeks." Marcus sounded tired and broken.

Two weeks? She had no awareness of anything since… her stomach churned at the memory and not in an entirely bad way. "Did I.. did I kill him?"

Marcus shook his head, "Don't worry about him now Elsa, we got him to a hospital, he's alive"

Elsa breathed a sigh of relief and was glad that relief was what she felt, that despite her violent urges, she was thankful she hadn't killed him. "He was a very bad person," she wasn't trying to defend her actions but she had seen that man's darkest thoughts and she didn't want him to be able to direct those intentions at anyone else in the future, anyone that couldn't defend themselves.

"The police are aware of his current situation, they will deal with him once he has – recovered," Hesper spoke, choosing her words carefully. "No-one will believe his story of how he received his – injuries," the careful phrasing was evident once more.

Elsa closed her eyes and tried not to remember but the images were too strong. She loathed the pleasure she felt at the memory of spilling the vile man's blood and hated the fact that she wished she could have had just one taste, just a little bit. If she was in hospital and they were taking care of her, why had they not fixed her, why was she still having these thoughts?

"What is wrong with me?" Elsa demanded.

"There's nothing wrong with you." Hesper said, "As such."

"What do you remember?" Marcus asked, "After you left the house?"

Elsa frowned, she wanted answers not questions. "I just ran," she said, "I don't know how far, I had to get away from you before I…" She looked at her father as she remembered with shock what had happened when he'd found her in the alleyway, about to do the unthinkable. "You shot me!" she exclaimed, "How did you find me?"

Marcus looked pained as he resumed his seat at the side of her bed. "We have ways of tracking people like you. I had to stop you," he said, "I couldn't let you... you were..."

Elsa looked back to her father. People like you she thought what do you mean by that Dad? Psychopaths? Freaks? Mindless killers? "You shot me." She was not accusing, there was no blame in her voice, just curiosity.

"You were not yet at full strength," Marcus began and she let that comment pass too, trying to hold back the avalanche of questions crashing through her mind long enough to let her father explain, "I tranquillised you."

"Tranquillised?"

Hesper spoke again, her voice like velvet in Elsa's ear but still making Elsa jump, she'd almost forgotten that Hesper was there so still and quiet was her presence. "You've been tranquillised ever since," she said, "Enough to kill a rhinoceros a hundred times over, but you're too strong for it now."

Marcus, took a deep breath. "I have a lot I need to tell you."

"I'm listening." Elsa said, her mind screaming as she tried to remain calm. Hesper left the room silently, moving with a fluid grace that Elsa could not help but watch.

"I have kept a lot of things from you over the years Elsa, " Marcus began, "I thought I was protecting you but now," he shook his head, "This is all my fault," he said sadly, "I should have realised what was happening to you but I didn't want to see it."

"See what?" Elsa asked, "Dad, please just tell me what is happening?"

"Firstly, I have lied to you about myself, about what I do for a living" Marcus looked her in the eyes as he spoke and she felt his guilt and his pain. She was aware too that she could still smell his blood and hear the beat of his heart but it was like background noise now and she didn't feel the hunger and the terrible violent urges she had before.

"You're a salesman," she said, as if saying it herself out loud would make it continue to be true, "You sell medical equipment."

Marcus shook his head, "Not exactly," he said. "Well, not at all; I work for an organisation called Haven."

"I've never heard of it."

"No-one has unless they work for them too."

"Why would you lie to me about that?" Elsa asked, confused, "What do Haven do? Is it some kind of secret government thing, or military?"

"Neither the government or the military know about us." Marcus stated simply.

"Why not?"

"Because of what we do," he replied. "And because of some of the people we employ. There are things in this world that most people know nothing about Elsa, the supernatural, the paranormal, pure evil – terrible things. Haven tracks these things, cleans up after them, protects those that need protecting and 'deals' with those that people need protecting from."

Elsa didn't miss the pause before the word 'deals', or the implication in her father's tone when he said it. "What are you talking about?" she asked, sensing his anguish and conflicting emotions. He didn't want to tell her these things, she could tell, she could feel his parental protective instinct in overdrive. "Tell me Dad," she said softly, "I need to know."

Marcus nodded and continued, "If you were to go on the internet Elsa, and look up demons for instance, you could get a list of demons in legend and folklore. I would estimate currently that about 80% of that list actually exist, or at least have existed at some point." He paused and massaged his temples for a moment, "and those are just the ones we know about."

Elsa studied her father. Her apparent newly developed the ability to read people, to know when they were lying and to sense their strongest emotions told her that her father was telling her the truth, no matter how ridiculous his words might sound to anyone other than her. "Go on." she said flatly.

"There are lots of other myths and legends that exist too, werewolves for example." He looked at Elsa, as if testing her reaction to see if she would believe him. She felt she shouldn't but somehow she did and she nodded for him to continue. "That's how I found you." he said, "I realised what had happened as soon as I saw your reaction to my blood, as soon as I looked into your eyes. I can't believe you managed to tear yourself away, you did so well." Elsa couldn't believe her father was praising her for just about managing not to kill him. "We have lots of different types of people working here at Haven, werewolves included. I called on a good friend to help me track you, like you he has a keen sense of smell and he moves pretty fast too."

"Like a bloodhound?" Elsa asked.

"Sort of, for reasons I'll get to in a minute, your smell was particularly pungent to my friend Gray so it wasn't hard to find you, thank goodness we got there in time." His eyes drifted for a moment and then he snapped back, "You see, not all the creatures we hunt were born that way, some of them are changed against their will and when that happens, when there is still a human part there, sometimes they decide that it is the human part that they want to hold onto. One of the things we do at Haven is help creatures that were once human control their darker urges and join us in protecting the human race from those that are less inclined to embrace a more chaste existence. Gray is one of those people, so is Hesper."

"Hesper is a werewolf?" Elsa knew there was something different about the woman but couldn't imagine her as the kind of creature she thought a werewolf might be.

"No, Hesper is a -" Marcus was struggling, Elsa felt he was trying to tell her something important but didn't know how, "I'm going to have to start at the beginning for this to have any hope of making sense."

Elsa nodded again, getting more confused by the second.

Marcus took a deep breath, "Your mother worked for Haven too, that's where we met." he said with a small smile, "I know I've told you before but you look so much like her."

Elsa felt the same pang she always did when she thought of the mother she'd never known. She'd seen photographs but found it hard to make the connection between those pictures and the living, breathing person her mother once was. There had always been a gap in her life where she wished the memory of her mother could be.

"Your mother didn't die during childbirth," Marcus said then, his expression distant, as if lost in his memories, "She was killed before you were born."

"Killed?" Elsa was horrified, violent images flashed through her mind like reflections on shards of a broken mirror.

"I should never have left her on her own," his eyes were full of tears, "I was part of a team hunting a particularly powerful and bloodthirsty group of vampires and we had information we thought would lead us straight to them."

"Vampires! Dad.." a horrible sense of realisation was creeping over her, crawling under her skin and snaking around her heart.

Marcus held up a hand to silence her, "They tricked us," he said quietly, "They killed your mother to send me a message, to warn me not to go after them." He closed his eyes to blink away tears, "I realised too late what was happening, I didn't get back in time. They were still standing over her when we arrived. We killed them all but it was too late for Sarah, she'd lost too much blood. We were able to save you though. We kept you under close observation here for the first year of your life, I was so afraid you may have been turned."

"Turned?" She questioned him although deep down she knew and her growing understanding was spreading like a poison through her body..

"Into one of them." Marcus said simply, "Vampires excrete a venom when they bite which can change humans into vampires too."

"Did Mum…?"

Marcus shook his head, "They took too much blood, there is a point beyond which no amount of vampire venom can bring you back from death and they knew exactly what they were doing. I have no doubt that had we not stopped them, they would have made sure you were dead too."

"But I was okay?"

"So we thought. You showed absolutely no signs of vampirism, you were a happy, healthy, normal little girl."

"I don't feel normal anymore." Elsa said, her mind reeling. So many things were beginning to click into place, so many feelings and horrible violent thoughts were suddenly explained

"I know, I know," Marcus nodded wearily, "It seems that the vampires venom has lain dormant in your system and for some reason it has now awoken."

"I'm a..." she couldn't bring herself to say what she knew to be true. She had a sudden flashback to the accident, to Kate's head lolling down towards her and the steady dripping of Kate's blood onto her face, trickling into her mouth. "Kate." she almost whispered, "The car didn't land upright in the accident, it was on its side. Kate was above me, when I woke up her blood was dripping onto my face, I tasted it in my mouth."

"You tasted human blood?" her father asked, "I should have thought of that, you were covered in blood but you weren't injured apart from the bruising. I saw the bruises myself, it doesn't make sense." he frowned, "As a vampire you shouldn't be so easily hurt, it should be virtually impossible to even break your skin."

"By the time we got home, the bruises were gone." Elsa murmured, "I have cut myself since but it healed."

"You didn't tell me?" her father's tone was questioning, "You must have been gradually becoming stronger. If I'd known..."

"If I'd known!" Elsa couldn't keep the accusation from her voice, "You never told me about these things Dad, I thought I was going mad!"

Marcus looked ashamed, "I'm sorry." he said, his eyes downcast, "Maybe human blood was the trigger, maybe that is when the change began."

Elsa was reeling. I am a vampire. I'm a vampire! She felt as if she were being sucked backwads into a black hole and the light that had been her life was getting smaller and smaller and further and further out of reach. "No," she said quietly through gritted teeth, her hands clenched into fists, gripping the sheets tightly until her nails pierced the fabric and began to dig cruelly into her palms, "This is not happening," Her voice was rising, "This is not happening to me!"

Marcus began to reach for her then pulled his hands back. She watched his every movement in slow motion. She could see that he was scared of her, the very moment when a concerned father's love was over-ridden by fear of the monster before him. She hated that she had caused that reaction and, in that moment, she hated that he reacted that way.

"Get out!' She snarled menacingly.

"Elsa…"

"GO!" She was struggling with every fibre of her being to control her anger and despair.

Marcus hesitated for a moment and then turned and walked for the door. He turned to her one more time as he left the room, "You are still my daughter Elsa, I will help you and I will always, always love you."

She saw the tears on his face as he closed the door and only then, when no one could see, did she let her own come.

# Sunlight? Crosses? Garlic?

---

*✶ A/N - For those following the soundtrack to this story, I'm going with 'Stall Out' by Mutemath as suggested by @Popping_Cherries - thanks for that! Enjoy folks :)**

Elsa had to cry herself out; she had to put a few more holes in the walls and shout and scream at the injustice of what had happened to her. She had to be restrained, sedated and finally soothed by Hesper who was wonderful and patient and so very, very strong. Until eventually, she stopped fighting. Until all she really wanted was for her father to hold her in his arms and tell her she was going to be all right. He sat on her bed and rocked her like he used to when she was little, her anger at him gone and his fear of her forgotten.

"I remember everything now," she said quietly, "About the night of the crash. I smelt petrol, the car was on fire and I knew we had to get out. I climbed out of the front window and I couldn't think how to get Grant and Kate out. I pushed the car Dad, I pushed it back upright! The doors were jammed but the windows were broken, I pulled them both out of the windows and carried them away from the car."

"You are very strong now Elsa," Marcus explained, gazing around the damaged room. He indicated to the broken manacles attached on the bed, "Thankfully by the time you were strong enough to break those, we had just about enough tranquiliser left to keep you out for another hour while we finally perfected your serum dose."

"Serum? Is that what Hesper's been injecting me with? I thought it was more sedative." The daily injections had been the least of Elsa's concerns over the last few days.

Marcus patiently explained, thankful that his daughter was talking to him again, "Part of my work here at Haven is to try and develop medications which make it easier for those with a taste for blood to avoid falling prey to temptation. We've had great success with vampires but each one is different and it takes time to get it right. Sometimes it works, sometimes it doesn't, it depends in part on how much they want to be saved. I could see that you wanted to be stopped, you would never have coped as long as you did or managed to turn away from me that day otherwise."

"How does it work?"

"You will have to be injected everyday, it won't stop you wanting blood or enjoying the thought of what it tastes like or how to get it, but it will stop you craving it to the point where you have to sacrifice your human side to obtain it."

"It will stop me killing?"

"You will stop you killing, the serum just boosts your willpower and dulls your senses a little. You have to understand Elsa that all vampires, pure born ones or once human ones, have the choice, no vampire has to kill humans, you can survive on any blood. Human blood just gives you the best hit, like a drug almost."

"I can smell blood," Elsa felt like a weight was being lifted from her shoulders as she could finally talk about how she'd been feeling. "And I can tell what people are feeling, and when they are lying."

"You will also find that it is very difficult for you to be hurt," her father said, "Not impossible, but very, very difficult."

Her mind was racing through all the vampire films she'd seen, all the myths and legends she'd read or heard of, "What about sunlight? Crosses? Garlic?" She felt foolish but she had to know.

"Crosses, garlic, stakes through the heart – all myths," Marcus said, "Sunlight can't kill you but bright, direct sunlight can make you feel very unwell."

"So I can still go out in the day?"

"I wouldn't recommend you stay too long on sunny days but yes, you can go out in the day. One benefit of this countries miserable weather is that bright sunny days are quite thin on the ground. Pure vampires cannot tolerate daylight well at all, but those that were once human can combat the problem very simply ," he gave a half smile, "Sun cream, very high factor."

Elsa raised her eyebrows, it was almost funny. "Sun cream," she said shaking her head, "This is crazy."

"You're taking it very well," her father said, which earned him another set of raised elbows. Elsa was very aware that up until very recently she had not been taking it well at all.

"In some ways it's almost a relief to have a reason for the way I was feeling," she admitted, "I thought I'd had some kind of head injury that had sent me mad and turned me into a potential murderer." she paused thoughtfully for a moment before continuing pensively, her relief at having answers clouded by what those answers were. "I am a potential murderer though

I suppose," she said, "Although I don't feel like I did before. I couldn't control it, the hunger. I guess that's the serum then?"

Marcus nodded and Elsa felt suddenly embarrassed admitting her desire to kill to her father. She realised with shock that she was not blushing. Her skin had always been so reactive to her emotions; any hint of embarrassment and she felt a heat creep into her face and knew her skin was glowing but now, nothing. Her fingertips reached self-consciously to her face, her skin was impossibly smooth and cool as marble. A question she didn't want to ask was screaming in her mind. She wasn't sure she wanted to know the answer to the question she knew she needed to ask, "Am I still... alive?"

She could feel her father's heart breaking as he struggled to find an answer. He swallowed hard before attempting to speak, "It's hard to explain," he said, "You breathe, your heart beats, you feel emotions – you do all of the things that a human being does," he was fighting against the tears she didn't think she could bear to see again, "But you aren't human anymore Elsa, your body doesn't need to do many of those things. They are habits, your body going through the motions. You won't need to eat, you won't be able to sleep, your skin will always be cold, you will never get sick." He placed a warm hand on her cold one once more, "It is virtually impossible now for any human being to hurt you and any injury you do receive will heal in next to no time. You won't grow old so in that sense you are very much alive but..." he couldn't find the words to explain further and she wasn't sure she was ready to hear it. Her head was reeling once more.

"Can I be hurt properly at all?" she asked, "I mean, can I be killed, can I die?" She felt his reluctance to answer, "Be honest with me Dad," she said, "You owe me that now." She hated to use his guilt against him but she had to know.

"There are - ways." He said heavily.

"How?"

"Elsa.."

"How?"

Marcus looked defeated and he couldn't look her in the eye, "Please don't make me talk to you about these things," he begged, "Hesper has offered to talk you through some of the more difficult aspects. I just – I can't, I'm sorry."

Elsa closed her eyes, "Stop saying sorry," she said and she tried to put a kindness and forgiveness in her tone as she knew that for all the mistakes her father had made, he had done everything because he loved her, she shouldn't be angry with him for that. "You didn't do this, you don't need to be sorry. It's just going to take me some time." She climbed off the bed and walked to the window, making a show of looking at the view without really seeing anything at all.

"Would you like me to get Hesper?" Marcus asked.

Elsa nodded and wondered if she would ever get all the answers she needed.

# As Normal A Life As Possible.

Elsa stayed in Haven's clinic for two more days, more for her own sanity than any physical reason. Physically she'd never felt or looked better, mentally she was still in pieces. Everything she thought she knew about her past, her present and her future had changed and she didn't have a clue how to start coming to terms with it all. All the stories she'd ever heard about vampires flashed through her mind like some kind of gothic horror movie marathon. Hesper spent hours sitting with her, patiently answering her questions, telling her what to expect from her new life. If life was what it could be called. Hesper was a vampire too but, like Elsa, she had been human once, a very long time ago. She explained that when she was changed, Haven didn't exist. As a new vampire she had no control over her hunger and had killed many people before the human part of her regained enough strength to make her want to stop. There had been no magic serum then to curb her cravings, only her own will power and this was what she still relied on now.

"And you will too," she said gently, "Eventually. Your body will gradually become immune to the serum, vampirism is a very resilient disease. By then, you will be strong enough to cope on your own."

Elsa was interested that Hesper referred to vampirism as a disease, as if it was simply an illness like the flu. "Why use the serum at all if I'm just going to become immune to it?" she asked.

"Because new vampires cannot cope without it, there is no way you would be able to stop yourself from killing. You would tear out the throat of the person you loved most in the world in a heartbeat in those first weeks or months, years even for some. We all react differently to the venom." Hesper sensed Elsa's fear and soothed her with as much warmth as the cool embrace of her arms could give, "You have already proven yourself so strong Elsa," she said, "I've never known a new vampire keep their teeth to themselves as long as you did." She smiled, revealing her own perfect white teeth. No fangs though; Elsa had been relieved to find this was another myth, they were retracted and only appeared when a vampire as about to feed from something living.

In many ways, Elsa didn't look physically any different to any other human being. But she saw the differences in herself when she looked in the mirror, so much so that she stopped bothering to look. She didn't need to check her appearance, brush her hair or apply make-up anymore. Her skin was perfect, her hair glossy, her appearance flawless in every way. It was very unsettling, she always been used to feeling a little plain, scruffy at times and her hair had always had a mind of its own. Hesper explained the purpose behind the subtle changes to her appearance and it reminded Elsa of John's strange behaviour on her last day at college before Haven, when he had voiced breathlessly how he wanted her and Sebastian had thought he was rescuing her when, in reality it was John he had saved.

"Vampires are predators Elsa, and we are exceptional ones because we make our prey want to be caught. No matter how frightened they are, or how much they want to live, ultimately they are drawn to us, they want to be near us, to have us take them." Her expression was almost wistful and Elsa felt she could see the faintest whisper of the killer Hesper had been.

Then her tranquil, serene expression returned once more, making Elsa feel instantly at ease. She liked the beautiful, calm vampire whose ability to control her urges and her acceptance of what she was despite what she had done in the past gave Elsa some hope.

There were moments when Elsa felt almost excited at her new abilities, amazed at her own strength and the keenness of her senses. There were times when she definitely did not. Hesper had carefully broken the news to Elsa that despite the fact that they were doing everything they could to stop her needing human blood, she needed blood of some kind to work alongside the serum to curb her cravings.

"Why do I have to have blood at all?" Elsa had questioned, "It's not like I'm going to starve to death."

"Not to death no," Hesper conceded, "But you would still starve. Imagine never having the one thing that could keep your body functioning, no amount of serum could fight the craving that would develop but by that point you wouldn't have the strength or ability to hunt or feed. You would become a husk, a dead shell and you would spend the rest of eternity starving for blood and unable to do anything about it."

"Oh." That did not sound good and Elsa wasn't sure she wanted to hear the answer to her next question, "So what do we do about it then?"

"We have a means of getting - supplies. It is not overly pleasant to feed this way but needs must," Hesper gave a ittle smile, "When blood bags get depressin, we hunt." Hesper's eyes glowed, Elsa's eyes did not.

"Hunt what?"

"Animals, large animals if possible but there aren't that many large predators in this country and it's more, shall we say, exhilarating to hunt a predator than it is to take down a cow."

Elsa grimaced but had to admit, the images flashing through her mind of hunting down large and dangerous prey did make her pulse quicken and her throat develop the now familiar dryness of her thirst for blood. The image of creeping up on a cow did not have quite the same effect.

"We can manage without feeding for a good few weeks at a time if we can access larger game," Hesper assured her, "There are opportunities to travel further afield, catch larger prey that will keep you going for longer. I will help you when you are ready."

"Er – thanks," Elsa said wondering how she was ever going to get used to these conversations. Her mind wandered to her friends at college and the conversations they would have about films, music, what they were going to do at the weekend and she imagined discussing holiday plans with them.

So what are your plans this summer Elsa?

Oh, nothing too exciting, I'm going to hunt mountain lions in the Rocky Mountains with someone from my Dad's work.

Elsa made a mental note to look up native predators in Britain. All she could think of offhand were foxes and she always been so against fox hunting...

All too soon, the time came for Elsa to go home. She had mixed feelings. There was a tension between her and her father that she wasn't sure she had the will or energy to overcome. She didn't blame him for what had happened to her but she was having a hard time coming to terms with the fact that he'd been lying to her for so many years. That every time he had gone away with work he had in fact been hunting vampires and other supernatural beings and helping people like her come to terms with their own nightmares whilst hers had lain inside her, a ticking time bomb she had no knowledge of and could not protect herself from. She knew he'd done what he felt was best and maybe if she couldn't feel the guilt and despair pouring from him every time he saw her, she would find it easier to be around him. Still, she was relieved to be leaving the clinic. She was eager to find some normality in all of this and felt that if she could go home, back to college even, she could try to forget what she had become. She injected herself daily with the serum which took the edge off her thirst for blood and Hesper had given her an emergency kit full of devices which looked just like the auto injectors carried by people with severe allergies.

"For emergencies only Elsa,' she warned, "The more you use the serum, the quicker you will become immune to it but there may be certain times, or certain humans, which will require an extra boost of willpower." She'd given Elsa a playful wink at this point, obviously far more at ease with what they were than Elsa ever thought she could be.

And so Elsa had argued her case with her father for going back to college. She had missed a lot of time with the aftermath of the accident and her time at Haven but she felt sure that she could catch up; Hesper had explained that everything about her was heightened now, including her mental abilities. Marcus didn't feel it was a good idea for her to be around so many people so soon but Hesper backed her up. Elsa had proven herself to be very strong and as long as she didn't suddenly become a straight A student overnight, no-one would suspect anything was amiss.

Marcus eventually relented because he did want her to have as normal a life as possible for as long as possible. She was never going to get any older but she could get away with looking young for long enough to get her through college and university, to enable her to experience achievements such as getting her driving license and embarking on a career; to allow her to enjoy an adult life as well as a teenage one. Elsa tried not to think about what would happen in future years when they could no longer explain why she never seemed to look any older but she did wonder when people would start to ask questions, her twenty-first birthday maybe? Definitely her thirtieth. She also tried not to think about watching her father grow older and older whilst she was eternally seventeen but these were the thoughts which invaded her mind at night when she was most aware of how she had changed, when sleep no longer came to her.

Marcus had fabricated quite a story to explain her absence from college and her strange behaviour before she left. Ironically, her cover story was the very thing she had feared when she hadn't known what was really happening to her. She had an undiagnosed head injury after the accident, which had caused her erratic and unusual behaviour. She had been rushed to a specialist hospital where they also diagnosed a rare blood disorder that explained her daily injections and emergency medication. Elsa had seen the forged medical records and was shocked at what her father was capable of doing. The college had not questioned him, no one appeared suspicious. Elsa was so aware of the lie she was scared it was written all over her face but her father, she thought bitterly, delivered it with ease as they sat in the college Dean's office the following day discussing her return to classes.

"There is another student in a similar position." the Dean said, looking down at some paperwork on his desk.

*I doubt it* Elsa thought darkly, averting her gaze from the pulse in his neck and resisting the urge to lick her lips.

The Dean had obviously found what he was looking for, "Yes, Sebastian Bennet has been off ill too, you can take the extra tuition together, support each other." Elsa fought to hide her surprise as Sebastian's name was mentioned. She remembered how he had looked the last day she'd seen him, so haggard and drained. She remembered looking into his eyes and how it had stabbed at her heart. The memory piqued her curiosity. Now that she knew she was able to read people so well she also knew that what she sensed from Sebastian was real and she wanted to know what it was in his life that was so terrible, what could cause him to feel such despair. She remembered too the underlying sense of danger that hung around Sebastian and she felt a faint hint of excitement at the thought of being near him. For the first time, she was relieved she could no longer blush as she was sure she would have gone bright red as she thought about him. She had been attracted to Sebastian since the very first day she'd seen him stalk into the canteen and it pleased her that she could still feel something as normal as the butterflies of a teenage crush.

So here she was, shaking the Dean's hand as he welcomed her back and told her that if she had any problems, his door was always open. Still self conscious at the coolness of her skin, Elsa was glad for the cold October weather which meant she could get away with keeping her gloves on.

It was half term but it was agreed that Elsa and Sebastian would go into college for some catch up classes before normal classes resumed in the first week of November. The thought of being alone in a classroom with Sebastian made Elsa feel nervous, none of their previous encounters had gone particularly well. At least she would only have two people to try not to kill though, Sebastian and the poor tutor given the job of running their study sessions when they should have been on a weeks break, the least Elsa could do was not kill them.

# I Need Some Fresh Air.

------------------------------------------------------------

✸ AN - for those following the soundtrack to this book, I've chosen Youre a Lie by the ever awesome Slash and Myles Kennedy to reflect Elsa's struggle with lying to her friend.*

Elsa's biggest challenge before she had college to focus on again, was keeping her mind occupied. She felt so alert all the time, so aware of everything going on around her. If she wanted to, she could count every particle of dust in the air in less time than it used to take the dust to make her sneeze. Her new abilities were taking some getting used to and she fluctuated between hating herself and being filled with awe and wonder at what she could do.

It was as she sat in her room during her second solid hour of testing how long she could hold her breath that she heard the front doorbell ring. To be more precise she had heard the sound of someone's fingertip hesitantly touch the doorbell without pushing it. Next she had heard their heart rate pick up a little and their teeth set together as they'd determined they would press the doorbell and then she'd heard the same fingertip jab at the button, holding it down just ever so slightly longer than was necessary before releasing. She knew who it was, the smell of Kate's blood was unmistakable to her, it was the only human blood she had ever tasted and

Elsa felt the strongest surge of hunger she'd experienced since leaving the clinic. She gripped the edge of her desk, jaw clenched and her fingers sunk easily into the wood, making it crack and splinter. It took a huge amount of self-control for Elsa to recover herself enough to administer one of her emergency doses of serum and once she had she felt strangely proud of herself. If she could be around Kate without slipping then there was hope for her yet, and everyone around her.

Elsa looked at herself in the mirror, something she generally preferred not to do now. She felt that she looked like a completely different person no matter how much her father tried to convince her she was the same Elsa to him. She didn't see how anyone could fail to notice how her eyes looked like they burned with flickers of incandescent flame but Hesper had assured her that humans were 'not very observant' and Elsa just had to hope that was true.

Satisfied that her urges were under control and she looked as normal as she could, Elsa turned her efforts to now behaving as normally as possible as she walked down the stairs to answer the door almost as soon as the doorbell was finished ringing, mere seconds had passed since she first heard Kate's finger hesitate.

Kate looked surprised to see the door opened so quickly and took an involuntary step back. "Er – hi Elsa," she said awkwardly.

Elsa read her friend carefully, Kate was feeling wary, undecided, confused. Elsa knew she had some ground to make up after their parting words a few weeks ago, Kate was unsure of where she stood and unsure of Elsa as she rightly should be.

"I am so sorry for what I said to you Kate," Elsa launched straight into the apology she had been rehearsing, "I wasn't myself, I didn't want anyone near me, I said the only thing I knew would make you go away but it wasn't me speaking I swear. I wasn't well, I just didn't realise. I promise you on my life I didn't mean it." She realised the 'on my life' bit didn't really mean much but hoped it made the whole thing more believable for Kate and she really was sorry, that much was true.

It was working, Elsa could feel Kate's wariness start to diminish and she suddenly felt full of warmth for her friend. She had always liked Kate, she was fun to be with, energetic and exuberant but now Elsa could really see into her heart and she realised she had vastly underestimated what a good, kind heart Kate had. Elsa had been so horrible to her and within a few short sentences she could already feel forgiveness emanating from Kate and even guilt that she had felt angry with Elsa in the first place.

"I, I should have realised you wouldn't behave like that unless there was something wrong," Kate stammered.

Elsa shook her head, dragging her friend into the house, careful to be gentle as she was aware that she really didn't know her own strength yet.

"Don't you dare feel bad for me," Elsa demanded, "I was a complete bitch to you and you didn't deserve it. I'll make it up to you, I promise." For starters I'm not going to try and bite you.

Kate was relaxing, "I wanted to visit you in the hospital," she said, "But your dad said you were really out of it and they didn't want to risk you getting any outside infections or anything." More stories Dad? Elsa thought but she beginning to accept that lies were a necessary part of her life now.

"I'm really glad you came round," Elsa said truthfully, she was eager to have her friend back if at all possible, it would make life seem that little bit more normal again, "Do you want a drink? I think Dad hid some chocolate cake in the kitchen somewhere."

"Okay, yes please," Kate gave a small smile, "I wasn't sure if you'd want to see me or not."

"Of course I do," Elsa asserted, "I'll never forgive myself for being so horrible to you, I had been wondering how to apologise, I thought you might never speak to me again."

Kate looked down, "I thought about it," she said honestly, "But I don't think it was your fault was it? Your dad told us how head injuries can affect personality and I did some research on the internet." Elsa was touched that rather than write her off as a nutcase, Kate had tried to find a way to explain her behaviour away. Kate continued, "And then he told us you were sick too, you've got something wrong with your blood?" She was frowning, Marcus had obviously avoided going into too much detail.

Elsa surprised herself at how easily she could lie, how much control she could have over her facial expressions and her tone of voice, "Yeah," she said, "It's a rare blood disorder with some ridiculously long name which I've got no hope of ever being able to pronounce or remember. I've got to have injections everyday." She pulled a face and Kate looked sympathetic.

"What does it do to you then, this blood disorder?" she asked, "You never seemed ill before."

"I know," Elsa said, her newly agile mind plotting believable answers before Kate's questions were even finished. "They think it's something that's been gradually getting worse as I've gotten older so it's sort of crept up on me without my noticing. Without the medication I'd be really lethargic and open to infection and apparently I'll be more sensitive to the sun so now I have to wear sun cream all year round."

"What a pain." Kate sympathised.

"Yup," Elsa agreed, pouring Kate a glass of juice from the fridge and handing it to her, "Looks like I'm going to have to rock the English Rose complexion from now on."

Kate grinned, "I wouldn't worry," she said, "Tango is so out of fashion these days."

Elsa returned the grin then stopped as she noticed a subtle change in Kate's expression, as if Kate had thought she'd noticed something but now wasn't sure.

"You look great actually Elsa," Kate said, the expression on her face remaining, "Really great."

"Thanks." Elsa said, making her voice sound as light and uninterested as possible. She turned her back to Kate quickly, rummaging in the cupboard, "I'm sure he hid that cake in here." She muttered, "Ah, here it is, do you want some?"

"Please," Kate answered as Elsa cut her a huge slice, "Aren't you having any?"

"There were two cakes in here this morning," Elsa lied again, "Trust me, I do not need anymore!"

Kate laughed and the atmosphere between them was relaxed as they sat at the kitchen table.

"So did you hear about Sebastian?" Kate asked her and Elsa's ears pricked.

"What about him?" She tried to sound disinterested.

"So you do still fancy him?" Kate said and Elsa scowled, Hesper was wrong about humans not being observant, she was going to have to very careful around Kate. Kate gave a knowing smile and continued, "The day you…"

"Flipped out," Elsa helped her.

"Yeah, well Sebastian was looking really rough and he just got up in the middle of history apparently and left without a word to anyone. Apparently he sped off on his motorbike and ended up at the Anvil." The Anvil was a pub in a bad part of town notorious for trouble. Elsa raised one eyebrow, something she realised she had never been able to do before. Kate nodded, "Exactly," she said, obviously pleased she had Elsa hooked on her story, "Anyway he got into a fight with some pretty big guys and got thrown out and that's the last anyone saw of him."

"How do you know all this?' Elsa asked, bemused as always by Kate's ability to find out virtually anything about virtually anyone in less time than it took most people to even realise anything was going on.

"Well Carrie Stokes' brother goes out with the sister of a guy that delivers there and he saw the whole thing." Ah, the good old local grapevine.

"Was Sebastian okay?" Elsa couldn't hide her concern.

"Elsa, he kicked ass!" Kate said enthusiastically before her expression became serious, "I'm not really sure he's someone you should be pursuing in a romantic sense," she said gravely, "Every girl likes a bad boy but he's something else, apparently two guys ended up in hospital and Sebastian walked away with barely a scratch."

"Didn't he get arrested?" Elsa asked.

"Are you kidding? Most of the regulars in that pub have records longer than, well a very long thing. The police weren't involved."

"Sebastian and I are going to be taking catch up classes together over half term and during frees when we all go back next week," Elsa said, "The college obviously don't know what happened or he would have been kicked out surely?"

"Well, I suppose since it wasn't reported to the police, there's no official proof." Kate reasoned, "But seriously Elsa, I think you should keep your distance from him, devastatingly attractive as he is, I think he's a bit dangerous."

Elsa looked thoughtful. She didn't think Sebastian was dangerous, she knew he was, and not just a bit either. The mystery surrounding him thickened and it intrigued her, she enjoyed the distraction.

"Earth to Elsa?" Kate waved a hand at her and Elsa returned her attention to her friend.

"You're probably right," she conceded, "We don't seem to get on very well anyway."

Kate seemed satisfied. "So I guess if you're trapped at college you're not going to have much free time over half term?"

"Probably not," Elsa admitted.

Kate looked at her watch, "I've got to go," she said, "Got to be back for dinner," she looked guiltily at the plate in front of her, empty save for a few crumbs of chocolate cake, "Not that I'm that hungry now."

Elsa was, she could feel her thirst growing gradually and was becoming more aware of Kate's scent and the warmth of her body. Damn, it hadn't even been that long since she injected herself. "Sure," she said, "It was really good to see you again, I'm glad we sorted things out."

"Me too," Kate smiled and leaned over to give Elsa a tight hug, Elsa felt her eyes roll as her face was pressed into the side of Kate's neck, the sound of the other girls pulse was deafening in her ears and against all her will, Elsa felt her lips parting.

"Hello Kate!" Marcus had walked into the kitchen, his voice was slightly too loud, the pitch slightly too high and he slammed his brief case down on the table as Kate pulled away from Elsa smiling with no idea how much danger she had put herself in. Elsa clenched her fists under the table, grateful to her father for his interruption and highly aware of the fear he was feeling. She hated knowing that she could scare people, especially her dad.

"Hello Mr Shaw, sorry, I'm just leaving." Kate remained completely oblivious to the tension in the room and Marcus smoothly placed himself between her and Elsa.

"No problem, good to see you Kate," he said.

"See you Elsa!' Kate said brightly.

"Bye," Elsa tried to sound relaxed but wasn't sure she was succeeding.

"Are you okay?" Kate's reaction told her she wasn't.

"Just feeling a bit woozy," That much was true, "Think I need a lie down, not quite one hundred percent yet."

Kate hovered as Elsa wished fervently she would leave.

"In that case," Marcus said lightly, guiding Kate out of the kitchen, "I'm going to have to kick you out Miss Owen and put my daughter to bed." His voice was jovial and Kate smiled, waving back at Elsa.

"Get some rest and take care," she said, "I'll call you."

It was all Elsa could do to keep her body still as she nodded, forcing a smile in return. She heard the front door open, then close moments later and her father was back in the kitchen concern etched on his face. "Are you ok?"

"I need some fresh air," Elsa said. Air that isn't filled with the smell of human blood.

"I don't think you should leave the house at the moment." Marcus spoke carefully and he backed away from her, "I'll get your medication."

Elsa hated that she made him feel that way, she wanted his help and his comfort but knew that right now she needed to keep her distance from him.

"I'll get it myself," she said and she disappeared in an instant, her movements too fast for her father to comprehend. In less than a second she was back and thrusting the box of auto-injectors at her father, "I need stronger doses before Monday," she said, her voice measured, her control returned, "I'm going out."

"Where?" Marcus asked, "What time will you be back?"

"I don't know," Elsa replied.

"Be careful," Marcus called after her helplessly.

"I won't hurt anyone," Elsa shouted back feeling suddenly angry, she wasn't intending on going anywhere where people were.

"That's not what I meant!" Marcus said quietly.

Elsa would have heard it had she been listening but she wasn't. She was wishing she had a motorbike, something that could move somewhere close to as fast as she could but without attracting the same attention. She had to keep her pace slow until she was sure no one could see her, before she could run at speeds no human could ever hope to achieve even with the most powerful motorbike in the world. She loved the speed, the feel of the air rushing past her skin, it calmed her down. But it was a risk, if anyone saw her she didn't want to think what it could mean. A motorbike might be the answer she was looking for.

# A Lot To Hide.

"**N**o." Elsa's father was shaking his head, "Absolutely not, they're dangerous."

"I'm dangerous," Elsa reminded him, twirling a fork in her hand before deftly weaving it in and out of her fingers, "And indestructible."

Marcus winced at the reminder, he seemed intent on ignoring the fact that his daughter was now a vampire as much as possible. Elsa was getting used to feeling his fear but occasionally she could sense something else just below the surface. She couldn't quite put her finger on it yet, although she was sure she would, she felt her abilities getting stronger and more finely tuned by the day. She knew her offhand remarks stung him and that she was acting like a stroppy teenager with a bad attitude but she reasoned that if her dad so desperately wanted a normal teenager then that was exactly what he was going to get.

"Please don't sculpt the cutlery," he asked.

"I'm getting a motorbike." Elsa stated.

"Why?" her father asked.

"Because I've always wanted one, because I like going fast and I can't go fast my way without drawing a certain amount of attention to myself." She pulled the elaborately bent fork back into shape and put it on the table, "Because I've got enough money saved to buy it without your help and because your previous arguments about them being dangerous and your worries of me getting hurt no longer apply."

Marcus looked at his daughter at a loss for something to say. Eventually he just shook his head and stood up from the kitchen table, "I'm going to work," he said, "We'll talk later. If you have any problems at college today, anything at all, leave immediately and call me."

"I'll be fine, There's only going to be three of us in the room and the new dose is much better," Elsa was referring to her emergency supply, which so far she had only had to use around Kate. After finding the serums effects lasted less than an hour at first, the new dose had seen Elsa through a whole film the previous day.

Marcus held his hands up as if in defence, "I'm just being your dad Elsa," he said, "Can't you let me be that still?"

Elsa frowned, "What do you mean?" she asked.

Marcus just sighed, "Never mind," he said, "I'll see you later?" It was a question rather than a statement, as Elsa didn't seem to run on a normal timetable anymore and was often nowhere to be found at dinnertime since she didn't really need to eat normal food.

"Sure," she said, "Dad?"

"Yes?"

"What exactly do you do at work?"

Marcus' face lit up slightly, "Why don't you come in one of the days this week when you're not in college and see for yourself?" he said.

"Okay." Elsa replied. She looked at the clock on the kitchen wall, "I'd better get going too." she said and disappeared before Marcus' eyes before reappearing a second later dressed and ready to go. He didn't even flinch, he was used to the speed at which vampires could move and Elsa was a little disappointed when her antics didn't get a reaction.

"Do you want me to drop you off?' her father asked, "It's pretty bright today."

"That'd be good thanks," Elsa said and she pulled a bottle of sun cream from her bag, spraying her face. "Weather report predicts rain later, I never thought I'd look forward to some miserable weather so much, all these frosty, sunny days are wearing me out."

Elsa was grateful that there were no other students around for her first day back, she was sure she would be the talk of the corridors and it was good to be able to find her bearings before that happened. She heard the distant scrape of a chair, and walked at as normal a pace as she could manage to her tutor room.

Sebastian was already there. She caught her breath when she saw him, it had been quite a while and she had forgotten the impact his sullen, hunched form could have on her. He didn't look up as she entered the room and slid into a chair at another table. If she thought she could sense he reluctance for social interaction before, she knew she could now.

Their tutor was talking. Elsa made all the right noises and facial expressions to appear as if she were engaged and paying attention but she wasn't at all. She didn't need to, she had already done all the reading she needed to do to catch up with what she had missed, sleepless nights and a new ability to not only speed read but also retain the information had proven very useful. Instead she focused on trying to read Sebastian.

He was making notes, his hand gripping the pencil as if it owed him something, his dark hair falling forward and obscuring his face. All she could see was the square set of his jaw, the muscles working furiously as if to stop his face twisting into a snarl. He gave the impression of concentrated work but she could tell it was anything but. He was unbelievably tense and when she tried to probe his emotions and his mind all she got was incessant static, a mess of noise and a tangle of every negative emotion possible.

Suddenly he looked up, his grey eyes met hers, his look one of accusation … leave me alone …

Elsa fought not to react, he hadn't spoken but she had definitely heard him somehow. She looked down at her notebook and heard his head turn back to look down at his own notes. She didn't look at him again.

Once their lesson was over, Sebastian stood and gathered his things. Elsa allowed herself to steel a look at him once more. For a split second there was a break in the static, like his guard had slipped, just for a moment. She gasped as the pain and sadness she'd felt from him before hit her like a train, so much more powerfully than she'd felt last time. His head snapped up and his eyes flashed dangerously. He shouldered his bag and left the room swiftly as Elsa scrambled to get her own belongings together and follow at a realistic speed.

She couldn't help herself, she had to know what was going on with him, "Sebastian wait!" she called out but he kept walking determinedly away from her so she picked up speed, trying to get close enough but not too close or too quickly to make him suspicious, "I just want to help!" What a ridiculous thing to say, she thought to herself, could I sound anymore like a stalker?

Sebastian turned suddenly, his strong hands pinning her against the wall, catching her by surprise. She allowed him to do it, not wanted to show him what she was capable of.

"Why won't you leave me alone like everyone else?" Sebastian snarled at her, "Why are you so desperate to be my friend?"

"Because I think you need one," she said, "Because I know you're not as bad as you want everyone to think you are."

"And what if I'm worse?"

"I don't think you're as bad as you think you are either." For the briefest moment she saw something other than fury in his eyes, the slightest flicker of muscles in his face softening. Anyone without her powers would have never noticed but she saw it and she knew she was right about him.

"Why do you hate yourself so much Sebastian, what can you have possibly done?"

He clenched his jaw, looking like he wanted to tear her apart.

"Stay away from me," he said menacingly and he stalked away.

Elsa let him go, his scent hung in the air and she knew she could follow him if she wanted to. She decided not to as she heard the sound of his motorbike roaring away, although she knew she could catch him up. She'd pushed him too much, she could feel his resolve slip slightly on occasion, as if he wanted to let her in but couldn't. She had also got a sense of just how dangerous he could be, flashes of violence slipping through the cracks in his mind. She needed to take more time with him, get more used to her own abilities so she could read him better. One thing she was becoming more and more sure of was that Sebastian had a lot to hide.

# Why Don't You Just Tell Me I Stink?

------

"I guess I expected it to be more.." Elsa struggled to find the right words so as not to offend her father. Marcus had seized upon his daughters interest in his work as an opportunity to once again find some common ground with her and taken her in with him for the day. So far she had not been overly impressed.

"High tech?" He offered.

"I suppose so, like a top secret government lab, all white and stainless steel with lots of serious people in white coats and futuristic technology."

Marcus raised an eyebrow, "You don't want much do you?" he said, his chair creaking as he stood. The office he had shown Elsa to was what she imagined a reclusive university lecturers would look like. Predominantly brown and grey with a tiny window that barely provided light, let alone ventilation, precarious looking shelves holding folder after folder and book after book, stacked untidily with pieces of crumpled paper sticking out all over the place. There were at least four used coffee mugs that she could see masquerading as penicillin experiments and countless further coffee mug stains on the desk, window ledge and collection of papers and folders that lay strewn across every available surface. A small dustbin was a volcano of discarded paper and other detritus erupting onto the floor and the computer keyboard looked like it had it's own ecosystem. In short, it was a pretty disgusting tip and had Elsa had to worry about illness and disease, she probably wouldn't have even walked through the door.

She clearly couldn't hide her distaste and she was frankly shocked that Marcus could work in such conditions. He caught her look and chuckled, "Come with me," he said, leading her out. Elsa followed him back out of his pokey office and down the corridor to the lift. Once inside, her father pushed the emergency call button and a female voice came through the small speaker.

"How can I help?"

"Facility floor please Carol," Marcus replied and Elsa frowned a silent question at him. He just grinned the way he always had when he teased her.

"Certainly Dr Shaw." The woman's voice said and the lift began to move.

Elsa raised an eyebrow, just as Marcus had done to her. She never used to be able to do it before her 'change'; she'd always wanted to be able to just raise one eyebrow.

"You wanted 'more'?" Marcus asked, "Just wait. We have to keep what we do very carefully hidden Elsa, most of this building is of no use to us whatsoever. We really only use one floor, the rest is designed to mislead unexpected visitors. My office," he used his fingers to make air quotes, "Is specifically designed to make people want to spend as little time in it as possible."

The lifted hummed to a stop and the doors opened with a hiss. They stepped into a corridor which had much more of the look Elsa had been expecting. Glass double doors at the end slid open silently and a figure approached them. Elsa's nostrils curled and she took a step back. Marcus placed a hand on her arm, "It's all right, no one here is a threat to you."

"He smells like raw meat, and wet dog," she whispered.

"I am sorry my scent offends you," The man said, "Vampires and werewolves do not mix well, your scent is difficult for me to cope with too, no offence."

"You heard me, sorry, I didn't mean to be rude." Elsa would have blushed if she still could.

"We both have a keen sense of hearing and smell," the stranger explained, "No apology necessary, I am pleased to meet you Elsa." He held out an inordinately large and hairy hand, which she shook as firmly as she could, trying not to wipe her hand on her jeans afterwards. He smiled, or at least bared his teeth in an attempt at a smile and turned to shake her father's hand.

"Gray, it's good to see you back," said Marcus, "Any problems?"

"Nothing I couldn't handle."

Elsa could believe it. Her father was not a small man but Gray, whose broad and muscular physique towered over him by a good foot, dwarfed him.

"I have just settled our newest arrival," Gray continued, "You'll forgive me if I don't accompany you to see him," Elsa saw the briefest flicker of his eyes darting to her. Why don't you just tell me I stink? she thought glumly. Gray left the way they had come and she wasn't overly sorry he wasn't joining them.

"It was Gray who helped me track you that day. This is where we had to bring you at first," Marcus explained as she followed him down the corridor and through another set of doors. They reached a large and formidable looking steel door and Marcus touched his hand to a small screen on the wall next to it. There was a mechanical clucking sound as the doors locking mechanism released and the door swung smoothly open. Marcus hesitated before entering, "If you want to, I will show you how new vampires usually behave," he said, "It may help you appreciate how strong you are and how far you've come but I will understand if you don't want to see. I'm aware it could also be upsetting to see where you've come from; although you did have much more control than the young man we have in here."

"I'll be ok," Elsa assured him, she felt that the more information she had, however hard, could only help her to process and begin to understand better what had happened to her.

Marcus nodded and she followed him in. They were in a very small room with a large mirrored wall in front of him; Elsa looked at her father confused.

"It's two way glass," he explained, "The room on the other side is completely sealed off so unless I press certain switches here," he indicated to a control panel to his right, "We can't see or hear anything. Even you can't."

He was right, Elsa was getting absolutely no sense at all that there was anyone in the room other than her father and herself.

Marcus flicked a switch and the glass changed subtly, their reflections faded to mere ghosts and it took on a lighter tint. Elsa could now see into the other room and her eyes were drawn to the top left hand corner where a figure was curled up, feet on the wall, hands on the ceiling, it's back to them. She could clearly see the tension in it's muscles, a miniscule and rapid trembling over it's whole body that she knew her father wouldn't be able to see. She couldn't sense any emotion through the glass, or hear any noise.

"This is Lucca, we picked him up in Italy a couple of days ago and Gray has been ensuring he got to us safely. We have been having a lot of problems in Europe recently with new vampires. We have a team investigating at the moment but the clean up operation is proving incredibly time consuming, which is unfortunately the most probable reason so many new vampires are being created, to keep us busy."

"Can he see or hear us?" Elsa asked.

"Not yet," Marcus said, "We've been letting him rest for a moment but he does need to get it out of his system so .." Marcus reached to the control panel again and flicked a different switch. The tone of the glass changed subtly again, Elsa and Marcus' reflections disappeared altogether and now it was as if there were no barrier between them and Lucca's hunched form at all.

She saw the change in his muscles in slow motion as it happened. He sensed the change in the room as they became visible to him within millionths of a second and his body reacted before he probably even realised that it was.

He turned his head, twisting his body at an impossible looking angle, his features distorted in a horrific snarl, his eyes dark and red rimmed, teeth bared. He crawled along the ceiling, spider like and contorted, his expression simultaneously agonised and malevolent, and threw himself violently against the glass. Elsa could not hear his tortured animalistic howls and screams but she could see the chaotic distortion of those sounds in the air and was thankful for the sound proof glass. She could see Lucca had a beautiful face, slim, angular features, long dark eyelashes, model-perfect lips, but it was ruined at that moment. She could dimly remember that feeling out of being completely out of control, giving in to the vampire within. The vampire was not a beautiful creature. It took Luca and it broke him apart piece by piece, reassembling him in a nightmare of thrashing limbs, teeth and clawing hands. He attacked the glass with every ounce of new vampire strength and hunger he had, every fibre of his being focused on one goal, blood.

Elsa drew her face closer to the glass in grotesque fascination and corrected her assessment – almost every fibre of his being. Lucca was still in there, she caught flashes of desperation, of the boy he really was who hated what he was doing and wanted to stop. She understood in that moment how once-human vampires could be saved, how she was saved; they wanted it, they wanted more than anything to be saved. The serum allowed that want to override the need for blood so that they could push the vampire down and allow the human to shine back through.

All this Elsa saw and understood within a matter of seconds. Marcus' hand had barley left the control panel and he had just begun an involuntary jump back as Lucca hit the glass.

"He is fighting against the need for blood," Elsa observed as she could see that Luca was flying from one side of the room to the other, always coming back to the glass, trying to get at them, but also darting away as if human Lucca was trying to regain control.

Marcus nodded, "It is a good sign," he said, "Are you ok?"

"Yes," Elsa said, "It helps me to understand – things." She looked at her father raising one eyebrow once more, the other one this time, just because she could, "You never told me I could crawl on the ceiling." She said, "Have you been holding out on me Dad? What else can I do?"

# Good Evening Ladies.

------------------------------------------------

✱ AN - for those following the soundtrack to this book, I've chosen Hybrid Theory by Lnkin Park for this chapter :) *

She'd been flippant after watching Lucca, it was the way she often dealt with difficult emotions. Unfortunately, sleepless nights gave Elsa a lot of time to dwell on difficult emotions and one thing she had certainly found since her change was that vampirism was like having permanent PMT. She swung violently at times from awe and wonder at what she was capable of and revulsion and hatred for what she had become. She found herself wondering what her face had looked like when she had been crouched over that vile man in the alleyway when her father found her. Had her eyes flashed, dark and dangerous? Had her lips formed that vicious snarl? Had her features twisted into the same nightmare vision that Lucca had displayed? They were not nice thoughts.

With a sigh, Elsa opened her wardrobe, she was going out to a concert with Kate. One of their favourite bands was playing locally, it was too good an opportunity to miss out on so she packed her emergency serum doses in her bag, threw on some clothes and was out the door in seconds without bothering to check the mirror.

A couple of hours later they were pushing their way to the front of the heaving throng of rock fans to drool over the lead singer. The music was thumping and throbbing and with every sweaty body crushed so tightly together Elsa began to quickly fear she had bitten of more than she could chew, so to speak. She may not have needed to breath the air but the stuffiness of it and the heat was nauseating. Along with the pulse of the music, she could hear the beat of every heart in the room, calling to her seductively. Kate was excited, her hair clung to her face, which was beaded with sweat, Elsa was conscious that she was not sweating at all.

"This is awesome!" Kate screamed, jumping up and down with the beat. It was pretty cool, Elsa had discretely used a little of her new found strength to ease their passage through the crowd, they had never managed to get this close to the front before. She tried to shut out the pulsing sound of blood in the veins of unsuspecting humans all around her, remembering instead that she had her serum and that she could control her urges.

She tried to focus on the band and looked up straight at the lead singer, who was half way through a lead guitar solo when he caught her gaze. Their eyes locked, which shocked her, it was like he actually was looking at her. Actually he was staring at her. He stumbled on a note and was jolted back to his guitar playing. Elsa couldn't help but revel in the idea that she might actually be able to pull a rock star now. She quickly reminded herself though that it was only because of what she was.

She felt another set of eyes on her and turned to find a tall, lean and incredibly handsome man watching her with a predatory gaze. He really was striking with intricate tattoos covering most of the flesh he had on display, which was a fair amount as he wasn't wearing a top. He had dark, long hair, almost black eyes, a sexy shadow of stubble and a body that was extremely pleasing to the eye, enhanced by the tattoos that snaked around every perfectly sculpted muscle. Kate gave her an elbow and a wink, noticing the strangers stare but he was making Elsa feel uncomfortable.

There was something about his look, the way he was moving, the way he seemed to stand out from everyone else around him.

He wasn't sweating either. She concentrated and realised that she couldn't see the pulse of blood in his body, couldn't hear the drum beat of a human heart.

He leaned in close and despite the loud music, she could hear him clearly, his voice like the sound warm water running over ice, "Nice," he said, "Is she yours or can anyone play?"

Elsa stepped back, ensuring she was between the vampire and her friend, "She doesn't belong to anyone," she said in a low voice, knowing that he would hear her.

"Oh, you're one of those," he sounded disappointed, "What a shame, we could have had some fun with her." His gaze fell on Kate once more, "I don't mind playing with her by myself." he said, head tilted to one side.

"No." Elsa stated.

"No?" The vampire laughed, "I hardly think you are going to stop me, I like her. I want her." His voice had quickly lost its honeyed tone and his last sentence was delivered with a menace that filled Elsa with dread. She grabbed Kate's arm and began to pull her out of the crowd.

Kate resisted, "What are you doing?" she asked incredulously, "The bass player was looking right at me!"

Elsa dragged her out into the bar, "We're leaving," she said, "Just trust me, we need to go." She fumbled in her bag for her phone, intent on calling her father. She had no idea who the vampire was but he didn't seem to be the kind that wanted to reconnect with his human side.

"What happened?" Kate asked, "Did that bloke grope you? You should tell one of security. Being sexy is no excuse for being a perv." She folded her arms, looking concerned. Elsa's head snapped round, she knew that he was following them.

"Can we please go?" she implored and, without waiting for an answer, began pulling at Kate's arm again until they were outside.

"Elsa!"

"Good evening ladies." Elsa kicked herself. He was already outside. There was no one around but them; she'd dragged Kate into a perfect ambush. She positioned herself once more between Kate and the vampire but he just smiled and tutted at her as if she were a small child, walking towards them at a steady pace and backing them down an alleyway before Elsa realised what was happening. "Don't be silly now," he said, "I'm older and stronger and better at this than you."

Kate's demeanor had changed, Elsa could hear her pulse quicken and could smell the adrenaline in her blood; she was scared. Elsa didn't know what to do but she knew she had to protect her friend, she was desperately recalling everything Hesper had told her about vampires vulnerabilities, there weren't many. Could she do it? She knew she was unusually strong for a young vampire, Hesper had told her so, that could be her advantage.

"Kate," she said, trying to sound as calm as possible, "Run."

"I'm not leaving you," Kate whispered back her voice shaking.

"No, she's right Kate, it's more fun if you run, it gets the blood pumping." the vampire snarled, and Elsa could see the change in his eyes as he released himself to the thirst for blood. His skin changed colour to an ominous gray, the skin around his eyes almost purple, veins protruding in his temples and his neck. His lips curled back, his mouth opened and only then did the fangs appear. Kate screamed as he leapt.

Elsa threw herself in his path and his hands tore at her viciously, long nails gouging her skin. She didn't feel any pain, she knew what she had to do and she clung onto him, maneuvering herself behind him so that she could reach around his neck from behind. He had not expected this and did not react in time; she placed one hand on his head and twisted with all her strength, satisfied to hear a snap as his neck broke and the vampire dropped to the ground.

Kate stared at the scene that was unfolding in front of her, it had happened so fast she couldn't really register what had occurred. She had seen a blur of movement and now Elsa stood over the fallen stranger and his head was twisted at an impossible angle. She began to shake violently and mumble incoherently.

Elsa knew that the vampire would heal quickly; a broken neck would only give them minutes. She had no choice now; she grabbed Kate, swung her over her shoulder and ran.

# Knock Back A Triple Whiskey.

-------------------------------------------------------

It took her minutes to get home. Kate was clearly in shock and Elsa placed her carefully on the sofa then stood staring at her friend at a complete loss for what to do next. Would the vampire be able to follow her scent back here? How long would it take him to heal from a broken neck?

"Elsa?" Her father stood in the doorway and suddenly she was struck by how much she needed him in that moment. For all her strength, speed and invulnerability, when it came down to hoping to make any sense of the new life she'd been flung into and it's dangers, she was a lost little girl who still needed her daddy.

"Dad!" she cried, "Something happened." She looked back at Kate as if that was enough explanation for him and he quickly moved to the trembling girl and placed a soothing hand on her shoulder. Kate's glassy stare began to focus on him and she moved her mouth as if she was trying to speak.

"Get my bag from the hall Elsa," Marcus said with concern etched on his face, "I can make Kate comfortable then we'll talk." Elsa was holding his bag out to him before he'd even finished speaking. He took out the medical kit he always carried and proceeded to administer an injection to Kate, muttering calmly to her the whole time. Her breathing and trembling began to slow and her eyes became heavy; within second, Marcus was lying her down and covering her with a throw.

"It's a sedative," he explained, "You'd be surprised how often we need to calm civilians down in my job."

"Not after tonight I wouldn't." Elsa was pacing the living room, her fear beginning to give way to anger.

"What happened?" Marcus asked.

"There was a vampire at the gig," she said, her fists clenched, "He seemed to think I'd taken Kate along so I'd have something to snack on later and he wanted me to share."

Marcus went white, "And you got away?" he whispered, "How?"

"I broke his neck." Elsa said it matter-of-factly but as she did, the enormity of it hit her, "Oh god, I broke his neck, I broke his neck Dad!"

Marcus put his arms around her, "Shhhhh," he soothed, "It's ok. You did what you did to protect Kate, you didn't kill anyone and ultimately, you didn't hurt anyone."

"I felt his neck snap," she murmured into his shoulder, "I did that with my own hands and I didn't care, I didn't even hesitate."

Marcus pushed her gently away so he could look her in the eyes, "What you did Elsa, was control a dangerous situation without anyone getting hurt. That vampire will heal. You are incredibly lucky you were able to do what you did, you must be so much stronger than even Hesper thought. You're such a new vampire, I can only assume he must have been relatively new too."

"He seemed very assured and confident," said Elsa, doubting her father's assessment that the vampire was young, "Do you think he could follow us?"

Marcus shook his head, "I doubt it," he said, "Your scent won't linger long enough, by the time he wakes up there will be nothing to follow."

"You doubt it?" Elsa looked questioningly at her father, "You can't be sure?"

"Even if he did find his way here, he can't come in if he isn't invited."

Elsa was shocked, "That's a thing?" she asked.

"Oh yes," said Marcus, "I thought Hesper had filled you in on all this stuff?"

Elsa shook her head, "That one hadn't come up."

"Well, it's a thing," said Marcus, "You could come into this house because it's your home. Places like college and the concert venue are open to the public, you don't need an invite then but if you were to try and walk into a private home, you wouldn't be able to cross the threshold unless someone asked you to."

"Oh, well that's useful to know," Elsa was once again struck by how much she had to learn, "That could have caused me all sorts of awkward situations." She looked across at Kate who was sleeping but had a frown that suggested she was not sleeping soundly, "What am I going to tell her?"

"The sedative I gave her will also cause some amnesia," Marcus reassured her, "We'll tell her she fainted, that you called me and I picked you both up."

Elsa nodded. More lies she would have to tell her friend, the bigger the web got, the harder it would be to remember them and Elsa had a feeling this would not be the last time she would lie to Kate, "We should call her parents," she said.

"Lets just wait a little while longer," Marcus suggested, "Until we're sure we aren't going to get any – visitors." He stood up and motioned for Elsa to follow him to the kitchen, "I think you need a drink."

Elsa screwed up her nose, she had not yet brought herself to accept hunting lessons from Hesper and was surviving on a diet of hospital style blood bags, which did the job but were not a pleasant substitute for warm blood pumping from the vein.

"I mean a real drink," Marcus said, noticing her look and taking a bottle of whiskey out of one of the kitchen cupboards, "You may not need to drink for hydration Elsa but it doesn't mean that alcohol won't have the relaxing effect I think you need right now." He poured two sizable shots and handed one to his daughter.

She looked at him incredulously, "You don't want me to have a motorbike, which I am legally allowed to do, but you're happy for me to knock back a triple whiskey when I'm underage?" she asked.

Marcus shrugged, "You keep telling me," he said, "Things have changed. I need to stop wishing they hadn't and actually start helping you instead of expecting you to be exactly the same Elsa you always were."

Elsa took the glass and stared into the rich golden liquid inside. Her father's words stung, "You want your old daughter back," she said sadly.

Marcus put his hand under her chin and tilted her head up, looking at her earnestly, "No," he said, "I wish this hadn't happened to you, but don't you ever think that it changes the way I feel about you. You are my daughter and I love you no matter what. I don't think I've been doing a very good job of making that clear to you."

Elsa felt tears sting her eyes, "I thought you were scared of me, disgusted at what I'd become."

"No Elsa, I'm proud of you," Marcus insisted, "I was disgusted with myself for not seeing what was happening and helping you sooner. I was scared that you would blame me and hate me and I couldn't think of any reason why you shouldn't feel that way. You have handled this so much better than I have."

"It wasn't your fault Dad," Elsa said quietly, feeling like a weight had been lifted as she hugged her father, "I know I've been difficult since – I could have handled it better too."

Marcus hugged her back and then chinked his glass against hers, "So what we have here then, sounds like a perfectly normal father daughter relationship to me," he grinned but his eyes were brimming with tears too.

"Cheers to that," Elsa agreed and they both took a long drink, Elsa enjoying the warmth of the whiskey flowing down her throat and trying not to think that it reminded her of blood, it had been a while since her last injection, "Are there many vampires just wandering around in public like that?" she asked.

"Not really," said Marcus, "There are three types of vampire in this world. Those like you who embrace their human side and choose not to feed on human blood; vampires who feed on humans but stay under the radar, keeping their activities discreet and relatively humane; and finally there are those who believe that vampires are at the top of the food chain and everything else is merely there to provide them with food and entertainment."

"The one I met tonight definitely fits in that category," Elsa said.

"And that is the category that Haven is most concerned with," said Marcus, "They are driven by a need for all vampires to follow their thinking and they will stop at nothing to recruit others to their cause. They make new vampires and train them in their beliefs and they have been known to try and turn vampires that we have rehabilitated back to more bloodthirsty pursuits."

"That doesn't sound good." Elsa thought about Lucca and how easy it would be for a vampire like the one she had met tonight to make him forget his human side.

"It's not," Marcus agreed, "And where there is one vampire with those kinds of beliefs, there will be more, which is why I need to put my work head on now and ask you to tell me everything you can remember about the man you met tonight."

# From The Roaring Flames Of Hell.

✱ AN - For those of you following the soundtrack to this book, it has to be Bring Me Back To Life by Evanessence for this one :) *

Kate remembered nothing about their encounter with the vampire. Her mother went into fuss overdrive, believing her daughter had fainted and convincing herself it had something to do with the head injury she'd sustained after their car accident. That seemed so long ago to Elsa now.

At any rate, Kate was immediately put under house arrest 'for her own protection' and Elsa was left without her friend for a few days. This meant no one to talk to and alhough she couldn't share many of her new worries with Kate, she did wish she could talk to her about Sebastian and his continued black mood and aversion to her company. The further he pushed her away, the more she found she wanted to know about him. She'd almost forgotten that she fancied him at all; he had become a research project of sorts.

Her other research project was herself. After watching Lucca climbing across the ceiling and realising the possibilities of her own strength when she'd fought with the vampire that had tried to attack Kate, Elsa had spent a lot of time talking to Hesper about exactly what she was and was not capable of. It turned out the 'was not' list was pretty damn short.

Today she was trying to take her mind off the fact that it was her dads birthday, a painful reminder that everyone she loved was continuing to age without her and that her friends and family would eventually be gone, leaving her alone and eternally seventeen. Elsa had discovered some empty industrial buildings just outside of town, nice and remote with no one around. In the spirit of research, she decided this would be the perfect place to explore some of her new talents. She had made her way to the highest pint of the building she could find, deftly climbing the outside of the building. Spiderman has nothing on me.

Elsa stood on the edge of the roof on the tips of her toes. Her balance was perfect and she felt totally confident. She leaned forward as far as she could without falling and smiled to herself, marveling at how easy it was, secure in the knowledge that even if she did fall, she would be fine. Broken bones would heal and she would feel very little pain. A fall from this height couldn't kill her. Hesper had told her there were only two kown ways to kill a vampire. You must remove either the heart or the head completely from the body ... Elsa could see why her dad hadn't wanted to talk to her about it. It was exhilarating leaning into the empty air, knowing she couldn't really be hurt didn't stop it being exciting, but still the idea of even a little bit of pain in the event of a fall made her ensure she kept her balance. She knew though, that if she was careful, she should simply be able to jump from this height and land perfectly on the ground below as if she had just hopped off a step. She lifted one foot off the roof and spread her arms then, because she couldn't resist trying it at least once, she jumped.

There was a whooshing noise and a body slammed into her from nowhere, strong arms grabbed her tightly and all of a sudden she was being unceremoniously dumped inside the building on a dusty floor.

"What the hell were you doing? Trying to kill yourself?" her would be saviour was stood over her, his face contorted in anger.

"Sebastian?"

He clenched his fists obviously furious but that was not what was holding Elsa's attention. It was the two huge, black feathered wings sprouting from his back, arching up above his head and reaching right down to the floor. There as a sheen of sweat on his skin, his features were more prominent somehow, more angular, and there were ridges on his back where the smoother contour of his spine should have been. But those wings, Elsa thought they were the most breathtaking thing she had ever seen.

"Are you an angel?" she asked breathlessly, he looked so beautiful standing in shadow with just a dim light shining through a grimy window to highlight the contours of his body and the glossy black feathers of his wings.

His fists unclenched, his shoulders dropped and she could hear his heart rate slow and feel the utter despair he was feeling inside so keenly it broke her heart. He turned away from her.

"I'm the devil Elsa," he said. "You need to leave now."

"I'm not leaving," she said, standing up, "Devils don't save people who throw themselves off buildings."

"I should have let you fall," he said, "Now I have to leave again just when things were becoming more normal."

"What do you mean? You don't have to go anywhere, I won't tell anyone about your..." she wasn't quite sure what to say. "What were you doing there anyway, when I jumped?"

"I live here," he said, "I heard something on the roof and got there just in time to see you throw yourself off." he looked at her with a pained expression on his face, "Why would you do that?" he asked, "You've got everything to live for, you're young and beautiful, you've got friends and family, no worries, no responsibilities, a future. You have no idea what it is truly like to have no reason to live and every reason to die."

"I wasn't trying to…" Elsa shook her head, "That's how you feel?" she asked quietly.

"It's what I deserve."

"But you're still alive?"

Sebastian gave a bitter laugh, "Oh, I've tried." he said and he picked up a can from a workbench, emptying it's liquid contents all over the floor. "If my appearance won't convince you to stay away from me, maybe this will."

He placed a hand in his pocket and drew out a lighter, lighting it and throwing it to the floor. He did not flinch as the flames engulfed him and held her gaze through the golden shimmer of flame looking all at once both defiant and utterly, hopelessly lost.

"I've tried everything," he said simply, "I can't die."

Elsa did not look away, she could barely breath but she did not hesitate and stepped forward reaching her hand into the flames until she was just inches from touching Sebastian's chest, where she could see the pulse of his heart beating powerfully beneath his skin. "Then we are more alike than you realise," she said softly, wincing slightly as she withdrew her hand and held it up for him to see as the blistered skin healed and became cool and ivory smooth once more. Sebastian stepped back, his eyes searching hers, his expression one of shock and confusion.

"You are … like me?" It was a question tinged with hope and Elsa felt so powerfully his anguish she could hardly bear to be near him. Suddenly aware of the ridiculous picture they must present, he with his enormous, black wings curved about his shoulders and she standing on the other side of the flames looking like Joan of Arc at the stake, she stepped back, broke his gaze and turned away, "I am similar to you in many ways I think," she said, so much about Sebastian beginning to make sense to her now, "but not quite the same."

She looked back to see Sebastian turn away from her, walking to the edge of the room, his wings retreating back into his body leaving only two angry red welts down his shoulder blades. The ridges in his spie had smoothed and, as he sat on the floor, his back against the wall, Elsa could see that his features had also returned to normal. Her senses were reeling; she had not expected to meet anyone out here and had foolishly left her medication at home. The beat of Sebastian's heart was sending pulses of heat through her body. She could smell him, his fear and loathing of himself, his adrenalin, his sweat, and his deep, deep sadness. She could smell his blood. She forced herself to walk towards him once more, trying not to inhale his scent as she sat on the floor near to him, but not close. The fire continued to burn, the shadows it threw highlighting his features, making him look like a beautiful, perfect statue carved by a tortured hand.

"Explain this to me," he asked quietly, "What are you? What am I? Are there others?"

"I don't know what you are," she answered truthfully, "I, apparently, am a vampire." She saw his muscles tighten, so aware was she of him now she could virtually hear the friction of muscle fibres moving against one another. She expected him to look at her in horror, to get up and walk away, to never look back but instead he simply looked at her and asked, "Have you killed people?"

"No - almost," her answer was delivered quickly and she looked to the floor, not wanting to remember but somehow knowing that Sebastian needed to know everything, needed to know he wasn't alone, "Someone stopped me."

"Did you want to kill them?"

"Yes."

"Did they deserve to die?"

"Yes – I – I don't know."

"You need to know, it is the only way you can ever sleep at night."

"I don't sleep." She wanted to ask him why he had asked her the question, had he killed people? She wanted to ask but everything about him told her that she already knew the answer and that he might not be ready to go there yet.

They sat in silence for a few minutes and when Sebastian spoke again, it was as if his voice was far away, as if he was speaking from another time, another place, a place where Elsa could never go. "I crave the blood and flesh of humans everyday. I have forced myself, over many years, to control the hunger but I can only do it for so long, then it becomes too much and I know I will get to a point when I will lose control. When that happens I have to make sure I'm somewhere I can't hurt anyone who doesn't deserve it. The hunger has to be satisfied, the best I can do is try and use it to rid the world of people who have as little right to life as me." His jaw was set and he spoke through clenched teeth, his hands pulled once more into tight fists, "I remember little but I know that no matter what they've done, the people that I choose, I can never be sure they deserved to die like that."

Elsa wanted to speak, wanted to tell him that she understood how it felt, the need to kill no matter how much you didn't want to. But her head was throbbing in unison with the beat of Sebastian's heart. His blood was so powerful, the scent of it so much more intoxicating than any human.

Her own blood rushed in her ears and she closed her eyes, trying to breath steadily through the desire to tear out Sebastian's throat.

"Elsa, are you ok?" for the first time Elsa heard something other than sadness or anger in Sebastian's voice, he was concerned and the tentative touch of his hand on her arm sent a bolt of electricity through her body which snapped her out of her violent, lust for his blood. She jumped up.

"I'm sorry, I have to go." was all she could manage and it took all her strength to turn and run away. To Sebastian, one moment she was there, an angel emerging from the roaring flames of hell, the next she and the flames were gone, the sheer speed of her departure sucking the oxygen momentarily from the space where she had stood and stopping the fire in it's tracks. Sebastian sat in darkness, alone again and more confused than ever.

At home, Elsa began to breathe more easily as the serum did its work. As her mind cleared and she lay on the bed that was of little use to her anymore, images of Sebastian filled her thoughts. Could she tell her father about him? No, first she needed to know what he was; what if he was on the 'kill on sight' list her father had told her about? We have a ist of demons and supernatural beings that are too dangerous to be rehabilitated, that are beyond the help of Haven I'm afraid. She couldn't allow herself to imagine Sebastian dying, she wasn't even sure if he could be killed, he said he couldn't die but the organisation had found ways to rid the world of so many demons, maybe they had a way. Sebastian's desire to die terrified her; she would not risk introducing him to the very people that may be able to make it possible. She wanted so badly to tell him that there may be a way to stop his cravings, but she knew she couldn't give him that hope unless she was sure. She remembered him standing in the flames, his body so strong, his spirit so broken and she hated herself for leaving him behind. When he'd touched her, that split second his fingertips had made contact with her skin, she'd felt something so intense that the mere memory of it made her breath catch in her throat, her pulse quicken. The attraction she'd always felt towards him was now etched with white-hot flame into her very soul and somehow she knew there would never be anyone else for her but him. In each other they had understanding and hope for the future. She'd felt it and she'd sensed it in him to, hope that together they could be more than the monsters they feared they were.

# The Birds And The Bees.

-------------------------------------------------

✱ A/N - for those of you following the soundtrack to this book, it's Eternal Life by Jeff Buckley for this one! *

At breakfast the following morning Elsa was distracted by thoughts of Sebastian.

"Everything ok sweetheart?" Her father's voice interrupted the tangle of emotions and questions in her mind.

"Hmm? Yes fine," she said absently.

"It's just you're eating breakfast." Marcus nodded at the spoon in Elsa's hand, which contained a good serving of cereal and was dripping milk. He had not seen Elsa eat actual food since she'd come home from the clinic. The fact was, she only ate food now when people who expected it as normal behaviour were watching.

Elsa put the spoon down, she must have fixed herself breakfast on autopilot, an old habit that had crept back in whilst her mind was elsewhere. She couldn't help but smile, "I was miles away," she admitted.

"Anything I can help with?" Marcus asked earnestly.

"No, it's fine Dad, really. Just usual teenage angst." She stood up to exchange the pointless cereal for a blood bag from the fridge, which she decanted into a mug and popped in the microwave, a little trick Hesper had told her to make it more palatable. Her father didn't bat an eyelid at that but he was studying his daughter carefully.

"Boy problems?" he asked.

"You could say that," Elsa took a sip from her mug and allowed the warm blood to slide slowly and luxuriously down her throat.

A pained expression crossed Marcus' face, "That's something we need to talk about," he said.

Elsa rolled her eyes, "I don't need the birds and the bees talk Dad."

"That's not what I mean."

"Oh," Elsa hadn't even thought, her dad was worried she could hurt a potential boyfriend, or that she could draw them in against their will, "Ok I get it, it's nothing like that, nothing you need to worry about," she sighed, "Just someone I have to work with in history who is a bit difficult."

Marcus visibly relaxed, "Oh right," he said, "I'm sorry Elsa, you understand why I worry? I just don't want you to get hurt."

"Or anyone else," she said and Marcus looked stung. "Sorry Dad, I didn't mean it like that, I hadn't really thought about the effect I can have on boys or what it could lead to. I did need reminding, thanks."

"It's ok," he said and gave her a kiss on the forehead as he walked past her and into the hallway, picking up his keys and briefcase, "I'm off, have a good day today."

"You too," Elsa finished off her drink and rinsed the mug before putting it in the dishwasher. She didn't like putting a mug upside down in the dishwasher for the last bits of blood to drip out of it and onto the plates below, it just didn't seem right somehow. She had her suspicions that her father paid close attention to the mug she used and discreetly chose not to use it himself. To be fair to him she didn't bring it up, just made sure she always used the same mug.

Elsa arrived at college alone; Kate was taking a couple more days off after her doctor had advised rest following her mysterious and unexplained fainting episode. She had a free first but was planning to hit the library and get ahead start on next term so she could get away with skipping a few lessons if the fancy took her. She had her earphones in and Jeff Buckley's Eternal Life blasting into her ears, smiling to herself at the somewhat applicable lyrics. Eternal life is now on my trail, got my red glitter coffin man, just need one last nail. She was glad she didn't need a coffin but if she had, a sparkly red one would have been acceptable.

She sensed him as he appeared beside her and grabbed her arm, pulling her into an empty classroom. The touch of his hand, even through her layers of clothing, had no less impact. Her heart flipped, if that was still possible and the breath she didn't need caught in her throat. She pulled her earphones out and looked up into his steely glare, so he was still not happy to see her then.

"Have you said anything?" he demanded, releasing her arm and pacing between her and the door.

"Of course not," she said, "I told you I wouldn't, who'd believe me anyway?"

He relaxed slightly, stopped pacing and stole a look at her, the coldness giving way to a glimmer of hope.

"Did all of that really happen yesterday?" he asked, as if he dared not believe it.

Elsa perched on the edge of a table, "Yes," she said, "Now we both know, at least sort of know, what we are."

"You ran away." It was a statement, he wasn't asking her why.

"I had to," she patted the space on the table next to her, surprised at her own boldness and equally surprised when Sebastian actually sat there. She liked having him close to her, his smell was intoxicating. She was dosed up and in control, she could enjoy his aroma without feeling homicidal, "I was losing control of my need for blood, I might have hurt you."

Sebastian actually laughed then, just a short laugh but it was a sound she hadn't heard from him before. It changed his features, his demeanor, my god he's gorgeous. "You? Hurt me?" He shook his head and if the grin on his face hadn't been so wonderful to see, she would probably have been quite annoyed with him.

"You don't know much about vampires do you?" she asked.

"I don't know anything," he admitted, "I didn't know they even existed." He frowned at her, "Are you sure that's what you are? You walk around in daylight and I swear I saw you eating garlic bread the other day."

It was her turn to laugh whilst her brain also stored the knowledge that he had been watching her closely enough to notice what she had for lunch, "Myths," she said. Like she was the expert, it wasn't so long ago she would have had no clue herself, "Stakes and crosses are rubbish too apparently."

A few moments of silence followed, Sebastian was clearly not used to keeping a conversation going.

"What are you?" Elsa asked eventually and she could feel him stiffen.

"I don't know," he said, his voice low.

"Have you always been this way?"

"As long as I can remember."

"And you haven't met anyone else – like you?"

Sebastian shook his head, she could feel his walls coming down slightly, "I don't remember ever having any family, I've always been alone."

"How long?"

Sebastian looked into her eyes, as if he was searching for the assurance that he could tell her things he had never told anyone, "I'm pretty old," he said eventually.

Elsa stared straight back at him, "I'm pretty much immortal," she said casually, trying to lighten the mood and help him relax, "It's a recent development."

He smiled and her heart jumped again, she was so ridiculously pleased that she had made him smile.

"What do we do now?" he said, "You're a vampire and I'm a – whatever it is I am. Are there more like us?"

"There is so much I need to tell you," Elsa said with a grin and hesitated before placing her hand on Sebastian's arm, her face becoming serious. He flinched slightly but didn't move it away, "You're not alone anymore."

All at once his tumultuous emotions washed over her like a tidal wave, his defences cracked and it all flowed forward, making her gasp and release his arm to grip the table edge and steady herself.

Sebastian jumped up, concerned and stood in front of her suddenly, holding her shoulders, "Elsa, are you ok? I'm sorry."

She shook her head as the wave subsided and she regained control, "It's ok," she gasped, "I'm very sensitive to what people are feeling and you feel things so strongly, it took me off guard."

"I'm sorry," he said again, stepping back from her, "I've always been able to tell you were very in tune with the way I was feeling, I've worked really hard to keep myself closed off but when you said that; when you said I wasn't alone…" His voice trailed off.

"I'm fine," she insisted and loosened her grip on the table edge. Two fist sized chunks of table fell to the floor and Sebastian raised an eyebrow, "You are stronger than you look," he said.

"That's nothing, you should see what I did to the wall in the humanities corridor." She picked a large splinter from her palm and watched her skin close up almost instantly, she could feel Sebastian's eyes on her, "Pain has to be pretty intense for me to feel it," she said, "And I can heal from almost any injury."

"Almost any?"

"There are a couple of ways to deal with vampires on a more permanent basis if you need to," Elsa said, "They aren't all as nice as me you know."

"Have you always been this way?" Sebastian asked.

She shook her head, "It's a long story," she said, "One I'd like to tell you, if you want to hear it?"

"I – I do want to," Sebastian looked awkward, "I'm not very good at this."

"What, normal conversation?" Elsa asked, "Although I suppose it's not exactly normal conversation if you think about it." She could sense it was a struggle for him to let anyone in, to talk about the thoughts that clearly tortured him everyday, "Look, I have only just begun to get my head around what has happened to me over the last few months, you have obviously struggled for a lot longer. Maybe we could help each other? Maybe I could help you deal with some of the things that you find most difficult about what you are."

"How?"

"Like I said, there's a lot I need to tell you, too much to fit in one free lesson. I could come and see you back at your place later?" The words spilled out before she had chance to stop them. She had never in her life invited herself to the home of anyone she had an undeniable attraction to, she could never usually even pluck up the courage to talk to them.

Sebastian looked a little surprised, then confused, then – something else she couldn't put her finger on because her own emotions were wreaking havoc inside her.

"Sure," he said at last, stretching the word out slowly as if testing it's meaning and impact.

"Do you own the building?" Elsa asked.

"What?" Confusion again.

"If you do you have to invite me in."

"Oh, right. Er – no I don't own it but you were already inside."

"Good point," Elsa wrinkled her nose slightly in thought, "I still don't know exactly how it works, just keep your eye out for me, incase I can't get in."

Sebastian nodded and then looked down at his feet, "Thank you Elsa," he said quietly.

"What for?" she said.

"For not being afraid of me."

# You Like Bikes?

"So how do you survive without killing?"

Sebastian and Elsa were sat on the warehouse roof, their feet dangling over the edge. It was mid November and the nights drew in quickly; Sebastian's breath created a swirling mist in the icy air but neither of them were cold as they sat and talked for hours.

"My father keeps me supplied with blood bags," Elsa explained, she had already told Sebastian about Haven and her father's work there. He had been very interested in the idea that medications could be developed to curb blood lust, "And Hesper keeps offering to take me hunting."

"Hunting?"

"Yeh, like going on a safari or something and chasing down some lions," Elsa wrinkled her nose, "Part of me feels excited by the idea, but the part that feels disgusted keeps winning."

Sebastian laughed. Elsa adored the sound, she had definitely gone back into full crush mode and even if she hadn't, she was sure that the mere impact that Sebastian's presence seemed to have on her both physically and mentally would have drawn her in by now. It was like she had no control over it and she wondered if he had similar powers to her for attracting prey. She couldn't quite figure out how to ask him.

"How do you survive?" She asked and she felt the familiar tensing of muscles as his face clouded and he struggled to protect her from his emotions.

"I haven't found a way to survive without killing," he said and paused as if giving her chance to show her horror. She didn't, this was something she knew about Sebastian and in truth she had always known it. He was dangerous, she felt it strongly but just as strongly she felt the anguish it caused him and she knew that it was not the way he wanted to be. She couldn't be horrified with him, if she hadn't had the support of her father and Haven would she have been any different?

"It's ok," she said, "You can tell me, if I understand, maybe I can help." She had explained her reasons for not yet taking him to Haven. When Sebastian had asked what criteria had to be met to qualify for help she had to admit she wasn't sure. Vampires and werewolves that were once human could be put back in touch with their human side but neither she nor Sebastian knew if any part of him had ever been human and until she knew he wasn't one of the black listed supernatural beings that her father had mentioned, she wasn't going to risk his safety. The more she knew about Sebastian, the more chance she had of finding out what he was.

"I can last quite a while these days," Sebastian continued, "Two months, sometimes three. The hunger builds slowly and I've found ways of dulling it for as long as possible."

"Like what?"

Sebastian looked uncomfortable, "I'm not sure I want to talk about it." He said. Elsa didn't want to push him.

"Ok," she said, "What happens when you can't dull it anymore?"

"I go somewhere that I know I will find the people this world will miss the least. I can smell them out and after looking for as many decades as I have, you know the best places." He looked at her, his face pained, "I'm not ready to go into this," he said, "I don't want you to know…" his voice trailed off.

"I understand," Elsa said, wanting to reach out and touch him but painfully aware that she had no idea if that would be welcome.

"I'm going to ask my dad to take me into work with him again," she said, "There's a massive library there, I'll look up all the things you've told me and see if I can find out what you are and if it's safe to bring you in."

Sebastian nodded, "Thank you," he said, "I'm sorry I've been so rude to you in the past, I've always kept people at a distance because I didn't want to risk …"

"I get it," Elsa said, "I pushed everyone away at first, when I changed. Before I even understood what was happening I knew I was a danger to the people I cared about."

"I can't remember the last time I had someone to care about." Sebastian murmured and Elsa couldn't help wishing she might be someone he could have those feelings for.

"So," she said, hoping to lighten the mood slightly, "Decades? You said you were pretty old."

Sebastian seemed relieved to get off the topic of how dangerous he was, "My earliest clear memories are of the Second World War," he said and Elsa raised her eyebrows in surprise.

"No way? You lived through that?"

He nodded, "I don't really remember much of my early life, just little flashes here and there. I was eighteen before I first started thirsting for blood and the first few years after that are a blur mercifully. But the war; I think I remember because, as bloody and horrific as my life had been up to that point, there were many days when the things that men do to one another in war easily matched it." His eyes became distant as he remembered, "I didn't have to kill to feed, that was done for me, I just had to be in the right place, wearing the right uniform, blending into the grotesque tapestry of the battlefields."

"That sounds terrible." Elsa couldn't imagine what it must have been like, when learning about the war in history the sheer scale of death and destruction had always overwhelmed her.

"It was, but it was also some of the most free years of my life," Sebastian admitted, "I feel guilty now of course. The soldiers may have been dead already but they deserved respect and dignity. I wish I'd known what was really happening, in the death camps for example, there were people far more worthy of the end I could bring them."

They were both quiet for a moment reflecting on the atrocities that had been committed against so many innocent people. Elsa had a thought, "Why do you study history if you were there?"

Sebastian gave a wry smile, "I wasn't there for all of it Elsa, there's much more to history that the 1920's an onwards. We learn from our mistakes, and history contains a lot of them."

"I suppose it does," she agreed. She didn't want to stop talking to Sebastian, he had a beautiful way of talking and she loved the sound of his voice. She was starting to feel fidgety though, she found it difficult to keep still for long periods of time such were the unboundless limits of her energy these days.

"Am I boring you?" Sebastian asked, looking amused.

"Not at all!" Elsa insisted, "I just find it hard to sit still sometimes. I've got so much energy and if I wanted to, I could probably run faster than the fastest car or motorbike. It'd be a great way to expel some energy but it would probably create a bit of a scene," she sighed, "I have enough money saved for a motorbike but Dad doesn't want me to get one. I know he can't really stop me but I don't want to rub that in his face you know? He's struggled to deal with the change in our relationship over the last couple of months."

"You like bikes?" Sebastian's face lit up and Elsa's heart skipped, she'd all but forgotten they had that in common and it was one of the first things Kate had pointed out to her back on their first day of college. It seemed like a lifetime ago.

"Yeh," she said shyly, "I really think it would help curb my need for speed in a less supernatural way."

"Come with me," Sebastian stood up and motioned for her to follow him down into the warehouse. He led her to the ground floor where she couldn't help but gasp at what he showed her.

"You're a fan of Suzuki?" She asked, stating the obvious if the gleaming machines in front of her were anything to go by.

"Oh yeh," Sebastian said, looking the most animated she'd ever seen him as he caressed the chrome of the nearest motorcycle, a Suzuki Bandit and Elsa's dream bike.

She stared at it in wonder, "That is the exact bike I've always wanted," she said and Sebastian looked surprise but pleased.

"Really? It'd be perfect for you actually, particularly now. Not too big, not too small, not too fast but definitely fast enough."

"It's gorgeous," Elsa breathed.

"You're head's not turned by the Hayabusa then?" Sebastian asked, leading her to the bike that was clearly his pride and joy, "She's my baby."

"A bit much for me," Elsa laughed then looked wistful, "I'm so jealous." She ran her hand over the tank of the Bandit longingly.

"You want a ride?"

Elsa's head snapped up at the question. "Seriously?" she asked.

"Of course," Sebastian said easily, "You said you're a quick learner, you don't really have to worry about coming off and you also said you were feeling restless. We could ride out together." Elsa wasn't sure if she imagined the slight flicker of his eyes away from hers when he said that, the hint of a blush to his cheeks.

"I don't know, I wouldn't want to damage it," she hesitated.

"Don't worry about that," Sebastian said, "Anything's fixable and with your balance and agility, there's no way you're coming off. Come on, it can be my way of saying thanks."

Elsa couldn't resist, "Ok!" she said enthusiastically, "I'd love to."

"Great," Sebastian looked genuinely pleased and was the most relaxed she had ever seen him as he talked her through all the controls and exactly what she needed to do. She barely needed the instruction, as she got on the bike it was as if she had always known what to do and in no time at all she was exhilarated by the fierce buffeting of the cold wind against her body as she followed Sebastian's taillight into the night.

# He's Fine Once You Get Him Talking.

---

"He's watching you." Kate twirled her spoon in her hot chocolate and whispered furtively at Elsa, "You've been getting on a lot better lately I've noticed."

Elsa rolled her eyes, "He's not watching me Kate, he's probably wondering why you're watching him and whispering to me. Could you be any less discreet?" Sebastian was, as usual sat alone in the canteen pretending to read a textbook and, Elsa was sure, highly aware he was being talked about.

Kate stuck her tongue out at Elsa, "He is hot, we're agreed on that," she said, "But you know he's trouble right?"

Elsa did but she wasn't about to confide Sebastian's darkest secrets to anyone, even her closest friend, "He's not that bad once you get to know him," she said, trying not to sound too defensive, "He's really helped me catch up in history, he knows his stuff."

Kate looked doubtfully over at Sebastian's hunched form, "That's the only reason you've been spending time with him?" she asked.

"Of course," Elsa lied, "I've had a lot of time off, I need all the help I can get. His social skills might not be the best but honestly, he's fine once you get him talking."

Kate's face became serious, "Just be careful ok?" she said earnestly.

"Chill out!" Elsa laughed, taking a bite of her sandwich. It didn't really taste of anything to her and she certainly didn't need it but she had to keep up appearances. Lies, lies, lie;, story of her life these days.

Kate's mobile chirped, she looked at the screen and then up at Elsa, "I'll be back in a minute," she said, "Signal's rubbish in here," she left the canteen answering her phone as she went. Elsa thankfully got up to throw her tasteless sandwich in the bin.

She paused by Sebastian's table on her way and he looked up from his book as she did. His intense eyes were ringed with dark shadows, his jaw line dark with stubble and his cheeks were beginning to take on the slightly sunken look they had a few months ago. She knew now what that meant.

"Hey," she said, "Are you ok?"

"I'm fine," Sebastian said and as he looked down to his book, Elsa saw the flicker of a smile, "Once you get me talking."

Elsa sat down and placed a hand on the page he was reading, "I knew you were listening," she said, "I'm just trying to get her to back off, you know that."

Sebastian held his hands up in mock defence, "I'm not offended," he said, "I appreciate it."

Elsa sat back and studied him, she felt him tense under her gaze, "So back to my original question," she said, "Are you ok?"

He wouldn't look her in the eye, "I'm dealing with it," he said.

Elsa sighed, they'd spent a lot of time together over the last few weeks, she'd really hoped he would be more open with her but those walls were still there, as impenetrable as ever. She had poured over books and computer files in Haven's library until her father began to ask questions but she could find no clue as to what Sebastian might be or how Haven might be able to help him. She'd compiled a long list of demons that Haven considered too dangerous to rehabilitate and, as far as demons went, that was pretty much all of them. Demons were never human, they had no humanity to tap into. The ones whose existence had been confirmed were now either presumed extinct or on the 'kill on sight' list. The ones whose existence was not confirmed were being actively searched for across the world and current research suggested that if they did exist, they weren't the sort of creatures you'd be bringing home to meet your parents. None of these demons, confirmed or not, matched Sebastian in any way but their feeding habits.

Asides from demons, Elsa was sure Sebastian was not a vampire or a werewolf. She had searched winged supernatural beings and was quite disappointed to find that Pegasus, fairies and dragons did not exist. In fact it seemed that pretty much anything that had wings in folklore and mythology that was nice didn't really exist. There was something similar to a Harpie that had been found in Bulgaria in the 1970's but after that particular nest had been destroyed, there had been no further sightings. They had all been female so Elsa concluded that Sebastian was not a Harpie and she hadn't mentioned it to him either as she was sure he would not have appreciated the suggestion that closest thing she'd found to him so far was a wizened, ugly, old winged woman.

She had looked up creatures drawn to blood and flesh, a particularly unpleasant line of investigation as it also meant facing the fact that she came under that category. The Alan had caught her eye at first; they existed, they had wings and she liked the fact that they were called Alan. However they were clearly described as being hideous and deformed, two things that Sebastian most certainly was not. They were quite sad creatures really, who used blood to try and make children of their own. Haven did not exterminate them but 'managed' them and made sure they did not pose a risk to humans. The Alan had no interest in killing humans and, as much as he didn't want to, Sebastian did. Another one to strike off the list.

The Chupacabra had no wings and a preference for goats; The Lamia was killed on site due to its preference for children and again, it had no wings. There were reams and reams of creatures in folklore and legend that didn't exist and twice as many that did or at least used to. Nothing matched Sebastian, who continued to refuse to meet Elsa's steady gaze and ignored her sigh. He knew that she had spent hours searching for answers for him and he appreciated it hugely but there were things he still couldn't tell her. Things he didn't want her to have to know.

"You're never going to tell me are you?" she asked quietly.

"Tell you what?" Sebastian mumbled.

"How you 'deal' with it."

He did look up at her then and his eyes were pleading. She had become quite adept at shielding herself from the pain of his anguished emotions but in these rare moments when he felt them so strongly it was difficult and she struggled to keep her composure.

"I have never had anyone that I could talk to about this," he said, "About anything really. I am so thankful for the time and effort you've put in and I know you want to help." He had a defeated look, "You haven't run away from me yet Elsa but one day you will, you will find out how I deal with this and you will run away and you won't look back. I don't want that to happen yet."

Elsa didn't know what to say. That wasn't exactly what she had expected to hear.

"I'm not going to run away from you," she said softly and despite her usual avoidance of touching him, she placed her hand on his. He tensed and so did she but she didn't move her hand. He had basically just told her how much he wanted her around and she wanted him to know that she wanted to be around him just as much, maybe more. Inexplicably she felt he would never hurt her, she felt one hundred percent safe with him. She could hear the pounding of his heart, her senses tuned to the rush of blood in his veins and she felt dizzy; aware once again of the huge impact he had on her, her thoughts darted to the serum doses in her bag. The sudden feel of Sebastian's other hand on top of hers, the first time he had voluntarily and intentionally returned her touch, snapped her attention back to him and him alone. His hands were so warm and he was looking at her in a way she couldn't put her finger on; he almost looked frightened. He opened his mouth to speak.

"Elsa?" She had not even noticed Kate's approach but the momentary spell between her and Sebastian was instantly broken. He pulled his hands back so quickly she wondered if they were ever there at all. She spun round to face Kate's questioning glare. "Lunch is over, you're going to be late for maths." Kate's tone was bright but her look spoke volumes. Elsa realised with surprise that the canteen was virtually empty.

Sebastian had gotten to his feet and was scooping his books into his bag, "I've got to go," he mumbled, avoiding both Elsa and Kate's eyes as he hurriedly left the canteen.

Elsa stared dumbly at the space he had just occupied for a moment until Kate smacked her shoulder with the back of her hand, "What was that?" she asked incredulously.

"What?" said Elsa, flustered. She retrieved her own bag and checked her serum supply. Asides from the look Kate was giving her making her uncomfortable, she could smell the unmistakable aroma of her friends blood and the sound of it rushed in her ears. She was in control but she needed a dose and soon.

"I thought there was nothing going on with you two, you said he was just helping you catch up with history."

"He is," Elsa insisted, "There's nothing going on."

"Elsa, he was holding your hand and you had disappeared into each others longing gaze." Kate's disapproval was evident but already slightly softened.

"That is not what was happening," said Elsa, walking away from Kate, "Like you said, I'm late for maths."

Kate followed her, "I get it, he's gorgeous," she said, "I was a bit surprised that's all, I mean we both agreed he's bad news."

"Did we?" Elsa couldn't help herself; "I think I actually said he's not that bad once you get to know him."

Kate swung herself round in front of Elsa and gripped her shoulders, smiling. Elsa fought to stop her eyes settling on the pulse in her friends neck, focusing instead on her bright blue eyes which were sparkling with mirth, "He's a bad boy," Kate said, "Every girl loves a bad boy. Just be careful ok?" Her expression grew more serious, "We all dream of taming a wild one, I just don't think it happens that often in reality, I don't want to see you get hurt."

Elsa forced herself to smile, "You're worrying about nothing," she said, "As in there is NOTHING going on between me and Sebastian." She disengaged Kate's grip on her shoulders and continued walking turning briefly to call back to her friend, "Now I really need to get to maths, I'll see you later!"

"This conversation isn't over!" Kate called after her and Elsa had no doubt that it wasn't. She made her way quickly to the toilets and administered a top up dose of serum, it always seemed to be the smell of Kate or Sebastian that set her off. Leaning against the cool tiled wall, she absently stroked the back of her hand where she could still feel Sebastian's touch. What had that all been about? Had they really shared some kind of moment or was that just her own wishful thinking? Her mobile rung out, interrupting her thoughts.

"Hello?"

"Elsa, it's Dad." She hadn't recognized the number, he must have been calling from work.

"Hi Dad, everything ok?"

"Are you busy?" he asked. Elsa looked at her watch, she was already a good fifteen minutes late for her lesson.

"Apparently not," she answered, "What's up?"

"Would you be ok to pop in and see me at work?" Marcus had an edge of anxiety to his voice.

"Ok, now?" Elsa said warily.

"That'd be great."

"Why Dad, what's wrong?"

"It's fine love, I'll fill you in when you get here." She could tell he was holding back.

"Give me five minutes," she said.

"Elsa it takes a lot longer than that to get here, watch what you're doing." His usual fatherly tone crept back and Elsa felt relieved, it couldn't be anything too serious.

"I'll be fine Dad, I won't be long," she hung up, wondering what he wanted to talk to her about. She had been doing a lot of research on the companies computers, maybe he was suspicious. She hoped that wasn't it. With a sigh Elsa threw her bag on her shoulder and made her way out of the college grounds, why couldn't life ever be simple?

# Food And Entertainment.

-------------------------------------------------

Elsa couldn't shake the sensation of Sebastian's touch as she walked out of the lift and into the brightly lit, crisp white hallway of Haven's facility floor. Knowing she did not have to watch what she was doing here, she was outside her father's office in seconds, eager to find out what it was he had to talk to her about and maybe distract herself from some rather unwholesome thoughts about Sebastian.

This was, of course not the dilapidated, fetid petri dish of an office Marcus had shown her when she had first visited his workplace. This office was as clean and clinical as the rest of Haven and much more acceptable to Elsa's keen olafactory perception. Her eyes told her that Marcus was not in his office, her nose told her where to find him.

A few doors down she knocked on a clear glass door to get her father's attention. He was stood with Gray, the large werewolf she had met only briefly and who made her wish her sense of smell wasn't quite so enhanced. She told herself she would make a much better job of hiding her distaste this time; after all, if Gray hadn't tracked her down that night a few months previously, her answer to Sebastian's question of if she had ever killed anyone would have been entirely different. She had a lot to thank this quietly intimidating man for and she knew her father had a huge amount of respect for him.

Marcus smiled when he saw her, one of those smiles that didn't reach his eyes, he was clearly concerned and motioned for her to come in.

Both men were stood in front of a large piece of what looked like glass. It was completely see through but was clearly some kind of computer screen as there were various open files and images covering it, which Marcus seemed to be able to move about with just a small hand motion in the air in front of the screen. Elsa had seen gadgets like this on television and always assumed it was the over active imagination of writers and producers she was looking at; apparently it wasn't.

"Wow," she said appreciatively, "You guys must be funded by the same people as CSI Miami's crime lab." Gray gave her a quizzical look but said nothing, merely nodding politely to welcome her.

"I'm not even sure where all our funding comes from," Marcus admitted, "Come and look at this." He indicated to a collection of still photographs on the screen, "Recognise anyone?"

Elsa had already spotted him, the vampire she and Kate had met at the concert. He had clearly recovered well from the broken neck she'd given him as he was pictured, hands in pockets walking down a street. A long length, black jacket covered up his tattoos; the collar was turned up and he had sunglasses on so his eyes could not be seen but Elsa knew it was him. She recognized his build, the sharp line of his cheekbones and the set of his jaw. She pointed at his picture, "Him," she said, "That's the one that attacked us."

Marcus nodded, rubbing his jaw and looking thoughtful.

"So what else am I looking at here?" Elsa asked; there were other pictures and scanned images of notes and official looking files.

"We've been looking into groups of vampires across Europe that have been causing us a few – problems," Gray spoke in a low, gravelly voice that made Elsa wonder what he sounded like as a wolf, she was curious as to what a werewolf really looked like when they changed, she'd only ever seen the fake kind in books and films.

"So this guy is one of them?" she asked.

"It would appear so," said Marcus, "Which means they're set to become a problem here too." He pulled the vampire's picture into the middle of the screen and enlarged it, "This is Vincent Lissner. The first record we have of him was in Estonia about 50 years ago and he's popped up in various European countries more regularly over the last few years. Wherever he's been, dead bodies and young vampires are found; we believe he's a major part of the blood movement."

"The blood movement, is that what you were talking about when you told me about those vampires who see humans purely as food and entertainment?" Elsa was thinking back to the conversation she'd had with Marcus while Kate had lain sedated on their sofa.

"It is," Marcus confirmed, "They create new vampires and introduce them to savage feeding habits immediately, teach them that it's the only way to do things. It makes them much harder to rehabilitate."

"They also go after those vampires we have helped and try to bring them back on side," Gray added, "By force if necessary."

"That's what you mean by problems then," Elsa didn't like the sound of Vincent and his friends one bit.

"Exactly," said Marcus. He pulled out three more photographs and placed them alongside that of Vincent. The first was a tall, lean man with silver hair. He must have been in his fifties when he was turned but, like all vampires, had that oddly youthful look of perfection to him. His eyes were a piercing, icy blue and very few lines marred his distinguished features; he was handsome but his face was cruel.

"This is Elliot Holt, he's at a similar level to Vincent we think as he gets around a bit. Both he and Vincent seem to move from place to place setting up groups to do their bidding then moving onto their next target. These two are lower level." He pointed to a girl of about fifteen who had a real street urchin look about her. A cigarette hung out of her mouth, her scruffy hoody swamped her petite frame and she looked like she thought the world owed her something. Her face and hair belied the picture of a street hardened ruffian, her fair skin was like polished marble with a dusting of freckles, her green eyes glowed and her flaming red hair hung in perfect waves around her shoulders. She was a vampire masquerading as a teenage tear away.

"Maggie Stuart," said Marcus, "Turned by Vincent twenty years ago, when he says jump, she asks how high."

Finally he pointed to the fourth picture, "And this is Robert Armitage, he's pretty new, to being a vampire and to us. We only know he's linked because we've seen him with Maggie." Robert was not as obvious a vampire to Elsa as the other three. For starters he had heavily pockmarked skin that must have been that way before he was turned and his mousy coloured hair was thin and straggly. It was difficult to pin point his age but Elsa suspected that whilst Maggie was trying to pull off the street kid look, Robert had probably actually been one at some point, his teeth were visible and they didn't look like they'd had regular care from anything like a qualified dentist. Elsa couldn't help but wonder if his fangs matched his teeth or if they would be the pristine white fangs of any other vampire.

She indicated to the other pictures on the left of the screen, "Who are they?" she asked.

"We don't know yet," Gray said, "We're working on finding out."

"And are they all here? In this country?"

"Yes," Gray almost growled and a look of disgust contorted his features, "They're spreading like a disease."

Elsa would have flushed if she could, Gray was talking about vampires as if they were germs to be eradicated; she was a vampire and she didn't like the feeling that these people on the screen were 'her kind', or that anyone might ever refer to her that way.

Gray quickly realised he might have offended her, "I'm sorry Elsa," he said gruffly, "I didn't mean that to sound the way it did, not all vampires are like them I know. I just meant that type of vampire –"

Elsa stopped him, "It's ok Gray, I know what you meant," she shook off her discomfort and looked back at the screen, "What happens next?" she asked, "What is Haven going to do about them?"

"We need to get to the root of the problem," Marcus said, "There's no point taking the time to eliminate one small group while three more are being set up at the same time, we've been chasing our tails that way for too long. We need to find our way to the top and work back down and we need to do it soon, they are working faster and getting bolder." He zoomed in on a police file, "We've found three deaths in the last week where they haven't even attempted to hide the bite marks, it's like they want people to know what they are and what they are doing." A saddened expression crossed Marcus' face, "We're losing vampires to them too, a lot of hard and good work is being undone."

There were a few moments of silence. Well, almost silence. Elsa could hear the slightly too fast beat of her father's heart and smell the adrenaline in his blood. She could hear Gray's breathing and the faint bristle of his hairs brushing together as his muscles tense. Both men were angry and both were trying keep their anger under control, Marcus with slightly more success than Gray. Elsa could almost hear the wolf inside him howling to be let out and tear those vampires limb from limb; she suppressed a shudder.

Suddenly Elsa had a thought, "Does Vincent know who you are?" she asked her father. He jumped at the unexpected question, his mind had clearly been elsewhere.

"I don't know," he admitted, "Obviously, all of us at Haven do our best to keep our identities concealed but these groups have been turning vampires that we've worked with back to killing for blood, they are bound to have contact with vampires who would recognise some of us."

"What if Vincent does know who you are and he knows I'm your daughter, you haven't forgotten what I did to him?" She was worried that her encounter with Vincent might have put her father at higher risk.

"That was impressive," Gray's gruff voice sounded appreciative and he flashed her a toothy grin.

"Yes it was," Marcus smiled and almost looked proud. He glanced apologetically at his daughter, "I had already thought about that Elsa, that's one of the reasons I wanted to see you."

"Why are you looking at me like you're about to tell me something I won't like?" Elsa asked suspiciously.

"Because I don't want Vincent to make that link between us," Marcus said, "Which means you and I need to put a bit of distance between us while we know he's nearby."

"Meaning?" said Elsa, pretty sure she didn't really want to know.

"Hesper is taking Lucca away hunting for a couple of weeks." Marcus began.

"I'm not going." Elsa was adamant.

"Elsa please, it'd be good for you and there'd be no chance of you bumping into Vincent and no chance of him realising the link you have to Haven."

"I've got college, I've already had so much time off!" It was a weak argument.

"You've more than caught up and you know it, you don't fancy a free holiday?"

Elsa wasn't going to let him win her over that easily, "It's not a holiday, it's a hunting trip," she said, "I'm fine with the blood bags, I don't want to hunt animals Dad."

"It's just for two weeks," Marcus reasoned, "We know Vincent is due to leave the country before Christmas, I'm just trying to keep you safe, to keep both of us safe."

That stopped Elsa's argument in its tracks; she didn't want her father to be at risk because of her. If there was any chance of Vincent finding her then he would also find Marcus and that didn't bear thinking about. She was being selfish she realised; she didn't want to leave Sebastian when they were so close to, to whatever it was that might be going on between them. She was worried about Kate's safety too, what if Vincent found her? He had seemed very taken by the idea of feeding from her, who knew what lengths he'd go to for a gourmet meal, or to get back at Elsa for breaking his neck. "What about Kate, is she at risk?" she asked.

"We've got her under surveillance," Gray spoke up.

"Who?"

"Someone I trust, another werewolf," Gray said, "My brother in fact. Any vampire that goes anywhere near Kate will smell nothing but wolf, it will keep them away."

"How is that possible?" Elsa was picturing dogs marking their territory, "No, never mind, I don't want to know." She felt reassured that Gray was in charge of looking out for Kate and felt herself relenting, "Ok, I'll go, just for two weeks and just to keep you safe," she said to Marcus who looked relieved, "Can I have an hour or so to pack some things and call in on Kate?"

"Of course," Marcus said, "We can meet back here about six?"

Elsa nodded, she knew she could pack and be back in minutes but she had somewhere else she needed to go first.

*AN: Soooo pleased with all the reads I'm getting, thank you all. Please, please, please guys, if you like it, vote for it! Wattpad is not emailling me when people vote so I can only thank you personally if it happens while I'm online but believe me, all votes are so very much appreciated as are comments (which I will always reply to) and new followers (who I will always visit and thank). I like to make dedications to my supporters too :)
*

# Darkest Times.

------------------------------------------------

✶ AN - For those of you following the soundtrack to this book, my song choice for this chapter is Snuff by Slipknot.*

Elsa could sense Sebastian's presence as she reached the warehouse, but something wasn't quite right. Usually there was a strong sense of his power and danger but it was muted, muffled somehow. She frowned to herself and called out, "Sebastian?"

There was no reply so she had to follow her nose to find him. She could smell other things too. There was a strong smell of whiskey and she passed at least three empty bottles but it was another smell that was really making her nostrils curl. A chemical smell, and burning.

"Sebastian?" Worried, she picked up her pace but then she heard Sebastian's voice and it momentarily stopped her in her tracks.

"Elsa, you can't be here." That was all he said but his tone spoke volumes. He sounded weak, defeated almost and his words carried a warning. She could tell instantly that he really didn't want her there and that he didn't want her to see him the way he was, however that might be. She stepped quietly up to the door she knew he was behind and placed her palm on it, the faded, peeling paint flaking beneath her fingers.

"I am here," she said quietly, "You don't have to hide from me." There was a long silence. Elsa could feel his struggling emotions, he was desperately trying to hide them from her but something was stopping him. His heart rate was slow and she couldn't feel the usual heat that emanated from his body.

"Please, you have to go." He could barely get the words out.

"Sebastian, you're scaring me. What's going on? I've seen all the empty bottles if that's what you're worried about. Is that how you deal with things? You drink yourself unconscious? It's ok." She tried the door handle.

"No!" It took great effort for him to shout and she heard the sound of him dragging himself across the floor in attempt to stop her from coming in; this told her he wasn't even standing and that did it for her, she was going in whether he wanted her to or not.

The door flew open easily, the workbench and pair of large metal drums Sebastian had attempted to barricade the doorway with thrown to the side as if they weighed nothing.

He was crouched on the floor, his enormous black-feathered wings held like a shield around him. Elsa could see the ridges down his spine that told her his form had changed, he was the demon he never wanted her to see. His skin was wet with sweat and his body shuddered. He didn't lift his head and she moved quickly to crouch alongside him.

"Please Sebastian," she said, quietly and she repeated her previous affirmation to him, "You don't have to hide from me."

"You shouldn't have come here," his voice was a growl, low and dangerous, "I'm not just hiding from you Elsa, I'm trying to keep you safe." He was panting and he slowly lifted his head, revealing his face. His eyes were sunken and they glowed a deep, animalistic amber; his strong brow was more defined, his cheekbones protruding unnaturally and his mouth was a snarl of dangerous teeth. Veins protruded in his neck and every fibre of his being was struggling she realised, fighting not to attack. She could also tell that despite what his instincts were telling him to do, his senses and reactions were dulled. As her eyes travelled over his body she saw a tourniquet around one muscular bicep, a hypodermic needle on the floor. She looked around the room and saw other things that told her alcohol was not enough to help Sebastian stay in control of his monster and her eyes filled with tears. She didn't back away, didn't recoil at his appearance. Instead she reached out and brushed his face gently with her fingertips, "Oh Sebastian."

He flinched away but it was not a sharp reaction, his amber eyes were rolling back in his head, which began to loll to one side. Elsa realised the drugs he had pumped into himself were finally having the exact effect he wanted them to. She didn't know anything about drugs or taking them but a scan of the paraphernalia around the room suggest he had taken a large amount of whatever it was. He had intentionally overdosed because he knew it wouldn't kill him, just put him down for a while. Sebastian continued to sink towards the floor and his head fell into Elsa's lap. His features gradually began to soften and return to the tortured, handsome face she recognised so well, his wings slid back into his body and his breathing calmed. Elsa held his head in her lap and brushed his dark hair, wet with sweat, away from his eyes.

"I'm sorry," she said, tears rolling down her cheeks, "I didn't know it got like this for you."

"Go," his voice was barely a whisper and his eyes didn't open.

"No," Elsa sniffed, "I'm not leaving you like this."

"I don't want …. you…" he was slipping away and Elsa couldn't believe he wanted her to leave him alone.

"It doesn't scare me off Sebastian," she insisted, "I want to help you through this."

"You can't," his eyes opened slightly, they were still amber and they stared at her intently, "If you don't go now," he managed to get the words out with huge effort, "I don't want to ... see you .... again."

His words cut Elsa deeply. He really didn't want her help. She thought they'd grown close but if he couldn't trust her with his darkest times then they were not as close as she thought. She laid his head gently on the floor, his eyes had closed and they didn't open again. She wiped her own eyes dry, she didn't know if he could hear her anymore but she spoke to him anyway.

"I'll go," she said, "I know you've done this on your own before and you will again but you didn't have to Sebastian. You don't have to be alone anymore. And don't you dare be so arrogant as to think I was only trying to help you. I was doing this for me too, maybe I needed someone to talk to and share my darkest secrets with, someone who would understand. I really wanted that to be you." She got up and walked to the door, turning to look at his inert form once more before she left, "I'll be gone for a couple of weeks but I'll be back, you need to decide if you want me around or not Sebastian. I'm not one for half measures, you either trust me or you don't. You're a good person, stop punishing yourself." And with that she left using all the speed she could muster, so that she couldn't change her mind.

*AN - thank you all for your continued support and reads - keep voting folks and tell me your thoughts, I love to hear them :) *

# Nope, Not Bears.

"I'm still cross with you for leaving without saying goodbye, free holiday or not." Elsa was talking to Kate on Skype and Kate was doing her best fake disapproving look. The fact was she had been far too occupied with a new love interest to notice Elsa had gone until she text her when they'd arrived in Canada.

"I said I was sorry!" Elsa protested with a smile. She'd been in Canada a week now and it had been – an experience. The idea had been for Hesper to take Lucca and Elsa out into the wilderness and teach them to hunt down large game that could sustain a blood thirst for weeks. Lucca had been excited by the idea, back in Italy his father had owned a farm and butchered his own meat so the young vampire was no stranger to killing animals for food. Elsa however, was. She just couldn't face the thought of killing a bear, or whatever else they might hunt out in the vast Canadian wilds. She couldn't justify it to herself and she had pictures of picking fur out of her teeth afterwards that simply made the idea all the more unpalatable. So instead, she had used the time outside, away from prying eyes, to run and leap and climb. She was enjoying and embracing her new strengths and it was exhilarating.

She had really enjoyed Hesper and Lucca's company too. Far from the last time she had seen him, Lucca was a lovely young man who'd obviously been raised well. He had talked to her for hours in his broken English about his family back in Italy and how much he missed them and it made Elsa so grateful that, despite what she had become, she still had her same family and friends around her.

Hesper was hugely knowledgeable and taught them something new about being a vampire everyday. She told them tales of her past lives; how she had been around to see so many of history's landmark moments from the birth of the Industrial Revolution to the Great Fire of London. She was quiet, and patient and easily the most serene person Elsa had ever met.

"You're so lucky your dad has a job that takes him all over the world," Kate was saying, "I'd never want to go on a work trip with my dad, the most exciting place he's ever been is probably a B&B near head office."

"It's not like he always gets to take me along," Elsa was lying easily again, much to her own disgust, "Anyway, I've told you all about my week, now what's this about a new man?"

"Ah yes, he came into the restaurant a couple of weeks ago and I was serving his table. He was with friends and I did notice that he kept looking at me, every time I looked over, our eyes met," Kate's face was glowing, "When I took them the bill, he came to the till to pay it himself and asked me if I had a boyfriend!"

"You're not still holding a torch for Jacob Evans then?" Elsa teased.

Kate scrunched up her nose, "No way," she said, "You know his mum still chooses his clothes for him?"

Elsa laughed, "So, what's his name? Where's he from? How old is he? What are his intentions?"

"Aiden, local, didn't ask but think he's older and he intends to take me out tonight." Kate ticked of each answer on her fresh-for-a-date manicured fingers.

"Exciting stuff," Elsa said, "What does he look like?"

Kate rolled her eyes theatrically and fake swooned at the webcam, "Gorgeous!" she sighed, "A genuine tall, dark and handsome sex god."

Elsa blinked an image of Sebastian from her mind; she was trying not to drive herself mad wondering how he was, what he was doing and if he'd heard what she'd said to him before she left him lying on a warehouse floor the previous week. Would he want to see her when she got back?

"Speaking of which," Kate seemed to read Elsa's mind, "The ever mysterious Sebastian has disappeared again."

"Oh?" Elsa tried not to sound too interested, "When?"

"About the same time you did," Kate answered, "You didn't take him with you did you? You'd need to find a pretty big suitcase to smuggle him in and something tells me you haven't introduced him to your dad yet."

"Why would I need to introduce him to Dad?" Elsa asked defensively, "We're not an item Kate, I keep telling you that."

"Yeh, yeh, whatever you say," Kate waved her hand dismissive of Elsa's protests, "I've seen the way you look at him and more importantly, the way he looks at you."

"What do you mean?" Elsa couldn't help asking. Despite her friend's exuberant humour and dramatics, she did trust Kate's opinion and knew from experience just how observant she could be.

"He looks at you as if every time he sees you it's the first time." Kate said seriously.

Elsa didn't know what to say to that, it was a beautifully heart lifting thought but was that really what Kate was seeing? Kate must have sensed her discomfort and immediately tried to lift the mood again, "Plus the other week, when Steve came up to speak to you in the canteen, I seriously thought Sebastian wanted to actually tear out his throat!" She was grinning at what she thought was her humorously over-dramatic version of what she'd seen. In actual fact, Elsa thought, she probably wasn't far wrong.

She forced a smile to reassure her friend, "He probably genuinely forgets who I am each time he sees me and he looks at everyone like he wants to tear their throats out." Kate just raised her eyebrows so Elsa decided to deflect, "You have to Skype me again tomorrow and tell me how your date goes," she insisted.

"Try and stop me," said Kate and she looked at her watch, "Ohmygod, I've got to go and get ready!"

"What time is it there?" Elsa asked, amused.

"Three 'o'clock," said Kate.

"And what time are you going out?"

"Seven."

Elsa had to laugh, trust Kate to always raise her spirits, "Have a great night," she said, "I'll speak to you tomorrow, same time?"

"Same time," Kate nodded and disappeared from the screen. Elsa felt suddenly alone and homesick, her momentary respite from melancholy gone as soon as Kate's smiling face left her computer screen. She threw herself back on her bed and smothered herself with a pillow. Her father had told her that they thought Vincent was leaving the country in about five days and then she could go home just in time for the Christmas holidays to begin. She wondered if Sebastian would be back by the time she got home; she wondered where they went from where they had left off.

There was a knock on the door, "Come in," she muttered from under the pillow. She knew it was Lucca.

"Ciao Elsa," she could tell he was smiling from the tone of his voice and she removed the pillow from her face.

"Hi," she mumbled, sitting up, "What's up?"

"My question for you," Lucca said, "Who is Sebastian?" He had a slight twinkle to his eye and Elsa groaned inwardly, thankful for the millionth time that she could no longer blush and making a mental note that Lucca's room was next door and vampires had very good hearing.

"Can we talk about something else?" she asked, anxious to be distracted from thoughts of Sebastian while she had no way of knowing where he was or what he was doing.

"Come with Hesper and I today, it will take your mind of this Sebastian," Lucca offered but Elsa shook her head.

"No, thank you but I just can't get my head around the idea," she said, "I think I'll go for a run instead." Preferably up a mountain and off the other side...

"Back home, there was a girl," Lucca said, casting his eyes down to his hands. He was generally very positive of his new life and grateful for the help he had received to overcome his thirst for blood. He had already told Elsa how difficult it had been for him before Haven found him; unlike her, he had killed. Her heart broke for him, it wasn't his fault of course but the immense guilt ate away at him when he was alone. Hesper had really taken him under her wing and treated him like a son, her calming presence helped him and he hung on her every word.

"She wasn't … ?" she didn't know how to finish the question.

Lucca closed his eyes but shook his head slightly, "No, not her," he sighed, "She was beautiful, I think about her still, very often." He looked at Elsa earnestly, "I cannot go back, I cannot see her but you have a chance of that with Sebastian, yes?"

"I suppose I do," Elsa said, "I'm just not sure if he wants me to."

Lucca pulled a face, "Men do not know what they want," he said, "You have to tell him." He smiled, "Enjoy all the normal you can for as long as you can." he said and patted her leg in a brotherly way.

Elsa smiled back, "You're so wise Lucca," she said with mock reverence, "Are you sure you're not really one hundred years old?"

Lucca tapped the side of his head, "Here yes," he said, "Are you sure you will not come?" He stood to leave.

Elsa shook her head, "No, I'll catch up with you both later."

Lucca nodded and gave a small wave as he left the room, closing the door behind him and leaving Elsa to think about what he had said. Maybe Sebastian didn't really know what he wanted; he'd been alone for so long that pushing people away had become a habit that might be hard to break. Was she ready to put herself out there though? To risk him telling her he couldn't ever fully trust her, couldn't ever let her completely in? She had to smile at Lucca's suggestion that a relationship with Sebastian could be a slice of normal in the otherwise crazy pie that was her life. It was and would be anything but, she knew that, but who was to say what normal was anymore? She groaned out loud with frustration, the more she tried to think of answers, the more questions she came up with. That at least was normal behaviour she supposed, tearing her hair out over a man.

Elsa leaned over to her laptop and clicked on the internet page she had minimized when Kate had called. It was a page on big game hunting in Canada and she was trying to find an animal that would provide enough excitement to hunt without offending her morals. Dall sheep; no because they were sheep and she'd never seen a sheep do anything but stand around, it just wouldn't be a fair fight. They had pretty impressive horns but still, they were sheep. She ruled out the Alaska-Yukon moose on the same sort of basis. She always thought the name moose sounded kind of big and dopey and there was something about their big noses, they just looked so innocent and cuddly. Caribou and mountain goats were also off limits and as for bears, she'd loved Yogi Bear as a child and had watched old repeats of Gentle Ben with her dad on a Sunday morning. Nope, not bears.

Finally, at the end of the list came wolves and wolverines. Now that piqued her interest. Until she remembered that she knew a wolf, kind of. There was no way she'd be able to face Gray if she'd been hunting and drinking from wolves so that was another one crossed off. Wolverines though; she thought of the X-men character, he was pretty bad ass wasn't he? She did a quick search and pulled up an image of a wolverine. It looked like a cross between a very small bear and a beaver. Great.

Elsa closed her laptop and sighed melodramatically for nobody's benefit but her own. That was that then, time to find a mountain to run up.

# Merry Christmas.

------------------------------------------------

✱ AN - For those of you following the soundtrack to this book, I have chosen Chemical by Kubb to go with the later part of this chapter. Hopefully (if it works) you should find, to the right, a YouTube link to my own acoustic cover of this track, which is the version I hear in my head when I picture the final scenes of this chapter. Enjoy! Oh, and please feel free to vote, comment etc my lovely, lovely readers :) *

The warehouse was empty.

Elsa had returned from Canada three days previously and Kate had told her that there had been no sign of Sebastian in college before they'd broken up for the Christmas holidays. Still unsure of whether or not he had heard her little speech when she had last seen him, Elsa had gone to the warehouse and left him a note to let him know she was back. She'd driven herself insane for two days waiting to see or hear from him and now it was Christmas Eve and she'd given in and gone back to check that he wasn't ignoring her.

The fact that he wasn't there yet didn't really make her feel any better. Ok so he wasn't ignoring her note but where was he? She knew, or at least assumed he'd not been home as the room she'd left him in was still littered with empty bottles and syringes and the workbench and drums were still exactly where she'd thrown them. For want of anything better to do with her day, Elsa cleared up figuring that the last thing Sebastian needed when he got back from whatever dark place he'd had to go to was to clear up after the dark place he'd left behind. This done, she re-read her note.

Sebastian,

I'm home, come and find me if you want some company.

Elsa.

That was it. Should she write anything else? She took a pen out of her pocket and chewed the end thoughtfully. The note didn't refer to their last conversation and it didn't sound needy, but was it too abrupt? She'd meant it to sound light and friendly but now she wasn't sure. Finally she scribbled the words hope you're ok at the bottom and placed the note right in the middle of the floor where Sebastian would be sure to find it. She pulled the blankets straight over the mattress on the floor in the corner of the room that served as Sebastian's bed and hoped she hadn't over-stepped her boundaries, then left for home.

She opted for a slow walk, even though there was nobody around. She wanted to feel the icy December air on her skin and tried to remember what it felt like to feel the cold. Occasionally tiny snowflakes scurried around in the wind, chasing each other to the ground where they disappeared almost immediately. The sky overhead was heavy, maybe there would be a white Christmas this year.

Elsa phone chirped and she looked at the screen.

Having an outfit dilemma – help? xx

Kate was clearly preparing for another date with the dashing and romantic Aiden. Elsa had yet to meet him but she was already inclined to like him. Kate was in a permanent state of delirious excitement and anyone that had that effect on her friend was ok in Elsa's book. He seemed to have money whoever he was; Kate gushed about his flashy car and the swanky dates he'd taken her on. Tonight was a romantic meal at an Italian restaurant Elsa knew you had to take out a mortgage to eat at and it seemed Kate was in need of fashion advice. Why she was asking Elsa she had no idea.

Elsa picked up her pace and headed for Kate's. The snow began to fall more heavily, dusting the ground and leaving a fleeting record of Elsa's steps before erasing them with fresh flakes.

"So you see my problem?" Kate said, standing between two equally suitable outfits in Elsa's opinion.

"I really don't know why you're asking me," Elsa said, waving a hand at her own uniform of skinny jeans and t-shirt emblazoned with one of the many bands she loved.

"Yes but surely you can see that this coat doesn't go with this dress but the material of this dress will crease up under the coat and I'll look like a sack of spuds when I take it off at the restaurant?" Kate looked pleadingly at Elsa who shrugged apologetically. Kate sighed, "You're right," she said, as if Elsa had just given her the perfect answer, "Looks before comfort, I'll wear this one and leave the coat behind."

Elsa laughed, "You realise I had nothing to do with that decision?" she said.

"You did," Kate insisted, "I was reading your body language."

"Whatever you say," Elsa was sat on Kate's bed and she hugged her knees into her chest, resting her chin on them, "When do I get to meet this amazing new man of yours?" She asked.

"He's actually quite nervous about meeting my friends and family," said Kate, switching on her straighteners and pinning up a section of her honey blonde hair, "I did invite him round tomorrow evening to meet Grant and my folks but he looked like I'd asked him to announce our engagement!"

"I suppose meeting the family on Christmas day is quite a bit of pressure," Elsa reasoned.

"Yeh," Kate agreed, "It has only been a couple of weeks. I'd love you to meet him though."

"Maybe I could arrange to accidentally bump into you at some point?" Elsa suggested with a sly grin.

"Yes!" Kate said enthusiastically, "That's a great idea!"

"Not tonight though," Elsa said quickly, "I can think of absolutely no plausible reason for me to be in a ridiculously expensive restaurant on my own on Christmas Eve."

"Still heard nothing from Sebastian?"

Elsa stuck out her tongue, "Banned topic of conversation," she said.

"Fair enough," said Kate, "You know there are loads of guys at college just waiting for you to show some interest don't you?"

"No there is not."

"Yes, there is. It's like you've developed some kind of hidden man magnet lately, I swear you could have your pick at college if you could tear yourself away from Mr Moody Pants."

Elsa snorted a laugh; she could just picture Sebastian's face if he ever heard Kate call him that. Unfortunately picturing Sebastian's face with any expression just exacerbated her already bad mood and dampened the laughter almost immediately.

"Elsa." Kate put her straighteners down and sat opposite Elsa on the bed, her hair half up, half down.

"What?" Elsa couldn't help sounding sulky.

"No man is worth you feeling so miserable," said Kate kindly, "All I'm saying is that if you two aren't an item as you keep telling me, then there's no reason you shouldn't take a little light relief from some of the other gorgeous specimens of men that are out there," She placed a hand on either side of Elsa's face and touched her forehead to Elsa's, looking into her eyes intently, "There are other options," she said, as if talking to someone who was a little slow on the uptake. Then she pulled back and tilted her head to one side, looking at Elsa and frowning slightly.

"Have I got something on my face?" Elsa asked.

"No," said Kate and then shrugged and lowered her hands, "It's just your eyes looked funny."

Elsa tensed, "Most peoples probably do when you get that close," she said, attempting to brush Kate's comment off. She got up and made a show of looking at her watch, "I've got to get going," she said and gave Kate a brief hug, "Have fun tonight and we'll plan 'operation accidentally meet Aiden' soon."

"Ok," said Kate, "Have a lovely Christmas!"

"You too!" Elsa called back as she left, unsure of exactly how 'lovely' her Christmas could possibly be.

Her father did his best to ensure Christmas day was no different to any other year. His parents had passed away, he had no brothers and sisters and Elsa's mum's family were scattered all over the world, none of them lived close. It was always just the two of them and that was usually the way they liked it. Presents were exchanged and opened in the morning as they always were but Elsa didn't have her usual breakfast of chocolate, chocolate and more chocolate. Instead she settled on the sofa in her new fluffy dressing gown and slippers to watch rubbish Christmas television with a gently warmed mug of the red stuff.

Each year, she and her dad usually took it in turns to cook Christmas dinner for the two of them but there had been an unspoken agreement that Marcus would cook for himself. He did his best the whole day to keep spirits up but it just wasn't the same and by the time her father finally went to bed, Elsa was relieved to stop pretending everything was great when really she just wanted the whole day to be over.

It must have been well past midnight and Elsa was watching Miracle on 34th Street for the second time that day; it was one Christmas tradition that didn't have to change and that kid was just so damn cute. She looked out of the window at the snow, which had been falling steadily since the previous evening. A light dusting had now become a thick, luxurious blanket and, as the snowfall had now ceased, it glittered in the clear, bright moonlight and reminded her of the Christmas cards she would make as a child that were 90% glitter, 10% card.

She realised with a smile that there were still things she'd loved to do in the past that her new circumstances didn't change. In fact, as the cold no longer bothered her, the fun of being the first person to step out in fresh, perfect snow would be all the more pleasurable. She did stop to change out of her pyjamas, just incase anyone saw her and then ran out of the front door, reveling in every crunching footstep and threw herself down onto the snow to make a snow angel.

It was bliss; she could stay out in the snow as long as she wanted without getting cold. She lay in the angelic form she'd created in the snow and looked up at the sky. There were no clouds and she could pick out every single star sprinkled like icing sugar across the sky. For the first time in a while, the smile stayed on her face and she thought of her mother as she looked at the heavens.

"Merry Christmas." Elsa jumped up; she'd been so distracted she had somehow not noticed that she was no longer alone. Looking around her she quickly picked out a tall figure in the shadows.

Sebastian stepped forward so that the moonlight picked out his features more clearly. His face had lost its sunken look, his eyes were cast down and his hands were driven deep into his pockets. He looked nervous and uncomfortable.

"You're back," Elsa said and mentally slapped herself on the forehead, of course he was back, he was standing right there in front of her.

"I got your note," he said quietly.

"I didn't know when you were coming back," Elsa said, inside her head she was screaming. What do I say? What do I do?

"I know; I didn't really know either."

They were stood about a meter apart and a silence stood between them like a wall that Elsa was sure would need a sledgehammer to be broken down. As it turned out, it only took two words.

"I'm sorry." They both said it together and Sebastian's head snapped up, his intent grey eyes fixed on hers.

"Why are you sorry?" he asked.

"I shouldn't have pushed you to share every aspect of your life with me," Elsa said, "I had no right, I know how difficult you find it to let people get close."

Sebastian shook his head, his broad shoulders relaxing slightly, "I should have trusted you," he said, "You never once turned away from me, even that last night ...." his voice trailed off and his gaze turned to the ground once more, "I heard what you said before you left."

Elsa tensed, unsure of how he felt about what she said. She could remember it word for word and she'd meant it too, she wanted him to trust her completely because she wanted to be a part of his life, all of it.

"Did you leave because of me?" Sebastian asked with a pained expression.

"What? No!" Elsa assured him and her chest ached at the expression on his face, "I had to go away for a couple of weeks."

"Why?" Now he looked worried and Elsa was shocked by how open his emotions were all of a sudden, his worry was for her and that touched her deeply.

"Kate and I had a run in with a vampire a while back who's pretty bad news, my dad was worried he might come looking for me and link me to Haven. I went away until we knew he'd left the country, just to be on the safe side," she explained briefly, anxious to keep the conversation moving.

Sebastian frowned and stood up a little straighter, "You never told me," he said, sounding confused and a little annoyed.

Elsa's heart sank as what she'd just said hit her. She had been angry and hurt by Sebastian's reluctance to let her help him through his toughest times and yet she'd thought nothing of not mentioning her own problems to him. She opened her mouth to speak but Sebastian held up a hand to stop her, his expression already softening.

"I guess neither of us are that good at asking for help," he said an Elsa breathed a sigh of relief.

"I guess not," she said, wondering where the conversation could go next. Sebastian shifted his weight from one foot to the other and back again, she could feel him building up to something and she waited.

"I don't know how to stop punishing myself for what I am Elsa," he said finally, the raw honesty of his emotions crashing over Elsa and bringing her composure dangerously close to cracking, "But I do trust you."

"I trust you too," Her voice was barely a whisper an every fibre in her body tingled.

"I don't want to be alone," his voice was hoarse and he was struggling with something. Elsa knew what it was and she took a deep breath and closed the yawning space between them so quickly that the snow was whipped up and swirled briefly around their feet.

"You're not," she said and placed a hand on his chest where she could feel his heart pounding quickly and feel the intense heat of his body.

Before she even knew what was happening, his hand was at the back of her head, pulling her into a fierce kiss. She melted into him and her heart exploded with the force of both their emotions. Every previous contact she'd had with Sebastian had caused an intense reaction but they were nothing compare to this. The world could have imploded around them and she was sure that they would have remained, locked in this embrace, unaware that anything had ever happened. It was not gentle, his strong arms held her tightly, the sensation of his lips pressed hard on hers was deep and all consuming and she devoured it with a hunger she never knew she had. The smell of him was intoxicating, her head swam and, when he finally released her it was all she could do to remain standing, her head falling to his chest, rising and falling with his breath.

After a few seconds, his hand reached gently under her chin and he tilted her head up so that their eyes met once more. His were glowing amber and she realised his jacket had torn apart and his wings were folded around them. He was searching her face for her reaction, and she could tell he was scared. Her answer was to smile, to touch her hand to his face, trace his cheek bone with the tips of her fingers and kiss him again, this time more softly, their lips barely touching as she felt his quick intake of breath then a slow exhale as every muscle in his body relaxed.

"Elsa," he whispered against her lips and she moved her fingertips to his mouth. She didn't want him to speak, she could happily never say another word or do another thing in her life other than stand here in this moment with him, as snow began to fall once again inexplicably from a cloudless sky.

---

*  AN - Did I do that first kiss justice? I'm anxious to know as I put a lot of thought into it. Vote if you like it! *

# The Altar of Sebastian.

-------------------------------------------------

"Do you have somewhere you'd rather be?" Marcus was watching his daughter gaze wistfully out of the café window where they were grabbing some precious father daughter time on his lunch break. Things had been very quiet for the last few days; no Vincent, no suspicious deaths, no new vampires. It made him twitchy and kept him on edge; rather than rest he was treating it as the calm before the storm and had been working long hours since Christmas.

Elsa looked guilty, "No," she said, "Sorry I was just thinking."

"I could see that," said Marcus, "As opposed to listening, did you hear a word I just said?"

"Um…you lost track of Vincent in Germany and Elliot was last seen in Munich sooo …" she shrugged, "That's all I've got."

Marcus smiled wearily and rubbed the bridge of his nose, "So they're close to each other, probably in contact with each other again which is not a good thing. We've identified some more members of their group but things have gone really quiet. I don't like it."

"Why not, quiet's good surely?" Elsa was trying to remain focused but all she really wanted to do was run out of the café as fast as she could and go to Sebastian. Her body tingled at the thought of him. They had been unsure of each other, after that first kiss, Sebastian was not used to letting people close and Elsa was trying to hold herself back, take it slowly and give him chance to get used to things but it was so very, very hard. She'd seen him once more since that night and it had been awkward, no more kissing and she got the distinct sense that his walls were going up again. It was so frustrating.

"Quiet is never good," Marcus said, bringing her thoughts back to their conversation once again, "You've got to be really aware of what's going on around you Elsa, something is brewing, I can feel it and I'm worried about you."

Elsa placed a hand on her fathers arm, "I don't think you need to be," she said, "If Vincent wanted to get back at me for what happened at that concert, if he knew where to find me, surely he'd have done it by now? He's obviously focused on whatever diabolical plans he has been cooking up with the blood movement and besides, Haven are all over that aren't they? You've got eyes on so many factions of that group there's nothing they could do without you guys knowing."

"We have no idea how big they are or how far they reach," Marcus said, "We only know what we know and who's to say how much of the picture we're missing?"

"Wow, you really are having a glass half empty kind of day aren't you?" Elsa said, sitting back, "Are you going to be working all through New Year? All work and no play makes Marcus Shaw a dull daddy."

He couldn't help but smile, "Well unless you're planning to spend New Year with me, I'll probably work yes."

Elsa stuttered; did her father want her to spend New Year with him? "I – er ..."

"Relax," he said, "I am sure you have plans with Kate, don't you worry about your poor old dad, I never bother with New Year, you know that."

Elsa still felt guilty, "You shouldn't always spend it on your own," she said.

"I won't be on my own," he reasoned, "Gray and Hesper will probably be there, neither of them seem to follow traditional holidays anymore."

Elsa smiled, "Just try and have some fun," she pleaded.

"I'll try," Marcus promised and he stood up, pulling on his coat, "I'd better get back," he said, "I'll be working late."

"I'm going out later myself," Elsa said lightly.

"Well tell Kate I said hi." Marcus leant down to kiss her forehead and left the café.

Elsa was seeing Kate next but that's not the 'out she'd been referring to. She thought it best not to mention who she was planning on seeing; introducing her dad to the idea of a potential new boyfriend would be bad enough but trying to explain Sebastian, well that still wasn't really an option.

Elsa stopped off at Kate's on her way to see Sebastian, she hadn't made any plans with him and she didn't want to push it but she didn't want to leave it too long before seeing him again and lose the momentum they'd gained on Christmas day all together. She needed some girly advice first and she knew Kate's was the best. She had managed to reduce her daily serum doses but still found she needed a booster before seeing her friend, just to be on the safe side. Kate's brother opened the door when she knocked.

"Hi Elsa," he said, standing aside to let her in, "How are you? I haven't seen you for ages."

"Good thanks," Elsa replied and returned his friendly hug, "How's your course going? And the new place?" Grant was in his second year at university and had recently moved into a flat with his girlfriend nearer campus.

"Great!" he said enthusiastically, "She let me put up Iron Maiden posters if I let her put flowery cushions on the bed so we're in a state of pretty much domestic harmony right now. The course is tough, especially after the time off I had to have at the beginning of the year but I'm coping."

"Glad to hear it," Elsa said smiling, "Don't let me forget to give you that CD back while you're home."

"No rush," Grant waved it off, "Kate's upstairs if you want to go up and if you can stand the toxic nail varnish fumes. All you can smell up there is perfume, and hairspray and other girly smells lately."

"I can hear you!" Kate's voice came floating own the stairs. Elsa had to admit, the smell of various chemicals wafting from Kate's room and through the house was making her nostrils curl but then she did have a particularly good sense of smell so she followed her nose up the stairs and tried not to show her distaste.

"Hi," she said, sticking her head around Kate's door. Kate waved her in, blowing on her scarlet nails.

"I have a plan," Kate said, as if they had already started having a conversation that Elsa wasn't aware of. She raised an eyebrow and waited for the punch line.

"Operation 'accidentally meet Aiden', remember?" Kate was waiting for Elsa to catch up.

"Oh right!" Elsa said, "What's the plan?"

"New Years Eve, everyone is out having fun right? Perfect opportunity to bump into people."

Elsa fiddled with the zip on her top, "Yeh, I might not be out for New Year."

Kate looked at her as if she'd just said she was going to commit murder, "It's New Year," she said, as if that was all the reason she needed for being so shocked at Elsa's simple suggestion that she might not be out, "What else could you possibly be doing?"

Elsa didn't answer, she didn't really know yet but she knew what she wanted to be doing and she also knew Sebastian was unlikely to want to hit the town.

Kate studied her for a moment then gasped, "You've got a man!" she squealed, "I knew it! Who, what, where when? Tell me everything." She grabbed Elsa's hands and bounced up and down with excitement.

"No, I – well, I don't really know…" Elsa sputtered.

Kate sat her down on the bed, "Oh. My. God. It's Sebastian isn't it?"

"When did you become a mind reader?" Elsa protested.

"So I'm right? When did he get back?"

"Christmas day, he came to see me."

"And?"

"And we-"

"You kissed!" Kate was beyond excited; Elsa began to honestly worry that she might actually burst.

"Why don't you tell me what's going on?" She said laughing, "You seem to have figured it all out."

"I'm sorry," said Kate, calming herself down, "You tell me."

Elsa sighed, "There's not great deal else to tell," she said, "We kissed, it was good," she indulged her friend, "It was really good." She rolled her eyes, "But he finds it difficult to let people in you know, he's a bit of a closed book and I know he's holding back on me. It's been a little awkward since. I'm not sure what to do."

"He is an unusual case," Kate said thoughtfully, "Are you sure you want to pursue this?"

"He's really not what people think he is," Elsa insisted, "He's had a hard time that's all. I've seen a side of him he doesn't show to anyone else."

"Then it sounds like you're off to a good start," said Kate kindly, "My advice? Be honest with, tell him how you feel, tell him what you want but let him know that there's no rush, no pressure. If he's wary then maybe it'll help if he knows exactly where he stands."

"I could be setting myself up for a fall." Elsa said.

"So what?' Kate said brightly, "At least you'll know you tried. I can tell this is not a casual thing for you Elsa, I've known you long enough. If you think it's worth the risk then go for it. You'll always wonder what if otherwise and I'm here for you no matter how it goes."

Elsa smiled, Kate was right, "You give the best advice," she said, hugging her friend.

"I know," said Kate matter-of-factly, "And you can repay me by finding a way to bump into Aiden and I tomorrow night!"

Elsa grimaced, "I don't know what's happening tomorrow night yet."

"I know, just try though ok? I'll let you know where we are." Kate suddenly jumped as if she'd remembered something, "Oh, I have a photo of him!" she said pulling out her phone, "Here, I took it on Christmas Eve."

Elsa took the phone. On the screen was a picture of Kate looking radiant and happy, her head tilted towards Aiden. He was undeniably attractive; dark, close cropped hair, designer stubble, flashing hazel eyes. He too was smiling but Elsa wasn't entirely sure what to make of it. He looked sort of triumphant, like he'd was the only one laughing at a joke nobody else got. Maybe the picture just caught him at an odd moment.

"Hot right?" Kate was anxious for Elsa's reaction and she had to agree he was indeed hot.

"Hot," she said, forcing a smile, "Can't wait to meet him." She now felt more strongly that she needed to meet him sooner rather than later, she felt protective of Kate all of a sudden and wanted to make sure this Aiden was everything Kate seemed to think he was.

"So you'll try and come out tomorrow?" Kate's tone was hopeful.

"Ok, I'll see what I can do," Elsa relented; "Now I'm going to go and throw myself at the altar of Sebastian and see what happens."

"Good luck!" Kate blew her a kiss and returned to examining her fingernails as Elsa left, unable to shake a feeling of unease. Whether it was about the photo of Aiden or the fact that she was going to see Sebastian with her heart firmly plastered on her sleeve she wasn't sure but there was only one way to find out.

*AN - Keep voting guys, I'm getting a lot of reads which is great, but without the votes I'm worried that people might be reading and not really enjoying? Hopefully you are all enjoying reading as much as I'm enjoying writing - thank you for all your support! *

Oh, btw - do we think Elsa should be concerned about the mysterious Aiden? What are your thoughts? ;)

# Adrenaline Rush.

------------------------------------------------

✱ AN - For those of you following the soundtrack to this book I have chosen Superhuman by Velvet Revolver for this chapter - it had to be really :) *

It was dark when Elsa reached the warehouse, she knew that was the way Sebastian preferred it and she figured she needed all the help she could get.

She didn't call out when she arrived like she normally would but headed to the room that Sebastian called home and paused before setting her shoulders and knocking on the door.

She listened intently and heard his breathing, his pulse and his tension; he hadn't heard her approach.

"Sebastian, it's me, Elsa," she said and she heard him walking to the door. It opened and he looked surprised.

"Did we_?" he began. He was dressed in jeans and a t-shirt that clung in all the right places, his feet were bare, his hair was tousled and he ran a hand through it. She wanted to pounce on him right then and there.

Elsa stopped him mid question, "No, we did not arrange to meet, I'm sorry for turning up unannounced but it's not like you have a phone and I wanted to talk to you."

Sebastian looked a little confused, he looked like he'd been asleep, "I have a phone."

"Not what I wanted to talk about," Elsa said, "Can I come in?"

He stood aside then, "Sure, come in." She felt him tense and draw in his breath as she walked past him. Not good.

"Is everything ok?" he asked, leaning on the edge of a workbench, arms folded.

"Yes, no, I mean, yes it is." Elsa felt suddenly flustered and began to pace. She didn't realise she was moving at vampire speed until Sebastian reached out to stop her.

"Woah," he said, "I can barely follow you when you go that fast, what's wrong?" He removed the hand that had held her arm for a moment and looked awkward.

"That's what's wrong!" Elsa said, stepping towards him, "I thought things had changed between us, maybe moved forward? Now you're pulling back again and I'm not sure what I did wrong."

Sebastian dropped his head and didn't say anything or a few seconds that felt like an eternity to Elsa, "You didn't do anything wrong," he said finally, "I'm sorry."

"Sorry for what? Sorry for kissing me?"

"No!" His head snapped up and Elsa felt her heart leap.

"No?" she said.

"No. I am not sorry about that, I'm just sorry I'm really not very good at this," he looked pained, "I don't want to hurt you."

"What do you mean?" Elsa asked, "Pulling away from me will hurt me Sebastian and that's what I've been feeling you do."

He shook his head looking frustrated, "I don't mean emotionally Elsa."

She was momentarily confused and then his meaning dawned on her, "Oh."

"I trust you and I want to be with you, I do," She felt the honesty in his words and it was the sweetest sound she had ever heard, "But I can't always control myself," he continued, "When my emotions run high, when I get an adrenaline rush or anything like that, it's harder for me to control the monster inside me."

Despite what he was saying, Elsa was smiling, "Do I give you an adrenaline rush?" she asked slyly.

Sebastian looked at her imploringly, "Please Elsa, I'm being serious."

"I know, I'm sorry," Elsa stepped closer again but Sebastian stood up and walked over to the other side of the room.

"The fact is you do give me an adrenaline rush," he said, "When we were kissing, my wings, my eyes, I had no control over that, it was all I could do to hold the rest back."

"But you did hold it back." Elsa said turning towards him but respecting the distance he'd put between them for now.

"What if I can't always?" He looked slightly embarrassed and if she could have, Elsa would have blushed too, she was enough in tune with Sebastian's thoughts and feelings to know what he was thinking.

"I don't believe you would ever hurt me," she said, trying to put him at ease, "I really don't and, if things ever did get out of control you know I can handle myself."

Sebastian looked doubtful and Elsa sighed, "You've not seen anywhere near half of what I can do," she said, "So I can move fast, learn quickly and my senses are heightened even more than yours but I'm strong too, really strong and don't forget, virtually indestructible." Now she began to move closer to him, "I know that I could fight you off if I had to but I also know that I won't have to because I don't think your monster is as bad as you think he is Sebastian, I think you are stronger than him." She was standing directly in front of him now and he hadn't moved.

"What if I'm not?" he said and she could feel his burning desire to believe what she was saying.

"You are," she was so close now she could feel his warm breath on her face.

"I've done terrible things Elsa, you don't know what I'm capable of," he still wouldn't meet her eyes.

"I know you," she said and her voice was almost a whisper, "And you are not the sum of the things you've done; please don't push me away."

He closed his eyes and touched his forehead to hers, "I don't want to."

She leaned up towards him, "Then don't." She felt suddenly confident and as his hands tried to push her back she resisted him, instead forcing him swiftly back against the wall. He gasped and finally his eyes met hers, glowing a fiery amber.

"I told you," she said, her own eyes glinting, "I'm strong."

He studied her face for a moment as she pinned him against the wall, he was trying to decide what to do, whether to give in or hold back. His walls were crumbling once more and she knew she had to just hold his gaze, to let him know that she wasn't scared of him and he didn't have to be scared either.

It worked; he gathered her up in his arms and kissed her deeply, finally releasing himself to what they both wanted.

"You think I can control myself around you," he growled as their lips parted, his hand ran from her waist, around her back and up to her neck with a firm pressure and he looked at her hungrily, "I am never so out of control as I am around you." And he was kissing her again and she surrendered to it fully, her own animalistic desires taking over. She too felt out of control but in the most wonderful way possible. She slid her hands under his t-shirt enjoy the full impact of her skin on his and he groaned. She felt empowered, as if she was winning a great battle and she pulled him in even closer, pressing her body against his.

Sebastian scooped her up off her feet and moved across the room as she wrapped her legs around his waist and the kiss became deeper and more and more heated. He sat her on the edge of a bench and she was dimly aware of the crash of various items as they scattered onto the floor. Her arm shot out to steady herself and a set of metal shelves went flying across the room. She felt the wall buckle against her back but she didn't care. She was completely lost in Sebastian and he in her. There was only one way this was going to end.

*AN - Sorry to stop it there folks but this is in the teen fiction category! I'm working hard to portray these (clears throat) 'romantic' scenes between Elsa and Sebastian in the right way - let me know what you think! *

# Sebastian.

Sebastian was sleeping. Elsa watched him as she couldn't sleep herself and she loved the fact that he was relaxed for once and looked peaceful. She drank in each contour of his body that was highlighted by the pale moonlight filtering through a small, grimy window. Her eyes traced the raised scars that ran down each shoulder blade, the only scars that remained on his body. She remembered with smile and a touch of embarrassment how carried away she'd really gotten just a couple of hours ago. She'd bitten Sebastian, tasted his blood, she couldn't help herself. He had barely noticed and certainly didn't seem to mind and it had tasted so, so good. Nothing like human blood, it was like an elixir that fuelled the fire already burning deep inside her and Sebastian had been worried about hurting her! Any marks she'd caused were long gone as were any he'd inflicted on her but she didn't recall any pain at all. She felt perfect, everything felt perfect.

As always, Elsa found it difficult to stay still for long. She used all her stealth to slide off the mattress that was Sebastian's bed, dress quickly and quietly as only she could and creep out onto the roof. She wanted to feel the fresh, icy cold air and remind herself that this was all real. She fished her phone out of her jeans pocket to text her dad, it was pretty late now and she didn't want him asking questions about where she was. As it was, he had already text her.

Gray and I ended up travelling to London following a lead, staying down here tonight, might even go out for a pint ;) x

She typed a reply and then opened a message from Kate.

Going to new club tomorrow night, Robots In Disguise playing so now you HAVE to come! Hope your talk went the way you wanted, let me know ASAP I must know EVERYTHING xx

Elsa grinned to herself, her evening hadn't gone exactly the way she'd thought it would that was for sure, but the last thing she was going to do was fill Kate in on everything that had happened. She replied that she'd try and make it to the club and idly wondered if Sebastian would want to go, she loved the band that were playing and it could be fun …

She sensed him behind her and turned. He looked nervous and unsure.

"I thought you'd gone," he said and suddenly for all his size and strength and danger, he appeared vulnerable.

Elsa was next to him in less than a second and wrapped her arms around his waist, feeling him relax to her touch, He was wearing only his jeans, which hung low on his hips, "I'm sorry," she said, "I didn't want to disturb you, I don't sleep and I find it hard to keep still for too long."

"You don't sleep?" He asked as he brushed her hair over her ear, "I didn't know that."

"I guess we still have some things to learn about each other," she said with a grin, "Not much mind."

Sebastian looked sheepish, "I don't normally, I mean I wouldn't ..."

"No, me neither," Elsa admitted, "So not that kind of girl! I hope you don't think ..." neither of them seemed to be able to get a full sentence out.

"Of course not," Sebastian insisted, knowing exactly what she was trying to say, "Ours is a unique situation I suppose, we both have other things driving us, other parts of us that take over occasionally?" He looked at her hopefully, he wanted her to agree with him, he wanted to know that she was ok with what had happened.

"You're telling me," Elsa said and he looked at first relieved and then worried. He pushed her back to arms length to look her over.

"I didn't hurt you?" he asked, concern etched on his features.

"What? No!" Elsa said, "To be honest I was more worried I'd hurt you."

He pulled her back closed and wrapped her in his arms, "How could you possibly hurt me?" he asked.

Elsa buried her face in his chest, not wanting to look him in the eye, "My teeth," came her muffled reply. She heard Sebastian laugh and he released her then swung his arm over her shoulder and began to walk her back inside.

"Don't you worry about that," he said, "It was different I'll admit but I'm not complaining."

Elsa stopped him and looked at him intently, "Really?"

He looked back just as intently, "Really, it's just part of who you are Elsa. You have accepted everything that I am, I feel the same way about you." He took her hand and pulled at her gently to follow him once more, "Come on, I want to show you something."

Intrigued, Elsa followed him back down to his room and took in the scene of devastation. What sparse furniture there had been in the room was scattered, some of it just plain broken. The bench Sebastian had originally deposited her on had one buckled leg and the corrugated metal wall behind it had a dent in it that was roughly her size. That was nothing compared to the brick wall on the other side of the room that, which had chunks missing from it.

"You wanted to show me what a mess we made?" she asked.

Sebastian laughed, "No," he said, fishing through the debris until he found a battered box, "This is what I wanted to show you." He passed her the box and she looked at him questioningly, "Open it," he urged.

Elsa took the box to Sebastian's bed and sat down with her legs crossed before taking the lid off. Inside was a small collection of items, a few passports, various pieces of paper and the occasional dog-eared photograph.

"What's all this?" she asked, picking up the oldest looking passport and opening it to the page which held a black and white photograph of a very serious looking Sebastian, wearing a suit with his hair slicked into a side parting.

"It's me," Sebastian said simply, "I have to re-start my identity every few years, move somewhere that people won't recognise me and start again. That box contains everything that has ever proven who I am and everything I've kept to remember my life so far. You wanted me to let you in? Pretty much everything I can tell you starts in this box."

Elsa was taken aback that he was sharing it with her. He sat down next to her and pulled a photograph out of the box. It showed a group of men in old army uniforms, all looking relaxed and smiling at the camera.

"My platoon during the war," Sebastian said and turned it over to show names written on the back that corresponded with each soldier on the front, "I didn't spend a long time with them, for obvious reasons I had to go AWOL eventually and after that I just moved from platoon to platoon, army to army. I could usually slot in somewhere and make myself useful for a while without raising too much suspicion. But these guys were my first platoon and that camaraderie was the closest I ever got to the feeling of family, I wanted to makes sure I never forgot their names."

Elsa opened another passport and couldn't help laughing at Sebastian's long hair and sideburns, "Duuude," she teased showing him the picture.

"In my defence, it was the sixties," he said, "The passports help me keep track of where I've been and who I've been."

"Who you've been?"

"I do have to change my surname at least," he said, "But I keep Sebastian because I know that is the name my mother gave me."

"How do you know that?" Elsa asked, she clearly remembered him saying he couldn't remember his family and didn't know exactly when he was born. There was no birth certificate in the box but he pulled out a scrap of paper. It was faded but some of the writing was still readable, "My son, Sebastian, he is innocent," Elsa read quietly.

"It gets more and more faded each year," he said and, more than she ever had before, Elsa could feel a crushing sadness flow from his heart, "One day the words will be gone and that's why I will always keep my first name."

Elsa wanted to cry, but she felt she had no right. She thought of all the times she'd felt so hard done to because of the turn her life had taken and she was ashamed. She still had so much to be thankful for and happy about and all Sebastian had was a box of snap-shots and other scraps of his existence.

"I'm not showing you this to upset you or make you feel guilty," Sebastian said softly, his hand stroking her back, "I showed you because I wanted to prove that I'm all in. I'm with you Elsa and I want you to know everything about me if that's what you want."

"It is," Elsa sniffed.

"Ok then," Sebastian shuffled back so his back was against the wall, stretched out his legs and beckoned Elsa over. She slid across and snuggled up alongside him, bringing the box with her. Sebastian talked her through every photo, every scrap of paper, every memory and then she talked to him, mostly about her mother, what little she knew. Eventually the sun began to rise and Elsa realised that the small amount of Sebastian's blood that she had tasted had kept her sated for hours but now she needed her serum and a warm mug of human blood.

"I'm going to have to go home," she sighed regretfully, her head leaning on Sebastian's shoulder.

He planted a kiss on top of her head, "You don't have your serum with you do you?"

"No," Elsa said, "And I'm a bit peckish."

"Can't really help you there unless you fancy a bacon sandwich?" Sebastian stood up, stretched and grabbed his t-shirt, pulling it on. Elsa pouted and he grinned shyly, offering his hand to pull her up from the mattress.

She took it, "Have you ever thought about getting an actual bed?" she asked.

"Not really," Sebastian admitted.

"Have you ever thought about living in an actual house?"

"Places like this serve my purposes," he explained, "Having a mortgage or a landlord can be a bit awkward for me and I don't think I'd make a great neighbour do you?" He looked at her with a glint in his eye, "Besides, no one tends to bother me out here. Well, no one used to bother me out here."

Elsa pretended to look offended, "Well if I'm bothering you…"

"You know you're not." Sebastian smiled and she knew she would never get tired of seeing him do that.

"There is one more thing I wanted to talk to you about before I go," she said, remembering Kate's text.

Sebastian assumed an expression of mock panic, "Look what happened last time you said you wanted to talk," he said, indicating the ruined room, "If that's where this talk is going, let me just move a few things first."

Elsa grinned, shaking her head, "Speaking of which," she said, "You know we have kind of skipped a few normal relationship steps here."

"A few," Sebastian agreed.

"So I was thinking maybe we could do something about that?" Elsa wasn't quite sure how to ask, which was silly considering everything they'd shared.

"Like?" Sebastian encouraged her.

"Kate is desperate for me to meet her new boyfriend and to be honest, I really want to meet him, I've seen photo's but there's just something that's ringing alarm bells for me. They're going to a club for New Year tomorrow night…"

"And you want to go." Sebastian said.

"Yes."

"And you want me to go with you?"

"Yes, but only if you want to, no pressure or anything. I just, well, I have to lie to Kate all the time and I'd like to be able to tell her the truth just this once, to tell her about you. Plus, I want your opinion on Aiden too, I want to check I'm not just imagining things. But you really don't have to come" Her words were tumbling out and Sebastian put his finger on her lips to stop her.

"I'll be there," he said simply and then, just to raise another smile from Elsa, "But if you could not tell Kate all the truth, I'd appreciate it."

# Interspecies Relationships.

------

*Please vote folks, my reads are shooting up which is great but I need votes and comments to keep me higher up the What's Hot chart :) Each vote only counts for that specific chapter so don't forget to click that vote button in each chapter you read! It is highly appreciated :) - feel free to nip back and vote on chapters you might have forgotten to before!*

For the first time in her life, as far as she could remember, Elsa was panicking about what to wear. Her wardrobe consisted of various pairs of jeans, a multitude of band t-shirts, her old school uniform, a few hoodies, three different colours of Converse trainers and a pair of Doc Martin boots. What the hell was she going to wear to a club on New Years Eve? After emptying the entire contents of her wardrobe onto the floor she was disappointed to discover that there were no long lost dresses she'd forgotten she had but she did find a pair of strappy kitten heels she'd once borrowed from Kate. She'd worn them to the party that had changed her life; the night she'd become a vampire.

Shaking the memory from her head, the shoes did at least prompt her to do the only thing sensible thing she could do at this point and ten minutes later she was at Kate's front door.

"Everyone's out," said Kate ushering her in, "So before we sort out your outfit you have to tell me how your talk with Sebastian went." She was clearly excited at the prospect of some gossip, "When I didn't hear from you yesterday I assumed no news was good news?"

Elsa was frantically trying to decide exactly what to tell Kate about her evening but she needn't have bothered. As usual Kate seemed to be the only person in the world that Elsa could communicate with telepathically, whether she wanted to or not.

"Oh my god!" Kate exclaimed, without a single word coming out of Elsa's mouth, "It went well didn't it? I mean it went really well!" She nodded as if to drive her point home, Elsa got it loud and clear and gently banged her head on the kitchen table.

"Kate, can't I have any secrets from you?" she asked, knowing that she did of course keep a lot of secrets from her closest friend.

"Nope," said Kate brightly, "I can't believe it though, you little minx! So that's it then, you two are a thing now? You'd better be if you did what I think you did. Was it good? You don't have to say. Yes you do, just don't give me all the gory details. On second thoughts do!"

Elsa laughed, "I'm not going to kiss and tell," she said and Kate pouted but didn't push her.

"Are you happy?" she asked instead.

"Very"

"And are you sure it's what you want?"

"Very," Elsa was smiling, "I want you to get to know him, the him that I see." Well, maybe not all of it, "He's coming out with me tonight."

Kate clapped her hands and jumped up, "Which makes the right outfit all the more important," she said and grabbed Elsa's hand, pulling her upstairs.

Elsa soon found herself in Kate's bedroom having various tiny scraps of fabric thrown in her direction with the insistence that she would look AMAZING in all of them.

Holding up a purple sparkly item, Elsa couldn't even decide which way up it was supposed to go and looked doubtfully at Kate, "I don't know," she said, "None of them feel me."

"You're just not used to getting dressed up," Kate insisted and she looked at all the items of clothing she'd selected so far and pulled a face, "No, you're right, they're not you." She looked suddenly triumphant, "I've got it!" She disappeared into the wardrobe again and reappeared with another dress. It was black, it was simple, it looked tiny, "Try it on," Kate thrust it towards Elsa's doubtful face. She took the dress and went to the bathroom; at least it was black.

Emerging minutes later, Elsa was feeling more confident. The dress fit perfectly and when she'd looked in the bathroom mirror she had to admit that what she could see looked, well, pretty good actually. Kate squealed when she came back into the bedroom, "That is perfect," she said, "You look great!"

Elsa looked in the full-length mirror and was pleasantly surprised at what she saw. She sometimes forgot how flawless her skin could be now, how she almost glowed at times. The dress was a stark contrast to her pale skin as was her dark hair that hung in loose, perfect waves over her shoulders. The effect was dramatic and the dress clung in all the right places, Elsa barely recognised herself.

She smoothed the material over her hips and turned to the side slightly, "Are you sure?" she asked Kate, "You don't mind me borrowing it?"

"Of course not," said Kate generously, "You look better than I do in it anyway. It suits your skin tone, your hair, your eyes," she studied Elsa as she did sometimes now, making Elsa feel very aware of how she knew her appearance had change over the last few months, "I swear, you'd look good in a bin bag these days." Kate said finally, "Ever since they diagnosed that blood disorder, you've looked positively radiant."

Elsa tried to laugh Kate's comments off, "So what your saying is I'd looked like hell for the seventeen years beforehand?" she said.

"No, of course not," said Kate, "But looking good just seems effortless to you now, you don't even have to try."

"Well now you know how I've felt standing next to you for years." Elsa wanted to get off the subject of her looks, "I need to get going, I thought I'd pop into my dad's work and wish him happy New Year before I go out later."

"Ok," Kate passed Elsa a bag to put the dress in, "I'll see you later then?"

"You will," Elsa assured her, "I'm looking forward to meeting Aiden."

Stepping into the lift at Haven, Elsa was aware of someone running in after her and grabbing the door as it was about to close. She knew instantly that it was a werewolf, the smell was unmistakable. As the door pulled back, a tall young man with sandy hair and an easy grin on his face stepped into the lift with her.

"Hi," he said, "Sorry, I'm in a bit of a rush or I'd have waited for the next one, I know I stink."

Elsa was taken aback at his forthright honesty and didn't quite know what to say. The young man laughed, "You're a vampire right?" he said, "And I'm a sweaty wolf so I know I smell pretty rank to you." He pushed a button, "Facility floor please."

"You don't smell that bad," Elsa said finally as the lift began to move, "I'm kind of getting used to it."

"You've spent time around wolves?" the stranger asked.

"Just one that works with my dad."

A look of realisation crossed the young man's face, "You're Marcus Shaw's daughter!" he said and held out a hand which Elsa shook. It was warm and he had a firm grip, Elsa couldn't help but notice the muscles that bulged beneath his shirt, "I'm Logan," he said, "Gray's brother." The lift stopped and Logan indicated for Elsa to step out first.

She smiled, his friendly nature was impossible to resist, "I'm Elsa," she said, "I would have never guessed you were Gray's brother." They began walking down the corridor together.

"I know, he's a bit of a moody arse at times but he's cool really." said Logan, "He takes life very seriously but then I suppose he sees some serious stuff."

"Are you the brother who has been looking out for my friend Kate?" Elsa asked.

"That's me," Logan replied, "I just made sure she smelled enough of wolf to put any opportunistic vampires off while you were away. Now I'm just keeping an eye on her from a distance."

"How did you do that?" Elsa asked, "Make her smell of wolf I mean." She'd been dying to know but couldn't bring herself to ask Gray, Logan seemed much more open to questions.

"I didn't wee in a big circle around her if that's what you're worried about!" Logan laughed.

"I didn't think that!" Elsa insisted, although the thought had entered her mind.

"I just broke into her house and rolled around in her clothes," Logan said, as if it was a completely normal thing to do, "Simple really."

Elsa couldn't decide if he was joking or not, the twinkle in his bright blue eyes seemed to be permanent and wolves were not as easy to read as humans. She shrugged, as long as Kate was safe she didn't really care how he' done it, "Well she doesn't smell anymore," she said.

"No, well that vampire's gone now isn't he? Plus she's got you back to protect her," Logan reasoned, "I hear you did a fairly good job last time."

"Pure luck I think," said Elsa, "You're still watching Kate?"

"Just some light surveillance," said Logan, "I'm kind of in training to work for Haven full time."

"Have you seen her new boyfriend?" Elsa asked.

A momentary dark look passed over Logan's face and he frowned, "You mean Aiden?" he said, as if the name left a bad taste in his mouth.

"What's your take on him?" Elsa was interested by Logan's expression, even on a werewolf she recognised a flash of jealousy when she saw it.

"I can't find anything on him," Logan said, obviously annoyed by the fact, "He seems to have money but I don't know where from, I haven't got a surname so it's hard to find out anything about him. He seems to treat her well, taking her out, spending his money on her and he hasn't really put a foot wrong as far as I can tell but…" He shrugged.

"But you don't like him?" Elsa prompted.

"No," Logan admitted, "There's just something about the way he carries himself, I can't put my finger on it."

"I haven't met him yet but I think I know what you mean," Elsa said, "I'm meeting them at a club tonight, Aiden doesn't know, apparently he is nervous about meeting Kate's friends and family so we thought we'd surprise him."

"I'll be there later too," Logan said, "I was told I could scale surveillance back but something about that dude just gets my hackles up." He was almost growling and Elsa smiled to herself. Definite jealousy, Logan had a thing for Kate! "Do you need someone to go with?" Logan asked then, though Elsa knew he was just being polite, it was not her he wanted to be there with.

"No, thanks," said Elsa, "I'll be with someone."

"Story of my life," Logan grinned, putting his hand to his heart as if his feelings were hurt. He paused at a turn in the corridor, "I'm going this way," he said, pointing a thumb to the left.

"I'm going that way," Elsa said, indicating to the right, "Maybe I'll see you later?"

"Sure, nice to meet you Elsa," Logan shook her hand again, Elsa found herself thinking how nice he seemed and how much happier she'd have been if Kate had shown her a picture with Logan's smiling eyes in it, rather than Aiden's.

"You too," she said, meaning it. She gave him a little wave then turned and walked two doors down to her father's office. The door was open and he was staring intently at his computer screen.

"Hi," Elsa said, knocking lightly on the door.

Marcus jumped, "Hi sweetheart," he said looking surprised, "Sorry, I was miles away, come in." He stood up and gave her a hug before pulling out a chair for her to sit down.

"I thought I'd pop in and wish you Happy New Year," said Elsa, "You know, just to remind you that it is New Years Eve and most people are planning a night out, not staring at a computer screen." She looked meaningfully at her father and he smiled back at her.

"I'm fine," he said, "There's been a couple of developments with the blood movement case, I'm just waiting for an email, some pictures of suspected affiliates," he minimised the email window he'd been staring at, "But a watched pot never boils does it? Do you want a drink?" Elsa was about to shake her head when he added, "We've got bags in the fridge."

"Oh, ok then," she said, "Probably a good idea to eat before I go out." She got up and followed her father a little way down the corridor to what looked like a staff room.

Marcus pointed her too the fridge and handed her a mug, "Where are you off to tonight then?"

"A new club in town," Elsa said, squeezing dark red blood from a blood bag into the mug before popping it in the microwave.

"A club?" Marcus raised his eyebrows to her as he filled the kettle and put it on to boil, "Is it under-eighteens night?"

Elsa rolled her eyes, "No Dad it's not," she said, "I'll be technically eighteen in a couple of months and I really don't think it matters under the circumstances does it?"

"I suppose not," Marcus relented, "I can't help it though, I'm still your dad. You going with Kate?"

"Yes," Elsa lied quickly, she didn't want to get into a conversation with her father about Sebastian now and besides, she would see Kate there. She convinced herself it wasn't a complete lie, "And I met Logan on the way up, he said he's going to come out tonight too."

Marcus smiled, "He doesn't have to do that," he said, "I think he might have a little crush on your friend."

"I think you might be right," Elsa agreed, sipping at the blood she'd taken out of the microwave. She remembered when she had been disgusted by her desire to drink blood, now it felt as normal to her as having a cup of tea and she didn't think she would ever tire of the taste of it as it ran smoothly down her throat, or the instant, mild feeling of euphoria that flooded her body when she drank. "Logan seems nice," she said, enjoying the warm tingle that was spreading through her body.

"He's a fine young man," Marcus said, "Kate could certainly do worse."

That surprised Elsa, "You'd approve of a werewolf dating a human?" she asked.

"Why not?" Marcus said, "Werewolves only lose control once a month, the rest of the time they are as good as human and they know exactly when they are going to change so it can be perfectly safe for them to have relationships with humans if that's what they both want."

Elsa was interested in her father's reasoning; knowing he wasn't against interspecies relationships was a start, maybe he could be introduced to the idea of her and Sebastian at some point. If Elsa could ever figure out exactly what Sebastian was.

"What are you smiling at?" Marcus asked, snapping her back from thoughts of Sebastian, she didn't realise she'd been smiling just thinking about him.

"Just looking forward to a good night out later," she said, unable to wipe the smile from her face. She tapped her mug against her father's, "Cheers Dad, Happy New Year."

*AN - Please keep the votes and comments coming if you're enjoying what you are reading, the more the merrier! Exciting developments are coming soon ;) *

# I Guess It Wasn't You We Needed To Be Worried About.

-------------------------------------------------

✱ AN - for those of you following the soundtrack to this book, I've chosen Voodoo by Robots In Disguise. A sexy track that perfectly matches the effect Elsa and Sebastina have on each other. Plus, it's the band I envision playing at the club in this chapter. Don't forget to vote folks! ✱

Elsa heard Sebastian walking up the front path before he knocked the door. It gave her enough time to slick on some mascara and run her fingers through her hair before seeing him. She checked herself in the mirror one last time, yes, it really was her. She shook her head thinking she would never get used to being confident that she looked good before she left the house.

It had surprised her when she heard Sebastian walking up to her house, they hadn't arranged for him to meet her at home, thank goodness her dad was at work, that would have been an interesting conversation to say the least.

When the knock at the door finally came, Elsa resisted the urge to fly to the door at her usual speed and instead took a deep breath and made her way downstairs at as close to a normal human speed as she could manage. It was ridiculous that she felt nervous after the previous evening but she did, her stomach was fluttering and flipping and she would have been sweating if she could.

She opened the door, "Hi," she said, as naturally as she could manage, "I wasn't expecting you to come to me." The sight of him took her breath away as it always did, he was wearing dark trousers, a dark, well fitted shirt with the sleeves rolled part way up and his hair had the 'just got out of bed' look she adored.

Sebastian didn't say anything for moment and Elsa wondered if she' offended him and searched her mind for something else to say. Then he stepped forward and pulled her towards him with one hand, the other gently tilting her face up towards his. He kissed her softly, letting it linger just long enough for her to get lost in it completely.

"You look beautiful," he breathed in her ear before he released her, "I know you didn't ask me to pick you up but I thought that if we were going to try and do something as normal as a date, I should do it properly."

Elsa gathered herself and stood aside to let him in, closing the door behind him, "You've certainly made a good start," she said.

"I'm a bit rusty," Sebastian admitted.

"Are you sure you want to do this?" Elsa said, "There's going to be a lot of people there, will you be ok?"

"I'll be fine," Sebastian said, "It'll be a good few weeks before crowds become a problem for me, right now I'm completely in control." He looked at her hungrily, "Well, maybe not completely." He had dug his hands into his pockets as if he was trying to stop himself from doing something that would distract them from leaving the house at all, Elsa felt her knees weaken slightly at the thought, "What about you anyway?" he asked, "Are you all serumed up?"

Elsa laughed, "Serumed up? Is that a word?" Sebastian shrugged. "I'll just go and do that now," Elsa said and before Sebastian even noticed she was gone, she was back, coat on, handbag in hand, "Shall we?"

"How do you move that fast?" Sebastian asked, shaking his head at her antics.

"Truthfully I have no idea," Elsa said, "It's just a perk I like to make use of every now and then, don't tell me you don't go for a little fly around just because you can." Sebastian smiled and took her arm as they walked down the path. Elsa realised he was leading her to a car, "I thought it would be a bike or a taxi," she said.

"Well looking at that dress, it's a good job I didn't bring the bike," Sebastian said, "I do have a car too, it just doesn't come out very often."

He certainly did have a car, an Aston Martin Vanquish no less. Elsa gasped, "Is this yours?" she asked incredulously.

"It is," Sebastian actually looked a bit embarrassed, "I bought it on impulse when I was in a rare good mood, it's a bit much really isn't it?"

"It's amazing,' Elsa ran her hand over the jet black paintwork, "Where have you been hiding it?"

"In storage," Sebastian said, "I've got a few cars and bikes, they're a bit of a weakness of mine."

"And you sleep on a mattress on a warehouse floor?" Elsa didn't understand the logic, "How do you afford this?"

"I've been around a long time," Sebastian shrugged, "And as you know, my living costs aren't exactly high." He opened the door for her and she got in, the car was even sexier on the inside, she could have quite happily lived in it. Sebastian got in the other side. He put his hands on the steering wheel but didn't start the car.

"Cars and bikes have always been my one treat to myself," he said, "The one bit of beauty I'd allow." He looked across at her, his gaze intense and honest, "Until you came along."

Elsa just wanted to devour him, that was twice he'd referred to her as beautiful, those walls of his were well and truly down and she was loving every minute of it. The serious nature of what he was saying was not lost on her though, this was all very new to him and she wanted him to know that she understood.

"You've punished yourself for long enough Sebastian," she said, squeezing his thigh and trying not to dwell on how rock hard it was, "Things are going to be different now I promise."

The club was packed. Elsa had not been so close to so many people since turning. She had underestimated the effect it could have on her, she'd been more worried about Sebastian but she now realised it was her that was going to find it difficult. She'd become over confident of her tolerance and had not bought any further serum doses with her. From the moment they walked into the club, her senses were assaulted by hundreds of hearts beating to the thud of the bass heavy dance music and the smell of so many different blood types, mixed with higher levels of adrenaline from the clubbers, many of whom she could tell were on drugs that had increased their heart rate, making them all the more appealing. She was at an all you can eat buffet featuring some of the most appealing foods she had ever been offered, young pumped up men and women distracted by their hedonistic pursuits and totally oblivious to the fact that there were predators in their midst.

She felt Sebastian's hand on the small of her back and tore her eyes away from the girl dancing in front of her. Sebastian was looking concerned, "Are you ok?" he asked. The music was loud but Elsa could hear him as clearly as she could hear the heightened pulse of the dancing girl. She shook her head and Sebastian took her hand firmly and guided her to the edge of the room and up a flight of stairs that led to a mezzanine floor where the chill out lounge was located. The leather sofas were all full but Sebastian simply glared at one unfortunate couple until they were convinced it was in their best interests to give up their seat. It didn't take long.

Once sat down and out of the crowd of writhing, heaving bodies on the dance floor, Elsa felt more in control, "I'm sorry," she said, "I guess it wasn't you we needed to be worried about."

"We don't have to stay," Sebastian offered.

"It's better up here," Elsa said, "I want to see Kate and Aiden."

"Are you sure? You were looking at some of those people down there as if they'd been dipped in chocolate and were wearing an 'eat me' sign." Sebastian was joking but there was truth in what he was saying an Elsa knew it.

"We don't have to stay long," she relented, "I really feel like I need to get a handle on this guy Kate's been seeing, I've got a bad feeling about him."

"Fair enough," Sebastian said, "We could stay up here, there's a good view of the club so it should be easy to spot them."

"Elsa?" The voice came from behind them and Elsa turned to find John Edwards smiling at her. Then he looked at Sebastian and Elsa saw a flash of disappointment cross his face followed by fear. Last time the three of them had met, Sebastian had thrown John across the corridor.

"Hi John," Elsa said, she hadn't liked the way John had behaved that day but she also knew it wasn't his fault. He'd been interested in her before she was a vampire and after, she knew it was a feature of vampirism that men could be drawn to her and have no control over it.

"I'm sorry, I didn't realise…" John took a step back and then turned and virtually ran away from them. Elsa had felt Sebastian tense beside her when John had approached, she had even heard the tiniest hint of a low growl from his throat and now she felt him relax a little as they watched John disappear down the stairs.

"It wasn't his fault," she said, noting Sebastian's still dark look, "It's because of what I am, he couldn't help the way he behaved." A sudden thought occurred to her, what if that was the only reason Sebastian wanted to be with her? The thought made her heart crack a little and the expression on her face must have been clear. Sebastian shook his head adamantly; she didn't have to say a word.

"It's not like that with me," he said.

"How can you know?" Elsa asked, unconvinced.

"You weren't a vampire before that car crash were you?" Sebastian was looking her directly in the eyes as if he was trying to convey something else to her than simply what he was saying.

"No." Elsa didn't understand what he was getting at.

"The first day of college, you were sat in the canteen, talking to Kate. I sensed you before I saw you and there was just something about you. I was drawn to you then, I had to leave the room." Elsa couldn't believe what she was hearing, "And then when you ended up sat next to me in history, I didn't know what to do, you had an effect on me I couldn't explain and I didn't know what it meant for either of us. That's why I pushed you away so much, I was afraid of what I was feeling. I was afraid of hurting you."

Sebastian looked away from her then as if he was embarrassed, "I had issues with John way before I caught him pawing over you in the corridor."

Elsa looked confused for a moment and then her quick mind made the connection it needed. She remembered the night of the party, her and John in the woods and that awful, uncomfortable kiss interrupted by the sound of something large in the trees, "That was you!" she exclaimed and Sebastian clearly knew what she was referring to. He looked sheepish but also a little defensive.

"I was just out minding my own business," he said, "Going for a little fly about, just because I can," He caught her eyes again then and gave a slight grin.

"Kate basically forced John on me," Elsa explained, "She was always trying to get me set up with someone."

"You didn't seem to be complaining too much," Elsa detected a strange edge to Sebastian's voice.

"You're not seriously jealous?" she asked shocked, "Of John Edwards?"

"I wanted to tear him apart." Sebastian said simply with a slight shrug of the shoulders. Coming from anyone else it would have been exaggerating for effect, coming from Sebastian it was a distinct possibility.

Elsa simply raised an eyebrow, "I was being polite," she said, "It was horrible and you," she poked him in the chest playfully, "Have absolutely nothing to worry about."

In one smooth movement, Sebastian pulled her into his lap and his mouth was on hers, igniting the fire inside her that smouldered whenever he was anywhere near her. The club melted away, the only heart she could hear was his, the only blood she could feel rushing through veins beneath the skin was his, the only scent in the room that could have any impact on her in that moment was his.

Sebastian broke the kiss first, breathing heavily. His eyes glowed amber and his face had changed subtly. Elsa bought her hand to his face, holding his gaze as he calmed himself.

"Maybe we should save that for later," Sebastian said finally and Elsa laughed.

"Nothing to worry about," she said again and then stood up from the sofa, pulling Sebastian to his feet too. They walked to the railings at the edge of the mezzanine floor and looked out over the crowd. Elsa forced herself to look only for Kate and her keen eyesight soon picked her friend out of the crowd. She was standing at the bar on the far side of the dance floor, gazing into the eyes of her male companion.

Aiden. Elsa's eyes narrowed as she watched them. Kate was clearly besotted but Aiden's body language rang alarm bells for Elsa straight away. She could see the stiffness in his muscles as he held Kate in his arms, the look of boredom on his face as Kate leaned up to speak in his ear and the predatory gazes he was throwing at other girls. Something was very wrong with the picture Elsa was seeing and when she looked to Sebastian for his opinion she could see that he was thinking the exact same thing.

"What do you want to do?" he asked.

"I guess we go over and say hello," Elsa sighed, wondering how she was going to deal with it.

As she turned to make her way to the stairs, Elsa felt her phone buzz in her bag. She paused to pull it out and looked at the screen, it was her dad. She held the phone up to her ear.

"Dad?"

"Elsa? Can you hear me? All I can hear is music."

"It's ok Dad, I can hear you, what's up?"

"Remember the intel I was waiting for? It finally arrived. They're using humans Elsa, it's something they've never done before."

Elsa was confused, "What do you mean?"

"I don't know if you can hear me Elsa, I'll send pictures. Just be aware, be on the look out. Love you." Marcus hung up. A second later Elsa's phone chirped with a photo message. Then another. And another. Each one was a photo, similar to the ones Elsa had been shown of the vampires in the blood movement that had been known to have been in the area. These pictures were different; the subjects were clearly humans, not vampires. Elsa didn't recognise any of them but something was eating at her as she scrolled through each one. Her phone beeped one last time with the final picture and as Elsa opened it the nagging feeling in her stomach exploded.

Aiden.

# Isn't He Great?

"Elsa what is it?" Sebastian had grabbed her arm, sensing the change in her, a split second later and she'd have been flying through the throng of clubbers to put herself between Aiden and Kate.

"Aiden," she said, showing him her phone, which beeped a low battery warning to her, "He works for them, the blood movement." She was seething with anger and could feel her fangs, she was heading for full on vampire in public and Sebastian saw immediately that she needed calming down. He pulled her close, her face buried into his chest to hide the raised veins around her dark, red-rimmed eyes. He lowered his head to whisper in her ear, knowing that she could hear him.

"You need to calm down Elsa, we can deal with this but not like that, not here. He's only human, but so is everybody else in this room, someone could get hurt." He continued holding her firmly, stroking her hair and she knew she could break away from him if she wanted to but she also knew he was right. With every ounce of self-control she had she pushed her anger down inside, quieting the roaring fire into ice cold steel. No one was going to hurt her friend.

She nodded finally and felt Sebastian's grip relax, he took her face gently in his hands and studied her eyes until he was satisfied she was in control. "What do you want to do?" he asked, "It's too public for either of us to really do our thing."

"We need to separate them," Elsa said, "Get Kate out of here safely without Aiden realising that we know."

"So you think you can control yourself enough to walk up and talk to this guy?" Sebastian looked doubtful.

"Can you?" Elsa turned the question round.

"I'll be fine unless he tried to hurt you," Sebastian said simply, "If that happens, I'll kill him and I don't care who's watching."

"Well same goes for me if he hurts Kate." Elsa stated, "Otherwise, I'm fine, totally in control."

"Ok then," Sebastian straightened up and rested a reassuring hand on the small of her back, "Let's go and 'accidentally' bump into your friend and her evil ass boyfriend."

Elsa was too focused on what she needed to do to allow the sweating, heaving mass of bodies to bother her as they pushed their way across the dance floor to the bar. They positioned themselves a short way down from Kate and Aiden and Elsa gave one last intent look to Sebastian who returned an almost imperceptible nod. Elsa turned and leaned across the bar as if she was ordering a drink then looked across and caught Kate's eye almost immediately, she'd already spotted them and gave Elsa a conspiratorial wink. Elsa played along, "Kate!" she shouted over, trying to inject as much surprise into her tone as possible, "Hi!"

Kate waved enthusiastically and tapped Aiden, encouraging him to turn and pointing across at Elsa and Sebastian. Aiden's eyes locked with Elsa's for a split second, empty and cold. Then he smiled and waved too, the chill gone so fast no human would have spotted it. Kate pushed her way towards them, dragging Aiden with her and gave Elsa an excited hug before leaning up to Aiden and shouting over the music, "This is Elsa," she gave Elsa a knowing and very poorly veiled look, "and Sebastian."

Aiden smiled down at Elsa, he was tall but not as tall and Sebastian and nowhere near as well built, if it came to it he would not be a problem. Elsa was positive he was human, no smell of wolf and clearly not a vampire.

"Nice to meet you both," he shouted. Elsa pretended to be having difficulty hearing. Frowning and holding a hand to her ear she pointed up towards the mezzanine floor. Kate nodded, understanding what Elsa was suggesting and leaned to talk into Aiden's ear once again. He too nodded and took her hand, motioning for Elsa and Sebastian to lead the way. Sebastian did not like having Aiden behind them, Elsa could feel his tension but he gave nothing away on the surface as they made their way back upstairs and away from the peak volume of the music.

As they walked Sebastian put his arm around Elsa's shoulder in pulled her in to whisper in her ear again, "How are you planning to separate them?" he asked.

"I don't know," Elsa whispered back, hoping he could hear her and knowing that Kate and Aiden couldn't, "Maybe you could go and get a drink and I could take a girly trip to the toilet with Kate? Then we could meet back up without Aiden." Sebastian gave her arm a small squeeze, he'd heard and understood.

Once sat down upstairs, Kate could barely contain her excitement, "It's great to see you both!" she said, throwing a generous smile in Sebastian's direction, "I knew you two were going to end up together." Elsa cringed but Sebastian played it perfectly smiling and throwing his arm around Elsa's shoulder.

"I'm feeling very lucky," he said, "I'm sure I don't deserve her." It was exactly the right thing to say and Elsa could see any small doubts Kate still had about Sebastian's suitability fading fast.

Turning to Aiden, Elsa switched on her own entirely false smile whilst imagining snapping his neck, "So you're the elusive Aiden?" she said, "I've heard a lot about you."

"All good I hope," he replied smoothly. If he was nervous or suspicious of Elsa, he didn't show it. Elsa could study him properly now he was close and not a single muscle fibre twitched to show even a tiny crack in his façade. He was good she'd give him that.

"Of course," she said, "In fact, Kate almost had me wondering if you were too good to be true." Not a flicker, Aiden's mask remained intact and there were no changes in his heart rate or blood pressure to suggest he was uncomfortable but Elsa felt Sebastian tense very slightly once again, he thought she was pushing it.

"Why don't I go and get us all a drink?" Sebastian offered, keeping to Elsa's plan.

Aiden held up a hand and stood, "This round's on me," he insisted to Elsa's surprise and pointed to the bottle Kate was holding, "Same again?"

"Please," Kate replied.

"Thanks Aiden," Elsa said, "I'll have the same as Kate please."

"Whatever you're having is fine," Sebastian added, "Thanks, do you need a hand?"

"No, I can manage four bottles," said Aiden, "I'm sure Kate wants to give you the third degree anyway mate." There was a subtle lack of friendliness in Aiden's voice as he called Sebastian 'mate' and Elsa could sense the inner growl she was sure Sebastian was trying to swallow as he kept the smile fixed on his face. Aiden winked at Kate and she smiled back at him adoringly; it was all Elsa could do not to shudder. She had to admit though, this was going better than she'd hoped, Aiden was willingly separating himself from Kate, which was going to make their job much easier.

Watching him disappear down the stairs to the bar, Kate sighed, "Isn't he great?" she asked, turning back to Elsa, her eyes shining.

Elsa wasn't sure exactly what to say, how could she tell Kate that the man she'd fallen for wasn't what he seemed to be? How could she explain everything she needed to explain and convince Kate to leave before Aiden got back with the drinks? Elsa thought back to some of her long conversations with Hesper about her abilities and the things she might be able to do as a vampire. There was something she could try but there was no guarantee it would work. Hesper had told her not all vampires could do it well but Elsa already knew that she could exert a strong pull over people if she needed to, John had been evidence of that. She took Kate's hands in her own and looked her friend directly in the eyes, trying to concentrate all of her will and intent into the words she was about to say.

"Kate, don't you think we should go outside and get some fresh air?" she asked, feeling Sebastian's eyes on her, he had no idea what she was trying to do.

Kate frowned at her, "What do you mean?" she asked, sounding confused. She did not break Elsa's gaze though so Elsa tried again.

"It's hot and stuffy in here, you aren't feeling to good are you? You want to go outside and get some fresh air."

Kate's expression became a little glazed, "It is hot in here," she said but her voice still had an edge of uncertainty, as if she didn't quite trust what she could hear herself saying.

"Really hot," Elsa agreed, "Aiden could meet us outside."

"He could, maybe we should get some air," Kate was beginning to sound more sure of herself and a sheen of sweat had appeared on her forehead. She wiped her brow with the back of her hand, "Do you mind if we nip out for some air?" she asked Elsa, as if she had just come up with the idea all by herself, "It's really stuffy in here, Aiden will meet us out there."

"No problem," said Elsa with relief, that had been easier than she'd thought and Sebastian looked suitably impressed. As they followed Kate out, he spoke to her in a low voice so that Kate couldn't hear.

"Don't get any ideas about trying that on me," he said with a grin.

Elsa returned her own mischievous smile, "I have other ways of getting around you," she said.

"Elsa!" Her head snapped round at the sound of someone calling her name and the three of them paused. Logan was pushing through the crowd towards them, "Fancy seeing you here," he said as he finally reached them.

"Logan, hi," Elsa was anxious to keep moving but also knew it was important that Logan understood the situation, he could be useful to them, "This is Logan, he works at my dad's place," she explained to Kate and Sebastian, "Logan this is Kate and Sebastian," she didn't give anymore details than that, knowing that Logan knew exactly who Kate was and not wanting to go into too much detail about Sebastian. Logan grinned widely and shook Kate's hand then turned to offer his hand to Sebastian. The smile on his face faded and his hand hesitated. Both Logan and Sebastian looked momentarily confused by each other, then a realisation crossed Sebastian's face as Logan's muscles tensed and he assumed a subtly more defensive position, Elsa sensed that if he could have raised his hackles at that point, he would have.

"Sebastian, take Kate out, I'll be with you in a minute," Elsa pushed Sebastian towards Kate, anxious to get him as far away from Logan as she could as quickly as possible.

"But," Sebastian began to protest, he didn't want to leave Elsa with this stranger and he certainly didn't want them to get separated. Elsa just gave him a look that she hoped explained everything. Of course it didn't, "Kate really needs to get some air, I will be out in a minute." Her tone made it clear she wouldn't take no for an answer, her eyes asked Sebastian to trust her. Finally, he did, taking Kate's arm and throwing a warning glare at Logan before leaving the club.

"What the hell was that?" Logan asked urgently.

"What?" Elsa wasn't sure exactly what Logan thought he'd picked up from Sebastian.

"That!" Logan pointed firmly at Sebastian's back as he and Kate pushed through the club doors on their way outside, "Because it's not human and it doesn't smell like anything I've ever come across before and believe me, Gray has come home smelling of some pretty weird stuff over the years."

"It's nothing to worry about," Elsa said, anxious to get him off the topic of Sebastian so she could fill him in on what was really happening.

"How the hell do you know?" Logan asked, "What is he? Because he smells bloody dangerous to me."

"I just know," Elsa said, "Please Logan, he's a friend, I trust him completely and that's all I can tell you right now, there's something more important and I don't have time…"

Logan's expression changed as he sensed her urgency, "What's wrong?"

"Have you seen the pictures my dad sent out?"

"What pictures?"

Elsa pulled her phone out of her bag, a second low battery warning was flashing but there was nothing she could do about that, "The blood movement have been recruiting humans to help them. I don't know how or why yet but look," she held up the photo of Aiden and Logan's eyes became immediately dark.

"Aiden," he snarled, his heart rate jumped and his fists clenched.

"He's at the bar," Elsa explained, "We were trying to get Kate out of here when you found us. You need to call this in to Haven and we need to get Kate as far away from him as possible. I don't know what his plan was but he's working for Vincent, it can't be good."

"I'm on it," Logan growled, "Get out of here but Elsa-" he hesitated.

"What?"

"Are you sure you're safe? With – whatever he is?"

"One hundred percent," Elsa said, "Please don't say anything to anyone at Haven, I'm going to sort it out, I just need to be careful. I really care about him Logan, he's a good guy I know he is. Trust me."

Logan hesitated for a moment, "Vampires are good judges of character right?" he asked, knowing the answer but needing to hear it from her.

"The best," Elsa said confidently, "Way better than wolves." She gave him a small, hopeful smiled and was grateful when he returned it.

"Go," he said simply and turned towards the bar.

Elsa put a hand on his shoulder, "Wait," she said, "There are other pictures, other humans working for the movement. Aiden might not be the only one here so you need to be careful. Don't approach him Logan, call it in."

Logan nodded taking out his phone, "Send me the pictures."

Elsa took his number and forwarded the files, conscious of how precious time was and cursing as her phone finally died. Depending on how busy the bar was Aiden may already be making his way back to where he was expecting to find them, every second she was stood with Logan was another second closer to Aiden spotting that they were gone and realising that they knew who he was and what he was there for. Finally confident that Logan had all the information she could give him, she gave him a quick hug, "Be careful," she said, "Tell my dad I'm on my way to Haven with Kate, just me. We'll catch up later ok?"

"Later," Logan agreed. His jaw was set, his eyes steely. He was furious that someone like Aiden had been allowed to get anywhere near Kate on his watch and determined to fix the problem one way or another. Elsa was worried about what he might do next but there was nothing more she could do, she had to get out to Sebastian and Kate and they had to get moving. There was no way of knowing exactly how many people in the club might be working for Vincent. It was a clever move by the blood movement, recruiting humans; supernatural beings were far easier for fellow supernatural's to spot. Humans were just, well, human's. Especially when they were as skilled at masking their emotions and true intentions as Aiden was, unless you knew they were there and you were looking for them, they would be hard to spot. Plus she had no way of looking over those pictures again now until she could charge up her phone. Hopefully there would be a suitable charger at her dad's office.

Elsa began to make her way to the club exit once more but a sudden strange sensation caused her to stop in her tracks. She put her hand to her chest, to the spot where her heart would have once been beating beneath her skin and felt an unusual pain. Not a sharp pain, but a dull ache and a sensation of – loss. It felt as if her heart was being sucked slowly from her chest and along with the feeling came a sudden gripping fear. Something was wrong.

*AN - I do like to leave a chapter on a cliffhanger! But don't worry, updates will be coming quicker as I'm off work for the next two weeks :) What do you think could be wrong? Can Logan get the message to Haven? Does Aiden know what Elsa and Sebastian are trying to do and could a mere human stop them even if he did? How are they going to explain all of this to Kate and will Logan tell Marcus about Sebastian? I have pretty much decided most of the answers to these questions but I'm always open to opinion and suggestion ;) Oh and don't forget to vote! *

# Not All Right.

------

> ✱ AN - For those of you following the soundtrack to this book, I've chosen Freak On A Leash By Korn - boom! ✱

Elsa was outside in a split second, not caring if anyone saw her move so fast. The street outside was deserted but Elsa could hear Kate's screams around the corner and was horrified to find her friend hunched over Sebastian's inert form on the ground. She could smell his blood and see the dark wet sheen on his black shirt and her world began to spin. Kneeling at his side, Elsa opened his shirt and placed her hands over what were clearly two gunshot wounds, close together right above his heart. She could hear his heart struggling but it was still beating and his blood pulsed from the wounds, seeping through her fingers with every beat his heart gave. Kate's screams faded into the background, there was only Sebastian.

Elsa had moved fast, her actions a blur but to her it felt like time had slowed down to crawl. The air had become thick and every movement she made felt like she was moving under water, pushing against an invisible force that wouldn't let her move fast enough. She would carry them both, she could do it, she wouldn't be able to move quite as fast but she could do it.

"Elsa," his voice was weak and he was trying to move his arm but couldn't, "I will be fine – Kate."

Elsa was momentarily confused but then it hit her. Sebastian had tried time and time again to kill himself. He couldn't die. He would be fine eventually. Despite that knowledge, the fact that he was lying bleeding on the pavement was still causing her indescribable fear and pain. Her head was telling her he would be okay, her heart was screaming in agony and she realised tears were streaming down her face.

"Kate," Sebastian repeated, his eyes driving his point home. Elsa finally began to take the whole scene in. Hardly a moment had passed but Sebastian was right, there was no time to waste. Something had gone wrong, someone knew they were trying to get away with Kate and Sebastian had been shot. Elsa could see no assailant and she needed to get Kate to safety.

"Did you see who did this?" she asked Sebastian urgently.

"Sniper. Don't know where it came from, you need to go. I can't move yet."

"I can carry you too."

"Faster without me." Elsa knew he was right.

"We need an ambulance!" Kate was shaking, clearly terrified and trying desperately to steady her hands enough to call for help on her phone. Elsa grabbed her hands.

"No!" Sebastian managed.

"No! Kate, no, look at me." Elsa said sharply. Kate's eyes were wild and wide but they fixed on Elsa's immediately, "You are calm, everything is going to be ok, we don't need an ambulance but we do need to leave, do you understand?"

Kate nodded, her breathing calming and her shudders subsiding. Elsa turned back to Sebastian, she hated to leave him like this but she knew she had to. She leaned down, her mouth close to his ear, "I'll come back for you," she said through fresh tears, "I lo-"

Elsa felt a thud against her back that threw her onto the pavement next to Sebastian and provoked fresh screams from Kate who backed herself against the wall in terror, her arms wrapped protectively over her head. Elsa's vampire senses could feel every part of what was happening in the minutest detail. The bullet that had torn through her back nicked her spine, which changed it's trajectory slightly and sent it through her left lung, shattering a few ribs before it exited through the front of her chest. She felt the skin explode as the bullet left her body, she felt her skull crack as her head hit the pavement and she felt the steady flow of blood oozing out of her chest. She felt something else too, she felt the heat of a chemical substance from the bullet begin to spread quickly and she realised that despite her strength, she was not going to be getting up from this gunshot. She couldn't move and she knew that the same thing must have happened to Sebastian. It was no normal bullet, there was a definite plan behind what was happening and there was now absolutely nothing she could do about it.

So when Aiden sauntered around the corner and crouched beside them smiling triumphantly, Elsa couldn't tear his throat out like she wanted to. When hands picked her up roughly and bundled her into a van with a hysterical Kate, she couldn't throw her captors across the street, grab Kate and run faster than any human could ever hope to follow. And when she saw the anguish on Sebastian's face, the faint amber glow in his eyes and the strain of his muscles as he tried desperately to move his body, and heard the agonized roar he let out as the van doors closed, she couldn't call out to him and tell him she would be all right. She was not all right. Nothing was all right.

*AN - A short one I know but that's because everything in the scene happens in a matter of seconds. Stick with it guys, the drama is not over yet! Vincents plan is unfolding and there are surprises to come :) Keep those votes and comments coming, you are all wonderful!*

# Monster.

------------------------------------------------

✱ The song for this chapter for those of you who like a tune while you read and are following the soundtrack is Slip To The Void by Alterbridge (God I am sooo in love with Myles Kennedys er - coughs - voice) The lyrics are fitting I feel and it has a certain desolate feeling to it which I feel works well with how Elsa is feeling here. Plus it starts off slowly then builds, like Elsa's hunger, fear and anger.*

What was that noise? It sounded like an animal of some kind, a small animal whimpering. It sounded afraid. It was disturbing her sleep. And boy did she need to sleep, every muscle ached, even her bones ached. Flu?

Sleep?

Elsa wanted to open her eyes, they should have been open but they weren't. I can't be asleep, I can't sleep! Panic gripped her like a vice. A vicious assault of memories attacked her, each flashing image tightening the grip of fear. Sebastian bleeding on the pavement, unable to move even as his wounds began to heal. Kate cowering in terror in the back of a van as Elsa gradually lost the ability to keep her eyes open and her mind clear. There had been nothing she could do. All her strength, all her invulnerability, speed, agility. It had served no purpose. They'd underestimated Aiden. It was not a mistake she would make again. *If I get the chance ....*

Kate! The whimpering was Kate! Elsa managed to crack her eyelids open a few millimetres, enough to begin to take in her surroundings through the veil of her eyelashes. It was like looking at an old photograph, grainy and faded at the edges. She remembered sitting with Sebastian, going through the photographs in his box and felt a tear escape the corner of her eye. She blinked it away, she had to concentrate on what was happening now. A twitch of her fingers told her she was coming round and she opened her eyes a little further, trying her hardest to turn her head and have a good look around.

The room she was in was square and had no visible windows on its bare, grey concrete walls. There was a door, also grey but darker. There was no handle and it looked like it was made of steel or some other type of metal. It looked strong. In the furthest corner from Elsa was Kate. She was pressed as far into the corner as she could go, her knees drawn up to her chest and her head resting on them with her arms wrapped around her shins. Her hair was disheveled and matted, her scuffed and bleeding knees showed through tears in her black tights and her dress was torn and bloodied.

Blood.

Elsa could smell it. It hit her all of a sudden and it terrified her. She could smell her own blood, Sebastian's and, most frightening, Kate's. But what terrified her most of all was that she wanted it. She was hungry, thirsty, starving in fact. There was no serum in her system, she had no idea how long they had been in that room and her need for blood was snaking through her system, invading every part of her, scratching incessantly at her thoughts trying to divert them from what she wanted to do. Escape. Save Kate.

Drink.

Elsa clenched her fists, feeling the sensation creep back into her body did not bring her relief because now she knew that once she could move again, Kate was in very real danger. Her eyes grew wider, the smell of the blood getting stronger with every second as her body too grew stronger. The smell of Sebastian's blood was old, almost rusty, as was her own. Kate's blood smelt sweet and fresh, what had they done to her?

"Kate." Elsa croaked. Her throat was dry, it felt like it had been rubbed with sandpaper.

Kate's head rose slowly, sluggishly. She was deathly pale, dark rings made her usually bright blue eyes stand out even though they were now dull and listless. Elsa felt fresh tears and clenched her fists even tighter as she saw teeth marks on her friends pale neck. Blood trickled invitingly from the puncture wounds, which were clearly designed to injure but not to kill. The purpose of those wounds had not been to feed from Kate, they had been to tempt Elsa. It was working.

"Elsa, what's happening?" Kate's voice was flat and her words drawn out. She had lost some blood, she was weak and exhausted. She would barely put up a fight. Perfect.

No!

Kate began to move, "Are you ok?" She was concerned for Elsa, she was going to try and move over to her.

"Don't!" Elsa manage to shout and Kate looked confused but froze, "Stay over there," Elsa continued, "Don't come anywhere near me." She obviously still had some influence over Kate's will as her friend sat back against the wall. Her hand absently went to her neck where she was bleeding and as she took it away, she looked at the bright red liquid on her fingertips and confusion was replace by blind fear.

"What did they do?" she screamed, trembling violently, her sluggishness forgotten. It was as if she too was only just remembering exactly what had happened, "You were shot! Oh my god, Elsa, you were shot! Sebastian was shot!" Kate began to scramble towards Elsa once more and as she got closer it took every ounce of the recovering strength Elsa had to drag herself up and move herself as far away from Kate as she could. It felt slow to her but she had clearly moved more quickly than Kate expected as she gaped at the spot where Elsa had been and then turned to see her crouched on the opposite side of the room from where Kate herself had just crawled.

"How did you - ?" Kate wasn't sure what had happened. She took in the blood stains on Elsa's exposed skin, "You are hurt, Elsa, let me see."

"I'm fine, it's nothing." The voice was low, it didn't sound like Elsa at all. Elsa's head was hanging down and Kate couldn't see her face but she knew she had seen Elsa get shot and she had stopped worrying about her own injuries, she just wanted her friend to be all right. She moved towards Elsa once more.

In a split second Kate was pinned hard against the wall, Elsa's hand at her throat. Her feet were off the floor and she grabbed at Elsa's hand with both of her own, choking as she kicked her feet wildly trying to find the floor.

Elsa looked at Kate, her head slightly tilted to one side. The vampire inside her saw prey, defenceless and already injured. An easy meal. Elsa saw her best friend, hurt and scared. Scared of her.

She had Kate at arms length, every fibre of her being fighting against her vampire. She wanted to let her go so badly. Kate's eyes were wide with terror, like an animal caught in a trap. She was staring into Elsa's red-rimmed, menacing dark eyes and watching as dry, cracked lips curled back revealing sharp fangs in a horrifying snarl.

Then as quickly as she'd been caught, Kate found herself slumped on the floor once more. Elsa had returned to her corner of the room and was curled up in a ball making some of the most awful pained sounds Kate had ever heard. Her hand went to her throat and she coughed, getting her breath back and recoiling from the thing she'd just seen.

"I'm sorry, I'm so sorry," The voice was Elsa's again, she was rocking herself and sobbing. Kate said nothing, she just stared at the girl she thought she'd known, unable to wrap her mind around everything that was happening and what she had just seen.

"Good evening ladies." Elsa raised her head slowly, her body had been weakened again by her recent activity. Through the fog of the smell of Kate's blood she recognised Vincent's voice. It sounded different, he wasn't in the room. A quick search bought her attention to tiny holes in the ceiling; his voice was coming through some kind of speaker system. Where the hell was he? She'd kill him this time, no hesitation, no regrets. For the first time since she'd become a vampire she knew she could kill with a clear conscience. Vincent had more than earned it. She would tear out his heart and watch him turn to dust.

Elsa looked across at Kate who flinched at her gaze, Elsa knew she still looked like a monster and she tore her eyes away from Kate's throat, looking up to the ceiling once more.

"Vincent!" she called out, "Let Kate go."

There was a lazy laugh, "I'm afraid that won't be possible." The voice held no mirth, it was flat, cold steel.

"What do you want?" Elsa hissed, her fingers digging into the concrete floor, not strong enough yet to break the surface.

"You," came the simple reply.

"Then why her?" Elsa didn't understand.

"You need to feed Elsa," Vincent explained, "You lost a lot of blood when you were shot, your wounds may be healing but you need to replenish your stock. You haven't had any serum for quite some time now, your true nature is taking over. Embrace it my love, it's what you are meant to be."

Elsa's head sagged, she knew what he was trying to do, "Not Kate, please." She would beg if she had to.

"Oh but, it's so much more fun this way, don't tell me you've never thought about it," he was taunting her.

"Elsa, what's going on?" Kate's voice was small, "What's happened to you?"

"Tell her Elsa," said Vincent, "Tell her how it's been a daily struggle not to tear into her throat with your teeth and drink her dry. Tell her what you are."

Elsa said nothing; the look on Kate's face tore at her heart.

"What is he talking about?" Kate's voice was almost a whisper.

"I won't do it." Elsa said flatly.

"Yes Elsa you will. The hunger will become too strong. You won't care who she is and afterwards, you'll want more. Marcus Shaw's daughter is coming home."

He knew who she was, he knew who her father was, everything they'd thought they'd hidden he knew.

As if reading her mind Vincent's voice came floating into the room once more, "Yes Elsa, I've always known. I knew before we met at that concert, I was there looking for you. I underestimated you that night so I thought

I'd put a bit more effort in this time. I even left the country to give you a bit of breathing room, let you get nice and relaxed."

Elsa's heart sank. She couldn't think of a way out. She didn't have the strength to break out of the room, she knew that, not without blood. Her phone had died back at the club, it couldn't be traced even if it was till intact which she highly doubted. She had no way of knowing where she was or if anyone would be able to find her. She was fighting her urge to drink from Kate with everything she had but she could feel her resistance failing. Vincent was right, the hunger would take over.

"Kate," she turned to look at her friend who looked back at her questioningly, fearfully.

"I need to tell you some things that are going to be hard to hear and hard to believe." All emotion had drained from Elsa's voice and she locked her eyes on Kate's, hoping that she could still influence her enough to make her believe, to give her at least a fighting chance, "But they are true and you will believe them. You will do exactly what I tell you to do, understand?"

Kate nodded her head, her eyes not leaving Elsa's.

"It won't work Elsa," Vincent mocking tone sounded from above, Elsa ignored him.

"I am a vampire," she continued, "A monster. I can normally control my need for blood but right now they have made it so that I can't. You are my best friend Kate and I love you but I will kill you if you don't kill me first." Her voice caught in her throat as Kate gazed at her impassively with no discernable reaction, "You need to try and fight back Kate do you understand? You have to do whatever you can think of to kill me. You won't be afraid, you will just know that you have to kill me. After a while I'll probably get back up and I'll come at you again but you have got to keep fighting, kill me again Kate and keep killing me for as long as it takes." Elsa could dimly hear Vincent's cruel laugh and tried to block it out, "Do you understand what I'm asking you to do?"

Kate nodded, her eyes glazed, "I'm going to kill you."

"That's right." Elsa leaned back against the wall, exhausted and tried to shut her ears to the sound of Kate's blood pumping through her veins. She would fight it for as long as she could and then she could only hope that she would be weak enough for Kate to fight her off. Deep down she knew that wouldn't be the case but she ignored the taunting of the vampire inside her. It couldn't be this way. Something had to happen. Something had to stop her from killing her best friend.

*AN - what do you think will happen, has Elsa got the strength to resist her need for blood? Is anyone going to come to her rescue? I'd love to hear your thoughts - and see your votes! :)*

# Gone.

-----------------------------------------------

*✱ AN - if you're followng the soundtrack then it's Long Hard Road Out Of Hell by Marilyn Manson and theSneaker Pimps for this chapter - enjoy!*

The vampire had no idea how long it had been. Her body was screaming at her, her throat was on fire and every muscle trembled. All she could here was the pulse of blood pumping through veins. She needed blood. She could smell it. She was past caring where it came from. Why hadn't she gone to the source of that smell before? She placed her hands down on the cool concrete floor and pushed her body upright. Through the curtain of her hair she could see the skin drawn tightly across her fingers. It looked grey and paper thin, severely dehydrated. She had to get blood.

Her bones and muscles stretched and creaked with effort as she turned her body towards that beautiful, sweet smell. Ah, there it was, she could see it now, a small human body sat in the corner, watching her every move through a glassy eyed stare. Fresh red blood seeped gently over the raised build up of darker, dried blood around puncture wounds to its neck and she could tell it was weak. Good, so was she, but she would still be the stronger force.

She leaned against the wall, using what strength she had in her legs to push herself up to standing. All she could hear was the human's breathing, shallow and rapid and it's pulse fluttering like a trapped butterfly. Its fight or flight response was engaged and it had nowhere to fly to. It would fight, of that she was sure, but it would lose.

As she began to shuffle towards it, her thin, cracked lips drew back over long, cruel fangs. She felt the skin of her lips split and the taste of her own blood made her smile. Yes, that's what she needed. The human, pushed itself as far against the wall as it could, looking wildly around for a weapon but there was none. It had only it's hands and that would never be enough. The human tensed its muscles, it was ready. The vampire smiled again, so was she.

The human fought more viciously than the vampire could have ever anticipated. Teeth, feet, hands; all flew at the vampire in an attack that had one aim, to kill. Momentarily stunned with the ferocity of its self-defence, the vampire stepped back but the human kept coming, fighting for its life with everything it had. The vampire was impressed but also ravenously hungry and quickly reassessed it's opponent. There was a rhythm to the blows and within seconds the vampire judged its gap and sent its prey flying across the room with one backhand swipe. The human hit the wall hard and slumped to the ground, a fresh wound to the temple gushing blood.

This sent the vampire into a frenzy, the smell of the blood as it pooled on the floor was almost too much and howling with hunger it descended on the tiny, broken figure on the floor.

A crash from behind it did not make the vampire pause and turn. Its focus was the warm, inviting pool of dark red life on the floor and nothing else. But it did feel the grip of strong hands pull it back, away from the human figure, away from its meal. Equally strong arms then encircled the vampire and held it close to a heaving, hard chest.

"Elsa, no!" a voice shouted, a voice the vampire recognised as it struggled against the grip of it's captor. But wait, this was a living, breathing creature, with blood flowing through its veins. The vampire sunk its teeth into the skin it was pressed against and finally, finally felt the heat of liquid life flowing past its lips and down its throat.

Sebastian.

Elsa felt as if an electric shock had passed through her body. She jerked back from her feeding with a force that almost broke Sebastian's grip. The taste of his blood awoke her and her mind was filled with the last moment she'd tasted it. Christmas night, in his bed.

"What's happening?" She was confused, afraid. Sebastian did not let her go and she looked around her, the memories returning. She had been captured, with Kate, she'd been so, so, hungry.

"It's ok," Sebastian was saying, "I'm here."

"Kate!" Elsa was panicking now.

"Elsa listen to me," She began to struggle against him but she was still so weak, Sebastian grabbed her shoulders and shook her hard, "Elsa look at me!" he shouted. She did, she looked straight into his burning amber eyes and all at once the world stopped. There was only him and he needed her to listen.

"I tracked you here as soon as I could move, Logan was hurt too, I had to leave him behind, he's going to tell your father what has happened and his brother can track me here. But they won't be here soon enough, you need to get out of here now." Sebastian was covered in blood and, Elsa realised, pieces of flesh. His wings were out, his brow and cheekbones prominent, his fingernails had become claws, he had been fighting his way to her and she could detect the blood of many different vampires and humans that had fallen to his rage along the way, "You need to get Kate out Elsa, she's hurt, I don't know how much time she has, you can move faster than me."

"I can't," Elsa whispered, "I'm not strong enough, I haven't fed."

Sebastian was thinking, his jaw set, "Feed from me," he said and as Elsa shook her head he shook her again, "You have to!" he shouted, "You can get Kate out faster and out of the three of us, I'm the only one that can't die, you can leave me here for now, I'll be all right but you both need to go!"

Elsa was sobbing now. She couldn't leave him again, she couldn't.

"You can," he whispered, pulling her in close, "We don't have time, please Elsa, feed." He maneuvered so that he was knelt on the floor, Elsa in his lap, he cradle her head onto his shoulder and gently pushed her towards his throat. She was so hungry and her head filled with the sound of his heart. What if she couldn't control herself? What if she simply carried on feeding, moving onto Kate when she'd finished with him? Wasn't that exactly what Vincent wanted? For her to drink live blood? Wasn't that exactly how he would claim her for the blood movement and take away the very last part of her that was Elsa?

"You can do it Elsa, you can control it, I trust you." Sebastian was saying. She wrapped her arms around his neck and felt herself giving in. Her need for blood was too much, she couldn't stop herself. As her teeth sank into Sebastian's flesh once more he gasped and she drank long and hard, her hands gripping him as she gulped his blood hungrily. It made her head swim as she felt the life come back to her dried and aching body. She felt him weaken as she grew stronger; it felt so different from any blood she had drunk before, her whole body was aflame, she had never felt so alive, so strong. So suddenly in control.

Her mind came into sharp focus and she released Sebastian who sank to the floor. He was still breathing and he would heal soon enough, she knew she had to focus on Kate but she felt so strong all of a sudden, maybe she could carry them both.

"I can take you both," She said kneeling down beside his slumped form, "I know I can."

Sebastian shook his head weakly, "It will slow you down, Vincent will be able to catch up with you, he's still alive, I couldn't find him before I found you. Get Kate out. Come back with Haven, I will be fine."

He was right, she knew it. Vincent could easily match her speed, he was older and stronger. But she felt so, different. Like she could do anything. Sebastian's blood had an effect on her like no other. She kissed him softly and whispered in his ear, she wasn't going to leave him without saying it this time, "I love you Sebastian and I will come back for you."

"I love you Elsa," he whispered back, "I know you will. Now run and don't stop." With that she turned to Kate. Her heartbeat was faint but she was still alive. Elsa picked her up, marveling at the ease with which she could lift her friend's body. And then she ran, faster than she ever had before. The corridors she ran down were a blur of cold concrete and mangled bodies. Humans torn to shreds, vampires with their hearts ripped out or their heads torn off. Despite her speed, her senses could take it all in. Every ragged wound, every headless corpse and it just made her love Sebastian even more. He'd done that to get to her, to save her and she'd do all that and more to get him back once she'd got Kate to safety.

The fact that Sebastian was not human, that he was what he was, made his blood different and the effect it had on Elsa was to amplify every ability she had. It took barely minutes for her to reach Haven's main building and she didn't even bother with the door. She scaled the outside wall and entered the clinic where she'd woken up so many months before through a window, shattering the glass into a million diamonds. A moment later, Hesper flew through the clinic doors and stopped in her tracks when she saw Elsa lowering Kate onto a bed.

"She's hurt," was all the explanation Elsa offered and Hesper asked no questions, simply attending immediately to Kate and calling for more staff to help her. Elsa didn't break stride, she was in her father's office in seconds finding him talking urgently to Gray on the phone.

"We're coming to you," he said, "Don't go in without us." He was dressed for combat in body armour and his head snapped up as Elsa entered, his face crumpling with relief, "Elsa, thank God!"

"Has Gray found it?" She asked before Marcus could hug her, she was only focused on one thing.

"Yes, we've got teams converging on the location now, we'll be ready to go in within the next five minutes."

"Too long." Elsa said simply and before Marcus could utter another word she was gone, the papers from his desk flying into the space she'd just occupied. He gaped after her, he had never seen her move that fast, she had literally vanished into thin air.

Elsa was going back, she would tear the place apart and everyone in it until she had Sebastian back. All in all from the moment she had left him on the floor of that room, less than ten minutes had passed but as soon as she entered the building, a fear gripped her heart. There had been noise and chaos when she'd left; she'd heard the cries of others in the building far away, panic and alarms. Now there was nothing, the dead made no sound and there were no signs of life. No alarms, no running feet, no one to try and stop her making her way straight back to the spot she had left Sebastian minutes before.

She stood in the room. There were scrapes and scratch marks on the wall and Kate's blood was still wet and glistening in the far corner. But there was no Sebastian. All that remained in the space where he had lain was a single black feather, tattered and torn and a piece of paper. She bent slowly, picked it up and felt her world fall away as she read the elegant, cursive script.

What an interesting turn of events wouldn't you say? Thank you for my present Elsa. I consider it a fair exchange. I do so like surprises – don't you?


The strength that Sebastian's blood had given her enabled her to crumple the paper into a fine dust. It meant that she could smash the solid concrete walls down in her rage and reduce the building in which she'd been imprisoned to rubble and dust. But it could not help her bring Sebastian back. He was gone and she had no idea where. And that was what broke her finally. That was what reduced her to a sobbing, anguished shell when Havens tactical assault teams finally reached their target and her father held her in his arms again, like he had when she'd first tried to come to terms with what she had become. Sebastian was gone, she had left him behind and now he was gone and she would never, ever forgive herself.

*AN - I want to thank you all my wonderful readers, voters and commenters as your support has seen this story climb up the hotlist to number 19 last time I checked! I'd love for it to get higher than 14 as that would put it on the first page of the vampire hot list and that is something I just never thought I'd see. So keep those votes coming and thank you so much!*

# Angels Exist?

Elsa stared at the wall. She was back at Haven, sat next to Kate's bed whose parents were probably frantic by now, wondering why she hadn't come home and unable to get hold of their daughter. Marcus would find a way to explain everything away, that's what Haven did. No one had witnessed the shootings outside the club; the shooter had used a silencer and everything had happened so fast. Logan had followed them out and smelt the blood, rounding the corner just as the van was pulling away. He'd been shot out of the van window as it drove away and thankfully his reflexes had been quick enough to stop him being seriously hurt. Sitting against the wall next to Sebastian with a bullet to the shoulder he had called Haven to tell them the situation had changed. By the time a team arrived to pick him up, Sebastian had recovered sufficiently to begin tracking the van and was long gone.

After receiving medical attention, Logan was able to pick up Sebastian's scent and track him in turn but everything had just happened that little bit too late, Vincent had been one tiny step ahead the whole time.

The tactical teams had returned to base with all the intelligence they could gather from the compound where Vincent had kept Elsa and Kate. Gray was heading the team analyzing all the data they'd collated; everyone was working around the clock to find Vincent. To find Sebastian.

Elsa had told Gray everything she knew, which wasn't much; she'd been out of it a lot of the time. Now she was waiting for her father. After his initial fear for her had been replaced by overwhelming relief that she was all right, slowly he'd become angry. Why had she gone running back to the compound alone? Anything could have happened. And who and what in the hell was Sebastian? She'd escaped for a few minutes to check on Kate but she would have to answer his questions soon, it might help to find Sebastian. It might also put him at further risk if he turned out to be a creature that Haven would exterminate without question. Despite her fear, she would tell her father whatever he needed to know, her priority was to find Sebastian, and she would worry about the rest later.

Kate looked deathly pale, her skin even whiter if possible than the crisp sheets she lay on. She had dressings on her head where it had been split open and Hesper had quietly informed Elsa that Kate's skull had been fractured quite badly. This head injury, along with the vampire bites that had been inflicted on her had resulted in huge blood loss and Kate had been close to death when Elsa had arrived at Haven. Hesper had treated her injuries with a transfusion of vampire blood that had sped up the healing process considerably. The swelling in Kate's brain had reduced dramatically and she was now breathing steadily on her own. This kind of treatment had its risks. It was a fine line but Hesper believed she had got the balance right; too little vampire blood would have left Kate battling her injuries alone, a battle she would have almost certainly lost; too much would have turned her into a vampire. A specially adapted dialysis machine was waiting to clean Kate's blood when she was stronger, to ensure the vampire blood transfusion left no lasting side effects other than Kate's full recovery.

They hadn't been able to use Elsa's blood to save Kate. Another thing for her to feel guilty about. Hers was contaminated, their words. Hesper had taken samples to analyze after they had all seen the extraordinary effect that drinking Sebastian's blood had on Elsa. All her abilities had been amplified, she'd been astonishingly strong and fast, even for a very old vampire. Hesper was one of the oldest vampires any of them knew and she'd never seen anything like it. Unfortunately Elsa had also metabolized the blood very quickly and the effects had now subsided. Now she felt empty, like the very last piece of Sebastian she had to hold onto was gone. They'd even taken that solitary feather that had lain on the cold concrete floor next to Vincent's taunting note.

Hesper entered the room silently. She placed a cool hand on Elsa's arm, "Your father is waiting in the library," she said and there was a kind tone to her voice. Elsa knew Hesper could feel the guilt that threatened to crush what was left of her spirit. She had left Sebastian twice, weak and wounded and now he was lost. She had almost killed her best friend and it was her fault Kate had been in danger in the first place. Elsa said nothing to Hesper, rising to leave the room without looking back at Kate. What she was going to say to her when she eventually came round, Elsa had no idea. There would be no way to erase her memory this time, it had been too long. She might well wake up and remember every last horrific detail. As she moved silently through Haven's eerily quiet corridors, Elsa's weary mind was running over everything she would need to tell her father and she barely even registered how she came to be stood at the library doorway, where she had spent so much time trying herself to find out exactly what Sebastian was.

Marcus was sat at one of the tables, his laptop open and piles of books and papers scattered across the tables surface. He looked tired.

"Dad," Elsa announced her presence, she had obviously entered too quickly and quietly for Marcus to notice.

"Elsa," Marcus stood and held out his arms, "I'm sorry if I was angry with you before, it wasn't fair."

Elsa moved into her fathers embrace, "It's ok," she mumbled, "I understand."

Marcus pulled a chair out and she sat down, "Why didn't you tell me about Sebastian before?" he asked gently. Elsa felt tears sting her eyes again, she'd felt so numb since she'd been back at Haven and she fought to keep her emotions in check, they wouldn't help her find Sebastian.

"I was scared," she admitted, "I thought he might be a demon, that you may have to destroy him. I tried to find out myself what he was but I couldn't, I don't know enough about this world."

"If he was all demon Elsa, you'd be dead by now. Logan didn't recognise his scent, neither did Gray and I trust his nose above anyone's. Sebastian is definitely something we haven't come across before but that doesn't mean we can't figure out what he is. If we can do that it might tell us why Vincent was suddenly so happy to take him in place of you."

"Why did he want me so badly? Why go to all that effort and risk just to convert one vampire to his movement?" Elsa asked.

Marcus was silent for a moment, clearly struggling internally with something. Finally he gave in, "There's something I haven't told you about Vincent," he said quietly, "When your mother was killed, we destroyed the vampires responsible, like I told you, but they were just the tip of the iceberg. The blood movement has been a very long-standing problem for us. Vincent was one of the vampires we were tracking when your mother died and I believe it was Vincent who sent those vampires after Sarah, after your mum. One of the group that we killed was his companion Ulric, they had travelled together for hundreds of years, they were friends, lovers, everything to each other. I believe that Vincent wanted to convert you to get his revenge on me for Ulric's death. It would have been hugely important to him and for him to happily abandon that plan and take Sebastian instead? Well, there must be a very good reason."

Elsa didn't know what to say. She felt angry that her father had not told her everything from the very start, maybe she would have been more alert, maybe she would have noticed she was being watched or followed and none of this might have happened. But they were just maybes and, maybe if she' told Marcus about Sebastian sooner things would have been different too. Once again, she kept her emotions in check. She shelved the information that Vincent had been involved with her mother's death along with his treatment of Kate, of Sebastian and of her. She would make him pay for everything he'd done but it would have to wait.

Marcus studied her face for a moment but she was giving nothing away. He continued, "I need you to tell me everything you can about Sebastian, everything."

She did. She told him how they had first met, how she'd been drawn to him even before she'd been changed and how he'd finally revealed himself to her and she to him for what they really were. She told him everything Sebastian had ever told her about his past, about the note from his mother, about the times he had killed and every way he'd tried to kill himself. And finally she told him how she'd drunk Sebastian's blood and the incredible affect it had had on her.

All the time she spoke, Marcus rifled through books and papers, moving between them and his laptop, typing, searching, reading. And every time she paused he would fire questions at her, "Does he feel pain? Can he be hurt? Does he just drink blood or does he eat his victims? She shuddered at the words.

"Dad, he is not a monster I don't care what you say." It was becoming difficult for her to remain neutral. It had been hours since Sebastian had been taken and her nerves felt frayed.

Marcus paused, "I'm sorry sweetheart, I can see how much you care for him, but I have to ask if we're going to help him." His voice was softer now, "Tell me about his wings." He looked back to his book.

"The first time I saw them, I thought he was an angel," she began and then jumped as her father slammed the book shut.

"A what?" he looked up at her sharply.

"An angel," she repeated, "They are huge and black but feathered, like I would have imagined an angels would be. You saw the feather he left behind didn't you?"

Marcus looked confused, he took off his glasses and rubbed the bridge of his nose between his thumb and forefinger, his eyes closed. "There is something," he said, "A possibility maybe but I never thought it could happen."

Elsa felt a flicker of hope, "What?"

"He could be a Nephilim, a product of a union between a demon and an angel."

"Angels exist?"

"We could never be sure, if they ever did, they certainly don't anymore," said Marcus, "I seem to remember a file..." he turned to the laptop again and began typing quickly. Elsa moved to stand behind him and could see he was logged into a secure part of Havens system, scanning through files for the key word 'angel'. After what seemed like an age, one file appeared on screen and Marcus clicked to open it. It was a scan of an old, yellowed hand written file, faded in places and difficult to read. A photo of a young woman, leaving a building with books clutched to her chest, looking up furtively as if she knew she was being watching, was attached to the top of the page and there were faded notes detailing times she had been seen and recording any observations made; '13/09/25 female, approximately 18-20 years old... tracking intermittently for five years.... has not aged visibly ... 04/03/26 scar apparent on left shoulder, right shoulder not visible ... 16/08/28 no set routine, careful not to be seen...'

"There's no record of her after 1928," Marcus murmured, "Do you know how old Sebastian is?"

"He thinks he was born in the late 1920's, he can't remember exactly."

Marcus clicked on a few pages, "There are medical records," he scanned the page and pointed to a section of text, reading out loud, "Jane Doe, approx 18-20 years of age admitted following sever beating. Incoherent on admission, refusing examinations, required heavy sedation. Evidence of violent sexual attack." he looked at Elsa, "It says she had large scars on both shoulder blades which appeared to be old wounds and that they were unable to complete treatment as the patient disappeared hours later." The scars sounded just like the ones she'd seen on Sebastian's shoulders.

Elsa looked back at her father and then again at the picture of the woman she was now sure was Sebastian's mother, "Is there a name?" she asked.

"There's a later record of a Sarah Bennet matching the same description being brought into hospital in the early stages of labour and disappearing as soon as she was left alone."

"Sebastian's surname is Bennet!" Elsa exclaimed, "She has to be Sebastian's mother, doesn't she?"

"It's looking that way." Marcus admitted.

"And Haven, back then, they thought she was an angel?"

"They thought she was the last one."

*AN - sorry it's taken longer than I intended, thanks for waiting patiently - don't forget to vote and I'd love to hear your comments on how the story is unfolding :)*

# Tell Her Everything.

✶ AN - the song for this chapter is No Sleep by The Cardigans*

"What do you mean the last one?" Elsa asked, "Sebastian can't die, demons can, surely the immortality will have come from his mother?"

"Sebastian is not an angel and he is not a demon," Marcus explained, "He is something else entirely and the normal laws of the supernatural don't apply to him. Angels could die if they were weak enough."

"What would have weakened her?"

"Angels were never meant to bear children Elsa, the attack by the demon, the pregnancy and the birth would have left her severely weakened. And angels had been dying off for years already."

Elsa thought about what she understood angels to be, "Is there a God?" she asked, "A heaven?"

"I have no idea," said Marcus, "The angels I am talking about are not the angels you will know from Bible stories. They are simply another type of supernatural being, an ancient race who were by nature good and pure. Maybe they were called angels because they resemble the beings from the

Bible; maybe the angels in the Bible are a writers creation based on sightings of the sort of being we know angels to be."

"Angels were very powerful at one time. They had the power to heal and they were considered guardians of the human race, protectors against demons and other threats. But the world, as we know, is not always a very nice place and it seemed that with every war, with every atrocity across the ages that humans could inflict on one another, angel's powers became weaker and weaker. They became less and less able to defend themselves against demon attacks and there are unproven accounts of children being born as a result of a demon and angel union."

Elsa seized on that piece of information, "You mean there could be other people out there like Sebastian?" she asked.

Marcus shook his head, "I suppose it is a remote possibility but all of the stories about such things happening," he hesitated, "Elsa, they are horrific."

"In what way?" Elsa didn't understand what her father was getting at.

"The children were abominations, they are reported as tearing their way out of their mothers abdomens, of being hideously deformed and, if they survived, they were destroyed immediately."

"Sebastian's mother survived his birth, he appeared human," Elsa said, "He didn't show any of his demon side until he was about eighteen."

"I can't explain why he is different Elsa," Marcus admitted, "Maybe the fact that he is more – normal – is actually a kind of birth defect. He should have been one of those awful creatures that feature in these old tales and he wasn't. Maybe he's an anomaly, a lucky accident of genetics."

They were both quiet for a moment. Discovering what Sebastian was, finding out who his mother was, none of it bought them any closer to finding him.

"This does help us understand why Vincent was so happy to take him." Marcus said finally, breaking the silence as if they'd continued the conversation in his head, "Vampires have long searched for hybrid creatures such as this, believing their blood to possess special powers. Your reaction to Sebastian's blood has proven this and Vincent would never pass up an opportunity to increase his own power and that of his followers and his children."

"His children?"

"When a vampire turns a human, that human is linked to them, dependent on them for support and teaching. The vampire has created a new vampire that they will nurture and teach in their own ways. We know what that means for Vincent."

Elsa fell silent once more. Not only were they no closer to finding Sebastian she now had images in her mind of what was surely happening to him. He couldn't die, she knew that, but Vincent would keep him constantly weak and drained of blood. He would be used as a food source and nothing more. He felt pain, he would know what was happening to him and be powerless to stop it. Every time he healed they would hurt him again, taking his blood and his strength for their own and keeping him as a shell, a vessel for their needs and wants. She couldn't bear it.

A noise broke through her despairing thoughts, a distinct scream that she recognised too well. Her father hadn't heard it all the way from the medical unit but she had. Kate was awake.

"Dad, Kate's come round, she's terrified," Elsa didn't know if she should go to her friend or if that would just make things worse.

"Go," Marcus said, "Tell her everything, we can't erase her memory, she will either accept what you have to say or not."

"What if she doesn't?" Elsa asked, "If she goes home ranting about vampires she'll be committed!"

"You have to make her understand," Marcus said, looking at Elsa with sympathy, "We all do. If we can't trust her to keep your secret, she won't be able to go home."

The reality of what her father was saying hit Elsa hard. Not only had she almost killed her friend, if she couldn't make her understand and accept her secret, Kate's life would be entirely ruined along with that of her family. She would never be able to go back. Elsa had to go to her, she had to try and make her understand.

"Will you come and tell me as soon as you find anything that might lead us to Vincent?" she asked.

Marcus nodded.

"I will be involved," she said and it wasn't a question, there was no way she was going to leave Sebastian again, if they found out where he was, she was going to get him and no one would get in her way.

Once again, Marcus silently nodded his understanding of what she was saying. His jaw was set, he did not want to agree, but he understood and he knew deep down that he was powerless to stop her.

Elsa moved quickly back to the medical unit. Kate was no longer screaming and as Elsa entered the room she saw Hesper stood over her friend, adjusting a drip.

"I've sedated her," Hesper explained, answering Elsa's unspoken questions, "She woke up with an instant recollection of what had happened and was extremely agitated. She is awake and will be able to speak to you and understand what you are saying but be careful Elsa, she is very fragile."

Elsa nodded and as Hesper glided silently from the room, she resumed her previous seat by Kate's bed and reached out to place her hand on Kate's.

Kate pulled her hand away with surprising speed for one so sedated. Stung, Elsa folded her hands in her lap. Kate's eyes were closed and she turned her head away from Elsa as if to try and shut her as far out of her consciousness as possible.

"Kate," Elsa said, "I'm so sorry, I don't know where to begin."

Kate said nothing, Elsa might as well have not been there at all.

"I know I hurt you," Elsa continued, "And scared you, I never wanted to do that. I can only tell you that it wasn't really me in that room Kate, the man that captured us did that to me to try and hurt my dad and I." She paused but there was still no reaction from Kate. Elsa wasn't sure where to go from there. Should she start from the beginning? Could Kate even begin to understand? It was going to sound ridiculous, I'm a vampire. Kate might have seen it with her own eyes but Elsa had had enough trouble coming to terms with it herself. As far as Kate was concerned, until being trapped in that room, vampires didn't exist.

"What are you?" Kate's voice was quiet, she slurred slightly but there was no disguising the contempt in her tone and Elsa could feel fear and confusion radiating from her friend. But she was speaking, she was engaging with Elsa and that was a start.

"I am a vampire," Elsa said, deciding brutal truth was the best angle, "I wasn't always, something happened to me that night we crashed. When I was a baby, before I was even born, my mother was attacked and killed by vampires. I survived and when I showed no symptoms of vampirism my father thought I'd had a lucky escape but it turns out that it just lay dormant in my system. When I came round in the car you and Grant were both unconscious. You were above me and bleeding, the blood dripped onto my face and that's what woke me up. I couldn't move and your blood dripped onto my lips. I tasted it without even realising what was happening and slowly, I began to change. All that time I was ill, all my strange behaviour was the change happening. I almost became a monster, like the monster you saw in that room. My dad saved me."

"Don't – exist," Kate's eyes were still screwed shut, as if looking at Elsa would make her have to believe what she was saying.

"That's what I thought too," Elsa said, "But we do and I am one. My dad works for an organisation called Haven. They have been protecting the human race from supernatural beings for thousands of years. He knew how to help me, they gave me medication to stop me craving blood so I could live as normal a life as possible. If a vampire wants to hold onto their humanity they can be saved Kate. That's what happened to me. The man that took us, he is also a vampire. His name is Vincent but he does not want his humanity back. He is the other kind of vampire that simply see humans as a food source and enjoy causing hurt and pain. He and my father have history, he wanted to force me to give up my humanity to hurt my dad. He kept you and I locked in that room and took away my medication. He hurt me so I lost a lot of blood. He tried to create a situation where my vampire side would take over and I would not be able to stop myself from hurting you."

"He succeeded." Kate opened her eyes and turned her head to look accusingly at Elsa, "You would have killed me."

"Not me," Elsa said pleadingly, "I would never hurt you Kate. What you saw, that thing that attacked you, was not me. It isn't what I want to be and you will never see it again, I promise you."

"You're right," Kate's voice was dead and she rolled onto her side, her back to Elsa, "I never want to see or speak to you again."

"Kate," Elsa begged, "Please, there's so much I need to explain to you, so much you need to understand."

"I don't want to hear it." Kate said coldly, "I want you to go away and leave me alone."

"I can't," Elsa said, her voice choked with emotion, "I need you to understand about Haven, about how important it is that no one knows about them and what they do and ..."

"Like anyone would believe me anyway," Kate spat, still with her back to Elsa, "I won't tell anyone your secret Elsa, I don't care about you or your father. I just want to go home to my family and try to forget either of you ever existed."

Elsa felt like Kate was stabbing her in the heart, "Kate-"

"Get out."

Elsa opened her mouth to speak again but she simply didn't know what to say. She could feel Kate's anger, her sense of betrayal, her confusion and pain. She searched for some indication that Kate could ever accept her for what she was and forgive her for what she'd done but she found none. Finally, defeated, Elsa stood and left the room. Standing against the wall in the corridor outside and listening to Kate sob into her pillow, Elsa felt completely lost. What was she supposed to do now? She'd lost the man she loved, her best friend and almost her own humanity. The weight of the guilt pressing down on her was becoming more and more unbearable. She needed a focus, something positive to do that might in some small way begin to fix the damage that had been done to her life and the lives of those closest to her. An image of Vincent formed in her mind. She had never felt such deep, burning hatred. He was at the centre of it all. He had been the cause of her mother's death, it was his fault she had become a vampire in the first place. He had used her friend to try and turn her from her humanity and he had taken Sebastian. He was the root of every evil that had occurred in her life since before she was even born. She would kill him, of that she had no doubt. That was her focus. She would not rest until she had found him and killed him.

*AN - I know you all want Sebastian found, there will be developments in the next chapter I promise!*

# I'm Coming For You.

------------------------------------------------

*✱ AN - welcome to all my new followers, I normally like to thank you personally but my laptop has died and I only have limited use of my boyfriends until mine is fixed :( I hope to speak to you all soon. So here is my next chapter :) hopefully I will update again in the week as I have a day off, so you might be getting two updates next weeks. Lot's of action coming soon!*

It was not long before Kate was well enough to go home. A story had been concocted regarding her twenty four hour disappearance and Hesper, posing as a police liaison officer, had convinced Kate's family to believe the weaker parts of the story in the way only vampires can. Elsa had kept her distance from Kate, hoping against hope that time would heal Kate's wounds and that one day she would get her friend back. Kate hadn't wanted Haven to arrange her transport home, not trusting that any of them were not monsters. She'd called herself a taxi and walked out of the door without looking back. She had, however, consented to seeing a counsellor that Marcus recommended; a human he assured her, who was trained to counsel those who had been through Kate's very specific type of trauma. Elsa saw this as a positive sign, Kate was at least willing to try and get her head around what had happened. Trying her best not to dwell on what she might have lost in Kate, Elsa was focussing all her energies instead on helping the various teams at Haven in whatever way possible to find Sebastian.

A forensics team had gone through every piece of evidence with a fine tooth comb in the two days that had now passed since Vincent had disappeared. Virtually all of the bodies at the compound had been identified and both Vincent and Aiden were unaccounted for, assuming Aiden had ever been there. The IT team were scouring every computer or other piece of electronic equipment that had been removed from the building and so far had come across only encryptions which were so sophisticated, they weren't sure they would ever be able to break them. Gray and his team had not found a scent trail to follow and there had been no sightings of Vincent or any of his known followers anywhere in the world that they were aware of. In short, they were drawing a blank on all fronts.

Hesper had a team working on samples of Sebastian's blood retrieved from both the compound and the scene of the shooting, as well of samples of Elsa's blood taken just before the effects of Sebastian's blood had completely worn off. Whilst this analysis was not going to help them find Sebastian, she hoped to discover exactly what type of demon was making up half of his genetics. With no angel DNA on record, there was no way to confirm that side of his parentage through science unfortunately. Hesper was also interested in what it was in Sebastian's blood that had amplified Elsa's powers so much, what was making him so valuable to Vincent. Elsa was comforted by the fact that Hesper was confident they would find Vincent and therefore Sebastian. Hesper was hoping her work would lead to finding a way to nullify the effects of Sebastian's blood on Vincent whilst also possibly recreating it's effects for the team that would descend on Vincent when he was found, giving them the advantage. When; Hesper had said when they find Vincent and Elsa was clinging onto that with everything she had

Elsa was taking a rare break from repeatedly asking each team if there was anything she could do or if they'd got any leads. She was alone in the staffroom, a mug of blood in her hands long gone cold, staring into the deep red liquid as if it could give her answer.

"Elsa, posso aiutare? I am so sorry, is there anything I can do?" Lucca had entered the room and she hadn't even noticde; he crouched in front of her and took her hands, "I came as soon as I heard, everyone who can help is here il mio amico."

Elsa had made a point of learning some Italian when she had been in Canada and she knew that Lucca was offering his help. Her father had impressed upon all the vampires associated with Haven the danger that Vincent presented and most of them, if not all, had rallied to the call. There would be a formidable force available to launch an assault on Vincent, if they could just determine where he was.

"Grazie Lucca," Elsa said, trying to raise a smile, "There are no leads yet I'm afraid."

Luca cast his eyes down, "Mi dispiace. They will find him, they have the best people here you know that, yes?" His eyes were focussed on hers intently once more and they glistened with emotion for her. This time Elsa did smile; Lucca was such a lovely young man, so free with his emotions and she knew he would do anything for those he cared about. It seemed he had come to care about her and everyone else at Haven too, as if he had taken them as his family because he no longer had his own around him.

"Grazie mille," She said softly, patting his small, slender hands before standing up, "I know we will find him." She downed the contents of her mug, cold and disgusting as it had become she knew she needed to eat even if she didn't need to sleep, she would need all of her strength to kill Vincent. Placing the mug in the sink, she heard her phone chirp in her pocket and took it out.

Library.

That was all her father's message said. It carried an urgency and Elsa felt hope jump in her chest, maybe they'd found something. She was there in a matter of seconds.

"What is it?" She asked.

Marcus looked excited, he introduced Elsa to a woman sat next to him, "Elsa, this is Katherine, she's agreed to help us."

Katherine was petite and olive skinned, with poker straight ebony hair broken only by a strip of bright white strands from her left temple. Her eyes were a deep brown and as Elsa looked into them she felt as if she could lose herself if the ages of wisdom and power that seemed to lie within. Katherine did not look old enough to have eyes like that; she was late thirties, early forties at the most. Her demeanour was calm and serene but not in the same way as Hesper. Hesper exuded acceptance of what she was and the past that lay behind her. This woman exuded confidence in the future, as if she knew she could face whatever may come.

"Pleased to meet you," Elsa said, holding out a hand for Katherine to shake. Katherine stood and took Elsa's hand in both of her own, a warm smile spreading across her face, making Elsa feel instantly at ease.

"Pleased to meet you Elsa," She said, "She really does look like Sarah." This comment was directed at Marcus who nodded, smiling.

"You knew my mother?" Elsa asked.

"Katherine is an old friend," Marcus explained, "She and your mother grew up together."

"She was like a sister to me," Katherine said, her eyes showing the pain she still felt that her friend was no longer with her.

"Excuse me for asking," said Elsa, "But why haven't I met you before? And how can you help with our situation now?"

"Both perfectly valid questions which require no apology," Katherine replied and she sat down, indicating for Elsa and Marcus to join her, "You have met me but you were too young to remember. When you were born, I helped your father for a while until we thought we were sure you had not been affected by the manner of your mother's passing. It became too painful for me to stay as you began to grow from a baby into a little girl. A little carbon copy of my Sarah. I carried a lot of guilt about your mother's death for a very long time, I still do."

"Why?"

"Because she called me the night she was attacked and I didn't get the call. She had been feeling some twinges, she thought she might be getting early contractions. I was going to be helping with your birth when the time came but when she needed me the most I wasn't there."

"That wasn't your fault." Marcus said softly.

"No it wasn't, but then it wasn't your fault either was it Marc? It does not stop these feelings we both have." Elsa was surprised to hear someone call her father Marc. She had never heard anyone call him that and felt as if she was getting a sudden glimpse into a past life she knew nothing about.

"Even if you had been there, surely there was nothing you could have done against a group of vampires?" Elsa said, trying herself to assuage some of the guilt Katherine felt.

Katherine smiled, a glint in her eye, "I may be a small woman," she said, "But you might be surprised at what I can do."

Elsa was confused; she was getting no sense of the supernatural from Katherine. Her heart was beating, she was not a vampire; she didn't smell like a werewolf and she just didn't seem to have anything about her that was out of the ordinary apart from the lock of white hair which was quite unusual, and those eyes...

"Katherine is Wiccan Elsa, she is a witch," Marcus explained.

Elsa looked at Katherine in surprise, a hundred questions flying into her mind.

"When all this is done I will answer any question you have," Katherine said, as if she knew exactly what was going on in Elsa's head, "But for now I get the feeling time is of the essence so suffice to say I do not wear a pointy hat and ride a broomstick, I do have a cauldron of sorts but it is usually filled with soup and I am not evil – oh and I don't cackle," Her smile faded, "But I can and I will do everything I can to help you find your friend."

"How?" Elsa asked, her heart feeling lighter by the second.

"I am hoping I can use a locator spell to find Sebastian."

"Hoping?" Elsa didn't like the uncertainty of the word.

"The closer the item or person you are trying to locate is, the more accurate the location I can find. Obviously at this point Vincent could be anywhere in the world with Sebastian so I may not be able to give you the exact co-ordinates of where they are but I should at least be able to give you somewhere to start looking."

Should, another word loaded with uncertainty, Elsa began to feel less confident as Katherine continued.

"The success or failure of this spell will hang on one thing," she said, "We cannot locate Vincent personally as we do not have anything personal to him. We were hoping, as you and Sebastian are close, you may have something of his we could use. His blood won't work; it has to be a personal item that he would attach emotional significance to, that is where the power for the spell will come from, the emotion."

Elsa's heart leapt, suddenly all of her confidence was back. The spell would work, they would find Sebastian. If there was one thing he had in abundance it was emotions, she felt them so strongly at times it was painful. And she also knew what she needed to bring to Katherine; she knew the exact item that Sebastian attached the most emotion to.

She jumped up, her eyes glowing, "I know just the thing!" she cried, "I'll be back in a few minutes, is that all you'll need? Just one item?"

"Just one," Katherine confirmed, "And we will find your Sebastian."

Elsa was already gone, heading to Sebastian's warehouse, to his tiny box of faded notes and photographs. *I'm coming for you Sebastian.* She thought the words as loudly and as clearly as she could, hoping in some way that wherever he was, he could hear them. *And I'm coming for you too Vincent.*

*AN - thank you so much fro reading - please leave your comments and votes, I really do appreciate them so much :)*

# Go To Him.

----

Marcus held the faded wartime photograph of Sebastian, looking on the face of the man his daughter loved for the first time and seeing just that, a man. No traces of the demon that lay inside him, the secret half of him that terrified Marcus. No sign that this young man could be a threat to Elsa in anyway. He sighed; he knew he couldn't tell Elsa what to do or hope to stop her feeling the way she so clearly did. He just wished she could have fallen for just about anyone else.

Elsa was oblivious to her father's thoughts, focussed as she was on Katherine, who was holding the fragile note in Sarah Bennett's delicate handwriting declaring her son's name and, for whatever reason she felt she needed to, his innocence. Katherine was sat in front of one of the large, glass computer monitors that Elsa had marvelled at the first time she had seen them. On the screen was a world map and Katherine seemed to be searching it, without actually touching anything. Her eyes were closed and she was muttering in a tongue Elsa did not understand as she held the note between the fingertips of both hands. The map began to move, slowly zooming in, landscape features gradually becoming clearer and larger, followed by cities and smaller towns. Areas were selected, then passed over in favour of others and gradually Elsa realised they were following a journey, the journey that must have been taken by Sebastian since his disappearance. Elsa watched intently, willing the map to stop, to show her that one place she wanted to know so desperately.

After what seemed like an age, the map stopped moving, the image settled and came into clearer focus. Katherine frowned and the muttering became faster, more urgent. The map did not move. Finally, Katherine opened her eyes and looked at the screen.

"It's the best I can do over that distance," she said, "Sebastian is within a twenty mile radius of this point as far as I can tell." He finger rested on the screen and Elsa searched the map for features or names she recognised.

"He's in North Africa?" she asked. Her keen mind and eyesight had been able to follow the quick movements of the map as Katherine had worked but she knew little of North Africa, "Where's Toubkal?" This was the only named place she could see on screen.

"The Atlas Mountains," Marcus said, "It's a national park near Marrakech."

"Morocco?"

Marcus nodded, "Toubkal is the highest peak in the Atlas range."

"So we have a twenty mile radius of mountains to search?" Elsa was worried, that sounded like searching for a needle in a haystack.

"It is not as bad as it sounds," Katherine spoke up, "It is not an area of high population which means if you can get me there I will be able to give you a much clearer location on Sebastian with very little interference. There are a series of mountain refuges dotted through the mountains; we may be looking at one of those?"

"Possibly," Marcus agreed, "It wouldn't be a problem for a group of vampires to discourage trekkers from using one particular refuge, we could get a good idea by talking to people who have trekked through the range in the last couple of days. Vincent will have picked the area for its remote location, it could be his undoing."

"It will be," said Elsa through gritted teeth, she could feel her fangs against her bottom lip and ran her tongue over them, they were a welcome reminder of her rage, a rage she would turn on Vincent at her earliest opportunity.

"We'll be taking a smaller team with it being so far away," Marcus was already planning what would need to be done in his mind as he spoke, "But we can pick up reinforcements from the local Haven branch once we're out there."

"How quickly can we get there?" Elsa asked, she'd run all the way if she had to.

"We could have everything in just a few hours, I'll make some calls. Let's get together in the meeting room in one hour." Marcus directed this at both Elsa and Katherine who nodded their agreement. Elsa's nerves tingled, the time was fast approaching; she would be with Sebastian again and Vincent was going to wish he'd never laid eyes on any member of her family.

An hour later Elsa was sat around a table with her father, Katherine, Hesper, Gray and two other people she was not familiar with.

"This is Rueben," Marcus introduced the man sat next to Gray. He was almost as big as Gray and clearly muscular, with close-cropped black hair and a square jaw. He was also a vampire, as was the woman sat next to him who Marcus introduced as Layla. She had flame red hair and flashing green eyes, with a dusting of freckles across her nose. She was small and wiry and it was clear to Elsa that she and Rueben were a couple, although for the purposes of this meeting they were all business. Marcus explained that both Layla and Rueben had a huge amount of experience with tactical assault, Elsa didn't ask where they had gained that experience from, she could tell they were old vampires and if her father trusted them then so did she.

"We are taking a small team from our own units," Layla explained in a lilting Irish accent, "And we have been promised reinforcements on arrival."

"You are joining us Elsa?" Rueben asked her in his quiet, unassuming voice. His accent was also Irish but softer than Layla's, as if he had been much longer away from his homelands. It was a voice that could fool a person into thinking there was nothing about this man to be afraid of, just as you realised he had already killed you.

"I am," she said determinedly, she sensed Rueben's doubt.

"Then you must follow my instructions," He gave no explanation as to why, nor did he invite any further discussion. Elsa simply nodded and Layla gave her a small smile and the slightest hint of a wink. Elsa could see who had the personality in this duo.

"Hesper, you have an update on your work?" Marcus asked.

"I believe I have synthesised a formula which can replicate the effects that Sebastian's blood had on Elsa," Hesper said, "We do not have time to adequately test it of course so I cannot guarantee how long the effects would last, I am concerned it may metabolise faster. Every vampire will have a set of readymade syringes, so they will be able to boost the dose if needed and if they are able. I am afraid it is not suitable for werewolves Gray."

"Gray will not be going in," said Marcus and he turned to Gray, "As strong and capable as you are my friend, any vampires we meet will be far more powerful than you have ever come across. We need your tracking skills but I won't risk your life in an unfair fight."

"You have my nose and my blood." Gray said, always a man of few words. Werewolf blood was poisonous to vampires and caused them excruciating and debilitating pain. All team members would be armed with bullets filled with werewolf blood in the hope of gaining further advantage over their foe. No-one mentioned that they had no idea if the blood would still be effective on vampires who had drunk from Sebastian, that was something they would have to find out as they went along.

"Logan wishes to come too I hear? Is he healed?" Katherine asked.

"Well enough," said Gray, "He will come, but he will stay with me."

"I think he's ready," said Marcus, "And I know there are certain things he's taken to heart shall we say? Don't let that heart do his thinking for him Gray, he must stay back with you." Gray nodded.

Elsa thought about what her father had said. She had spoken briefly with Logan since being back at Haven, it was not his injury that made him want revenge on Aiden and Vincent, it was Kate. He tried to hide his feelings but they were as plain to Elsa, and indeed to most people, as if he had hired a satellite and broadcast it to the world. He had feelings for Kate; he had visited her whilst she was still unconscious and he had kept his distance when he realised how frightened she was of the monsters she thought she saw all around her. It hurt him to think that she still didn't know who he was and he may never have a chance with her but it didn't stop him caring about her and wanting to tear out Aiden's throat with his own teeth next full moon.

A jet was waiting to fly them to Morocco both from and to private landing strips. No flight plan to be logged, no tickets, no passports; there would be no record anywhere of their trip and the intention was to get in and out of the country as quickly and quietly as possible. The only creature on earth that could sneak up on a vampire was a vampire. Once they had located Sebastian, they would have to assume that Vincent and any other vampires he had with him would be in the same location, they would go in expecting a fight and they were ready to give one.

"So we're all agreed, we get Sebastian out and the rest of the mission is to follow the NLP protocol?" Marcus asked. Everyone agreed; NLP – no live prisoners.

As they left the room, Elsa paused to walk with her father.

"What will you be doing Dad?" she asked.

"Co-ordinating," Marcus said, "Don't worry Elsa, I'm not an idiot, I know I'm no match for vampires that are super-charged on your boyfriends blood."

Elsa had been worrying. She knew her Dad had taken part in full combat missions in the past but, asides from the extra strength their adversary's would have on this occasion, he wasn't getting any younger and she worried about him. Knowing he would not be coming face to face with Vincent was a relief to her. She was not about to give Vincent the chance to take another parent from her.

Marcus grabbed her arm suddenly and held her back as the others walked on ahead.

"Sweetheart please, promise me you'll be careful," he said, his eyes full of fear, "I know you aren't a vulnerable little girl any more but you are still my little girl and I can't lose you. Not to him, not to anyone"

Elsa understood, "You won't," she said, "I promise." She hoped she sounded more confident than she felt. She knew the synthetic blood that Hesper had developed would give her back that feeling of invincibility she'd had at the compound after drinking from Sebastian but she also knew Vincent, and any other vampires they might come across would have it too. She was still a young vampire and Vincent had already proven he could, and would hurt her. She took confidence into the strength of her feelings for Sebastian, in her unwavering knowledge that they were meant to be together and that if there were any higher beings deciding their fate, that Sebastian had had more than his fair share of unhappiness. She made him happy and, if fate was fair, they would both be saved. She had to put her faith in fate and in the steely rage that flickered in her heart, waiting for her to fully ignite the flame and turn in on those that had wronged her, her family and the man she loved.

"Elsa, a very quick word," Now it was Hesper's turn to hold her back and Elsa glanced after the rest of the group, itching to follow them to the jet and get away as soon as possible, "It's about Sebastian."

That made Elsa stop and her father thoughtfully excused himself to catch up with the others, "What is it?" Elsa asked.

"I wanted you to know that I have also been trying to develop a serum for Sebastian, to curb his particular cravings," Hesper had a small smile on her face.

"Really? Has it worked?" Elsa was thrilled, the idea of being able to help Sebastian truly overcome the parts of himself that he loathed the most, well, it was so much more than she could have hoped for.

"I don't want to get your hopes up too much; obviously I can't test it until you bring him home." There it was again, Hesper's refusal to doubt that their rescue mission would succeed that so lifted Elsa's spirits, "But I'm hopeful I can, at the very least, dull his need for flesh and blood, give him some control."

Elsa threw her arms around Hesper's neck, surprising the elegant vampire, "Thank you so much!" she cried, "It means so much to me that you would do that, I know everyone else is unsure of him and what he is, I can feel it."

"And I can feel what you feel for him Elsa, he must be worth saving." Hesper kissed her lightly on the cheek, "Now go to him."

Elsa didn't need telling twice, she ran to catch the others up, thoughts of Sebastian filling her mind, thoughts of how happy he would be if his cravings could be curbed, if he could begin to find, even in a small way, the normal life he wanted so desperately.

"Heads up!" Her thoughts were interrupted as a bottle came flying at her head. She caught it without even thinking about it and looked over at the direction it had come from. Layla was stepping onto the jet and gave her a wave to hurry up, "It's hot over there," She shouted with a laugh, remarkably relaxed considering they were going to launch a full assault on a location they didn't yet know against an undetermined amount of super-strong vampires in a foreign country.

Elsa looked at the bottle; it was factor fifty sun cream. She smiled for the first time in days.

*AN - another update to come this weekend - action is going to kick off! Thanks for reading, I've had some really thoughtful comments too in the last couple of week - keep em coming! *

# That Level Of Violence.

----------------------------------------------------

Elsa was struck by how different the night sky looked in the mountains. She didn't live in a particularly built up area and always thought she could see the stars clearly back home, but this was something else. There wasn't a cloud in the sky and it brought to mind lyrics from a song by one of her favourite bands. The sky resembles a backlit canopy with holes punched in it. In reality, that description didn't even come close; it looked more like someone had dusted icing sugar across the sky. Maybe it was her keen vision, or maybe it was the complete lack of light pollution in the Atlas range but Elsa had never seen anything like it. She could see, she was sure, every single star it was possible to see and wondered if she was looking at galaxies further than any human being could ever hope to travel and stars that had long since died. Shooting stars were frequent, she'd counted so many she had no new wishes left for them; just the same one every time a tiny pin prick of light sped across the sky, *bring him back to me*.

It had been a quick and uneventful flight and there were no indications so far that anyone knew they had arrived; except of course the back up team which met them at the airfield. With Katherine's help, they now found themselves high in the mountains, looking down on a lone mountain refuge, usually popular with trekkers but, by all appearances, empty tonight. Haven's North African branch had been questioning people who had trekked the paths that passed the refuge and none of them could give a clear explanation as to why they had not stopped at that particular rest point. One party of six climbers had even risked continuing their trek in the dark after walking for hours, rather than stop for the night to rest. When asked why, they had looked confused and the best explanation they could come up with was that it had seemed like a good idea at the time. Dehydrated and with severely blistered feet, there was no way a group of experienced mountain walkers like those would have passed up the opportunity to rest at that refuge.

Katherine was certain that Sebastian was in there, not in the refuge itself but below ground. She could tell there was a network of rooms and tunnels below the surface, cut into the rock and had given them as clear a plan as she could of what they would be walking into. Every member of the team had memorised the floor plan, an easy task for a vampire. Katherine could also tell them that there were approximately thirty vampires in those rooms, but she could not tell them exactly where each vampire was, nor could she pinpoint Sebastian's exact location. But she had singled it down to four possible rooms, deep within the mountainside and furthest from any entrance they could determine; they were probably going to have to go through most of the thirty vampires inside to get to him.

Their assault team was now ten strong, with the addition of Marcus, Gray, Logan and Katherine back at a safe distance, co-coordinating three separate attacks on the refuge. They were at a disadvantage as far as manpower was concerned but they did have the element of surprise; at least they hoped they did. They also had Hesper's synthetic blood so they could match the power and ability of any vampire that had drunk from Sebastian, along with enough werewolf blood laced bullets to put all thirty vampires down ten times over.

A brief lesson was all that had been needed, Elsa was sniper accurate with her gun but she knew that her targets would be moving fast so there was still no guarantee she would hit everything she shot at. It didn't matter; she didn't want to shoot Vincent, she wanted to tear out his heart with her bare hands and watch him turn to dust.

She was itching to move. Sebastian was in there, so close, yet somehow still so far away. Everyone was getting into position. There were three possible means of gaining entrance; she would be going in through the back of the refuge and down into a storage cellar where Katherine believe they could gain access to one of the underground tunnels through wooden slatted paneling to one of the walls behind a pile of firewood. Elsa was amazed at how clear Katherine's description could be of this particular point when she couldn't determine exactly where Sebastian was. Katherine had explained that she had 'borrowed' the mind of a rat nesting in the woodpile and had gotten a pretty clear view. There was no way she could sneak into the mind of any of the vampires to find their locations, it would have been like knocking on the door to announce their presence before they went in. She had also told Elsa that Sebastian's mind was too weak to find, an admission from the witch that had opened the cracks in Elsa's heart just that little bit wider.

Logan's voice sounded in her ear, "Elsa, you ready?"

"I've been ready for days," Elsa impatiently muttered her reply to the air, knowing that a concealed microphone would pick it up and carry it back to Logan.

"Less than a minute now, take it easy, I wish I was going in with you."

Elsa and Logan had spoken on the jet on the way in; Logan definitely had his hackles up for Aiden and was frustrated he couldn't join the assault.

"Katherine has only picked up a few human's inside, we don't even know Aiden's one of them," Elsa reasoned.

"He's there," Logan replied, "I can feel it in my bones, especially the one in my arm that broke when he shot me."

"How do you know it was him?"

"I'm still alive, a vampire wouldn't have missed."

Elsa smiled to herself, she wouldn't want to be in Aiden's shoes if Logan did ever get hold of him.

"Ok Elsa, it's time." Logan's voice was all business now, "Layla and her team are about to breach the front. She'll be making some noise so as soon as you hear that, your team heads round the back. From then on it's one way communication only, unless your position is discovered by which point you can talk to us as much as you need to."

"I've got it Logan, we've been over this already." Elsa's jaw was clenched, her eyes scanning the darkness for evidence Layla's attack had begun. She reached into her pocket for the syringes Hesper had supplied each of them with and administered her first dose of synthetic blood. She felt the familiar surge coursing through her veins that she had felt after drinking from Sebastian, but more subtle this time. She could feel the strength build inside her but it was nothing like how she'd felt with Sebastian's real blood. That had left every fibre in her body feeling as if an electric current was pulsing through it; it had made her feel invincible. This time she felt a warmth yes, a gentle wave of power, but she realised with dismay that the impact was nowhere near what she'd had before. Oh well, it would have to do, there was nothing they could do about it -

"Now." That was all Logan said and as soon as Elsa heard the word, she saw flashes of light and heard three loud bangs. Layla's team were the diversion, hoping to draw most of the vampires to the front few rooms and tunnels, where they could be more easily picked off. Elsa was sure that whilst it might fool some of the refuge's inhabitants, it wouldn't fool Vincent. Elsa was part of Rueben's team and through the darkness she saw the smallest flick of his hand; the signal to move. He had been very clear, she was to stay behind him, he was the first point of attack should they encounter trouble. She had agreed; she would follow his orders until she saw Vincent but then no one was going to stop her doing what she needed to do.

They moved quickly to the rear entrance of the refuge. It wasn't guarded, something that told Elsa they weren't expecting visitors and reassured her somewhat. She could hear the commotion from the front of the building, shots fired, the sound of tearing flesh. Concentrating, she could hear the distant beat of human hearts and realised that it wasn't vampires who had been sent to meet the first wave of the attack. They'd sent the humans to their deaths instead to buy them time, which meant that both Elsa's team and the other group were more likely to meet the serious vampire threat. It was a blow to the plan but it was manageable; it also told them that whilst they might not have been expected at that exact moment in time, the blood movement vampires did have a contingency against possible attack. Typical of their kind, the human's were expendable, use them first.

Rueben led Elsa and another vampire, one that had joined them after their arrival, down into their first tunnel. Elsa had expected roughly cut tunnels, burrowing into the mountainside but that wasn't what they found. Like the compound where she and Kate had been held, the walls were smooth, grey concrete with neon strip lighting on the ceiling. This was no makeshift hideaway; this was a purpose built facility that had clearly been here for some time. It was likely that the vampires who were here now knew every corridor, every hiding place; another strike against Haven's assault that Elsa tried to put out of her mind.

Suddenly, three vampires rounded the corner, clearly surprised to find another three vampires, clad in black, that weren't supposed to be there.

Despite their surprise they quickly recovered and launched themselves at Rueben whose large frame virtually filled the narrow corridor. They were young vampires, possibly newborns but their strength was clear. Hatred burned in Elsa's heart; it was clear where their first meal had come from. Rueben quickly dispensed with one of them, a female. She flew at him, her fangs flashing and reached for his head, intent on ripping it from his body. Despite the fact that Elsa felt the synthetic blood had a weaker effect than Sebastian's, Rueben easily matched the woman's strength and ferocity. His hands reached her head before hers could make contact with his and, with the slightest of movements, he relieved her of her new vampire life to the sound of flesh tearing and bone snapping. She gave a howl that was quickly cut off, her body crumbled to dust in an instance and Rueben tossed her head onto the pile of ash without a second glance.

By this point, the other vampire working with Rueben and Elsa, a young, wiry-limbed Moroccan who had introduced himself as Nory, had placed a bullet in each of the other two attacking vampires, which had caused them to slump quickly to the floor. Rueben stepped over them to check around the corner for any further surprises then, satisfied there were none, instructed Elsa and Nory to keep look out.

Both of the stricken vampires were clearly in pain, the werewolf blood laced bullets lodged inside them had already begun to poison their systems and no amount of Sebastian's blood would save them. They were going to die but they were too young, too new to being vampires to realise. They were both male and one of them was screaming, a horrible high pitched sound as he clawed at his chest where the bullet had entered, ripping away pieces of his own skin trying to get the agonising bullet out. He was no good to anyone; Rueben thrust his hand into the vampire's chest and pulled out his heart, reducing what was left of the screaming clawing mess to dust. He threw the heart into the lap of the other vampire who was accepting his fate in a much quieter fashion. He was shaking as his body was rapidly succumbing to the poison in his system, his teeth gritted against the pain. Rueben held a gun to his head, pressing the muzzle hard against his skull.

"I will shoot you in the head," he said in his calm yet authoritative voice, "You won't die yet but the pain you feel now will be nothing compared to the pain of werewolf blood lodged directly in your brain. You will die in more pain than any being should ever be able to bear. Or, you will tell me where the demon is and I will rip out your heart now and all this will be over."

Elsa hung on every word, whilst keeping her gun trained down the corridor. The second vampire to die had made a lot of noise before Rueben silenced him, they could be about to receive more guests any minute.

The last vampire smiled through his pain, he was not as young as Elsa had first thought, he had more control, "Vincent will kill you all," he said simply, spitting the words through his teeth.

Rueben didn't give him another ultimatum; Elsa was beginning to see that when Rueben said something, he expected people to listen. He stared straight into the vampire's eyes as he pulled the trigger of his gun. All the guns except those of Layla's team were silenced and the popping sound was deceptively gentle. The vampire's body convulsed as the bullet hit and his eyes rolled back in his head as he fell back onto the floor. His body began to jerk violently and his mouth opened with the beginnings of a blood-curdling scream. Rueben stuffed the second vampire's heart into his open mouth before the sound could escape and the muffled shrieks followed them as Rueben moved ahead of Elsa and Nory and motioned for them to follow him down the corridor.

Elsa felt oddly calm. That level of violence may have bothered her once but it was part of her now. A part that she would prefer to keep buried yes, but she was growing to accept the vampire inside her and she needed it tonight. Without it she would never be able to do what needed to be done to get

Sebastian back and that was more important to her than anything. She just hoped she'd be able to find her humanity once again when all this was over.

*AN - a dedication for the first person to tell me the band and the song to match the lyrics quoted in the first paragraph ;) Don't forget those votes folks and thank you for your patience while I have been without internet *

# Piles Of Ash

---

✱ AN - If you're interested in the soundtrack to this book then it's Red Tape by Agent Provocateur for this chapter :) *

They were moving slowly and silently towards the first of the rooms that may hold Sebastian and had met no further resistance as yet. Far from easing their tension, this just concerned Elsa all the more. The sound of Layla's initial loud entrance had died down, only a couple of human heartbeats could be heard now, most of the human's that had been in Vincent's underground lair had given their lives for him. Logan had told them that Layla and her team of four were all safe and accounted for, moving to the second target location whilst a further team of three were zeroing in on a third possible location for Sebastian and had encountered no vampires at all. It was too quite, too calm and far, far too easy so far for anyone's liking. Three out of a possible thirty vampires were dead. That left at least twenty-seven vampires who now knew their security had been breached. Still not the best odds.

"Katherine thinks Sebastian has been moved. She's lost him." Logan's voice was urgent in Elsa's ear and she froze. Rueben and Nory looked at her, they'd heard it too. She was dying to ask questions but didn't want to compromise their position. Rueben motioned to Nory and signaled Elsa to stay put. The two men continued down the corridor to the next bend and checked that they were clear. Rueben looked back to Elsa and gave her an almost imperceptible nod.

Elsa whispered as quietly as she could, hoping Logan could hear her, "Does she have any idea of his last location? What does she mean lost?" She had to keep telling herself he couldn't be dead but the fear of it still snaked around her heart and began to squeeze tight.

"He began to move deeper underground and then she lost any connection," Logan replied, "She can't tell us why." There was a pause, "You know he isn't dead Elsa."

"What's the best guess on where to move forward?" She asked, ignoring Logan's last comment.

"From your location, moving through your original target you should be able to gain access to a door which leads further down into the mountainside; after that, we can't really help you. We'll instruct the other teams to meet you there, you'll have to move on as one unit."

"Understood." Elsa looked back down the corridor to Rueben who nodded his understanding and agreement. They continued to move silently and carefully down the corridor and through the door at the other end, which led them to their original target, a room that could have contained Sebastian. There was no ambush awaiting them but the smell of blood hit Elsa as soon as they entered. It was Sebastian's blood, she'd recognise it anywhere; he had been in this room!

Her eyes scanned the room and came to rest on two small drops of dark red blood. She moved over to it; the blood glistened slightly in the unforgiving glare of the strip lighting on the ceiling. It was still wet, only slightly congealed.

She glanced at Rueben and could see that he understood the significance; Sebastian had bled in that very spot just a few short moments ago.

Within less than a minute they had been joined by Layla and both teams of Haven vampires. There was one door leading to their new target and they all knew the likelihood of walking through it and straight into an ambush of almost thirty vampires was very high. Rueben spoke, his voice barely loud enough for them to hear.

"They have the numbers," he said, "Layla will blow the door and the rest of us will stay right back, with any luck they'll attack first."

"I doubt it," one of the new vampires said.

"Agreed," said Rueben, "But we don't have any other options. Layla, have you got any smoke bombs left?" Layla nodded, "Good, you know what to do. Once visibility is down, you and I will head the assault. Use your bullets first, get as many of them down as you can straight away, there will be time to go back and finish them off when we've secured the area. Layla and I will go straight through the middle. You two and you two," he signaled to Elsa, Nory and two other vampires, "Take the flanks and the rest of you the ceiling."

Everyone nodded; this was it and they all took their second dose of synthetic blood. Elsa was still stood by Sebastian's blood drops; she crouched down and touched her fingertips to the thick red liquid before bringing them to her lips. The effect of the synthetic blood was nothing compared to the hit she got now. Just those two tiny drops of almost congealed blood gave her more of a rush than both of the doses Hesper had given her. Everything around her slowed down, she could see ever particle of dust in the air, hear every muscle fibre in the other vampires tense as they readied themselves for what was to come, sense the electrical current of anticipation in the room. The combination of the synthetic blood and Sebastian's was making her stronger and more powerful than either could alone. She said nothing to the others, she would need that extra edge for Vincent and she didn't want Rueben to know her plans.

Everyone got into position; Layla laid charges around the door and retreated to a safe distance herself. She held up three fingers, then two, then one, then …

Elsa's focus snapped to the door as it was blown off it's hinges and she tipped her head mere millimeters to the left to avoid the chunk of molten metal that flew her way. A split second later, the corridor beyond the doorway was filled with smoke and they began to move forward. Nothing met them as they moved quickly down a flight of steps and the smoke began to clear. An open doorway at the bottom almost invited them in and a new flurry of smoke bombs gave them cover. At this point they split up as Rueben had instructed, moving at speeds faster than the human eye could comprehend. Elsa's eyes were not human, she could see everything that was happening in slow motion, analyse every move from every one of them and she could see now that their welcome party had finally arrived.

There were fifteen vampires in the room, they were high on Sebastian's blood and they were stronger and faster than Haven's vampires. Two of the North African vampires who had taken the right hand side of the room were quickly overcome by four of Vincent's team. They got a couple of shots off and one vampire fell to the floor, screaming in agony. The other three did not give the slightest reaction to their fallen comrade, tearing off the head of the shooter and turning his gun on his partner before there was time to blink. The second North African vampire fell to the ground next to the one his partner had shot, his body twisting, his face contorted but he defiantly refused to scream in pain. As his three assailants turned their attention to the vampires crawling along the ceiling, he used his final moments to put three bullets in the back of the one who had decapitated his friend. The other two turned back to consider finishing him off, snarling, their eyes glowing. But they didn't need to, the poison of the werewolf blood had overcome him and he could no longer raise the gun; they were free to get back in the fight.

Rueben and Layla were older and more experienced, the synthetic blood may not have had such a powerful effect as Sebastian's had on the enemy but they did have the advantage of their finely honed skills. Rueben thrust his hand into the chest of one vampire, detaching his heart and shoving it up into his throat where he could choke on it as he turned to ash, whilst simultaneously firing two bullets towards the ceiling, one for each of the vampires left from the fracas on the right hand side of the room. They dropped like stones, writhing to the floor as Layla fought off two more coming at them from directly ahead. As one clung to her back attempting to get a grip on her head, she punched a hole straight through the chest of another and it crumbled to dust around her arm. Elsa fired her gun once and hit the vampire clinging to Layla's back right in the middle of it's forehead, sending it flying back towards the wall. Layla gave her one nod before moving on and Elsa turned her focus back to Nory, who had lost his gun. They were being attacked by three vampires, two of whom were on Nory and one who was heading for Elsa. She saw Nory's gun on the floor and grabbed it. Standing up she held both arms out at shoulder height, firing one gun at the vampire heading for her, and one at a vampire she knew had just dropped from the ceiling to try and grab her from behind. The female vampire that had been flying towards her had done so at such a speed that when Elsa's bullet hit her, she was millimeters from the muzzle of the gun. She stopped in her tracks, her face a mask of shock. With barely a pause, Elsa followed through, shoving her gun, hand and arm straight through the vampire's chest. She felt the heart detach and pushed the whole mass out the other side before firing the gun again, this time hitting one of the vampires on Nory's back. Freed of one of his assailants, Nory ripped the head of the second and held his hand out for his gun. It was dripping with blood and flesh; Elsa gave a small smile, shrugged and handed it over.

Another quick glance around the room told her they were still only two team members down. They however, had managed to dispatch eleven of the enemy and the vampires who had scaled the ceiling were finishing off two more. The guns had been their advantage but a quick calculation told Elsa they were running very short of bullets now and she had no idea how many Layla's team had use on their original assault at the front of the building. There were possibly twelve or more vampires still in the building they hadn't even come across yet and their numbers were down to eight. They had the advantage in this room, but how long would it last?

The last vampire was crouched on the floor with three guns trained on him; Nory was wiping his gun on the clothes of the still twitching body of a not quite dead yet vampire, Rueben and Layla were covering the doorway leading out of the room and two of the North African vampires were covering the doorway they had entered through.

Elsa pressed her gun against the temple of their prisoner, "Where is Sebastian?" she hissed.

The vampire bared his teeth at Elsa and said nothing. Suddenly a shot was fired and the vampire jerked forward, howling to the floor. Rueben had fired from his position by the door and Elsa's eyes flashed at him.

"He can't tell us anything now!" she said angrily.

"He wasn't going to tell us anything anyway," said Rueben calmly, "We need to concentrate on the other twelve or more vampires that are still here."

He had made his point, they'd won the battle but the war was far from over. Elsa's nerves were on fire. The volatile mix of synthetic blood and Sebastian's was threatening to overcome her, she knew she' almost held back during the fight, what was she capable of with this cocktail inside her?

She felt like she could take on a hundred vampires alone with one hand tied behind her back.

"What do we do now?" one of the new vampires asked.

"We keep going," Rueben said, "Bullets?"

"I'm out," said Layla and five other heads nodded that they too were out of ammo. They collected up the guns of their fallen team members, emptied all their magazines and share out what they had left. Rueben and Layla tossed their empty guns to the floor; Elsa, Nory and the others each had one bullet.

"Six bullets, at least twelve enemy combatants," said Rueben, "Make them count."

Suddenly Elsa's ears pricked. She could hear something the others clearly couldn't yet, a very low, gentle hissing sound. Her eyes darted upwards and Rueben frowned at her.

"What is it?"

"I don't know," she said, "Something's coming."

They all looked up at the ceiling. They could see nothing, hear nothing but Elsa knew something was wrong. She could see tiny pinprick holes in the ceiling and realised they peppered the whole of the roof. She hadn't picked up on them before, they were barely noticeable in the concrete, even to a vampires eyes, and she wasn't sure even now if the others could see them, heightened as her senses were.

"How do you -?" Layla's question was cut short; they could all hear the hiss now and Elsa watched as tiny wisps of white smoke began to curl through the holes in the ceiling. Everyone around her began to cough and clutch at their throats and she watched in horror as first Nory, then his friends, Layla and finally Rueben fell to their knees, their eyes bulging. She could feel a burning in her throat but the gas did not seem to be having the same effect on her as it was having on the others. Blood began to weep from their eyes and ears, Layla coughed again and blood poured out of her mouth, down her chin and began to pool on the floor as she fell forward.

"No!" Elsa screamed and rushed to Layla's side but there was nothing she could do. The whole team were hemorrhaging blood at an unstoppable rate.

"It's attacking our hearts Elsa," Rueben managed to choke through the blood gushing over his lips, "We're –" he said no more, pitching backwards and falling silent. Elsa stood in the middle of the room, seven bodies worth of blood pooling around her feet, seven vampires dead. Within seconds, she was alone with seven piles of ash surrounding her and only Logan's voice in her ear.

"What's happening Elsa? What's going on?"

*A/N - tough one for me to write as I think I could have gotten quite attached to Rueben and Layla. Keep voting and commenting you lovely people, I'm at number 3! THANK YOU ALL!! Oh, and if any of you would like to recommend me to the Wattpad team for Devil Inside to be featured, I'd really appreciate it. I'm going to contact them myself too as this story is almost finished, it is my ultimate goal to be a featured writer :)

# Bodies.

------------------------------------------------

✱ AN - I've been dying to use this tune and finally the chapter has arrived - the song for this one is Let The Bodies Hit The FLoor by Drowning Pool :) 1

"Elsa!" Logan shouted down her ear again, it sounded like he was calling to her from the bottom of a deep hole. She had tunnel vision, unable to tear her eyes away from a small silver charm, a dragonfly that she remembered seeing around Layla's neck. It lay now amongst the blood and ash at Elsa's feet.

"What's happening Elsa?" Logan's voice was stern, he was trying to snap her back from wherever it was her mind had gone. It was as if a bomb had gone off, sending a ringing into her ears that blocked out all other sound. As her mind took in what had happened the ringing began to dissipate and Logan's voice began to get through to her.

"I -I don't know," she stuttered finally, stepping back from that surrounded her, "They're gone Logan."

"What do you mean gone? Where? Why won't anyone respond?"

"They're dead!" Elsa cried, as if the terrible reality of it had just hit her, "Everyone is dead!"

Logan swore, she heard him relay her message.

"Get the hell out of there Elsa! Now!" it was her father's voice in her ear this time but Elsa didn't respond. She was staring at the mess that used to be Rueben and Layla ... and Nory. Sebastian. She was so close to finding him. She'd promised herself she would never leave him behind again. Her mind was clearing, she could feel the effects of the synthetic blood still in her system, along with Sebastian's blood. She could do this.

"Elsa, move!" Her father's voice was desperate. Elsa reached up to her ear and removed the earpiece.

"I'm sorry Dad," she said as she threw the earpiece to the floor and then removed the small microphone. She wasn't going anywhere but forward, to find Sebastian.

A sound began to fill the room, the sound of someone clapping a slow and mocking clap. Elsa turned slowly to find Vincent leaning lazily in the doorway.

"I'm impressed," he said in his sarcastic drawl, his lips curled into a cruelly smug smile, "I don't know how you got his blood into your system but no matter, now I get to watch you get torn apart instead."

Sebastian's blood, that was what had saved her from the gas, none of the others had it in their system, only her. She clenched her fists and snarled back at Vincent but before she could move he stepped back and in his place appeared fifteen more vampires, drunk on Sebastian's blood and coming straight for her. Katherine had been four out.

Elsa went into autopilot and jumped to the ceiling, crawling across it at lightening speed and dropping down next to a gun she knew held one bullet. She grabbed it, aimed and fired with a speed she didn't even know she possessed and one of the fifteen fell as the werewolf blood bullet hit him in the eye and burrowed deep into his brain. She took a moment to register his face, it was unmistakably Aiden she had hit, Vincent must have changed him. She stored the memory of the shock on his handsome face as the bullet had plunged into his eye socket, pulverizing the eyeball and lodging into his brain before releasing its poison. Poison that she knew had come from Logan's blood. She would tell Logan about that later, it would make him smile.

Fourteen she counted down in her head, running full pelt at two more vampires, arm outstretched. Her hand plunged deep into the chest of the first, out the other side and into the chest of the second. With a flick she tore out both hearts and threw them to the floor, spinning around as the bodies turned to ash and reaching down to grab two more guns, one in each hand. Twelve.

From her crouched position on the floor she reached both arms up and fired at two vampires who were in the process of dropping down on her from the ceiling. Ten. As they fell, screeching in pain, she grabbed one and swung it by the feet, using it to swat away another vampire as if it were nothing but an annoying fly. It snarled and came straight back at her. She ran straight back at it and, just before they met, she dropped to the floor, taking its feet out from under it. It flipped over her head as she skidded onto her back, grabbed another gun, rolled onto her stomach and fired. The vampire was hit in mid air and dropped like a stone. Nine.

There were hands at her head, trying to twist it from her body. Elsa reached behind her and pulled the attacking vampire over her head with her hands around its neck. She squeezed with all her strength, felt its neck snap and shook it's limp body just once with such force, its flesh tore and its body flew across the room. The head was still in her hands and she threw it aside as four more vampires descended on her. Eight.

One of them had picked up a gun from the floor. Elsa knew it was an empty one, she knew exactly where each gun had fallen when her friends had died and she knew which ones had bullets in them. As the muzzle was pressed to her head she froze, letting them think they had her. The vampire with the gun smiled as the other three circled closely and the final four hung back, laughing.

Elsa smiled back; she had already grabbed the final two guns that had bullets when she'd skidded on her back across the floor. She knew she could move faster than these vampires, Sebastian's blood worked better for her than it did for anyone else and she had Hesper's formula too. She reached behind her back and pulled out both guns before the grinning vampire in front of her could even finish pulling the trigger on his empty gun. She darted to the side and punched holes straight through the hearts of two of the circling vampires, leading with the guns. She turned before the bodies had even had time to dissolve into ash and the bloodied muzzles of each gun fired at two of the vampires who had chose to hang back. The vampire who had tried to fire on her had just heard the click of his empty barrel and a flash of confusion appeared on his face as Elsa jumped high, free of the two bodies, which had now crumbled from around her arms. She kicked out hard and was satisfied when his head came clean off his body as her foot made contact with his face. Three.

No more bullets, three more vampires. She didn't need bullets; her whole body was on fire. She could feel Sebastian was close, if possible her senses were become even more heightened, she knew she could hear the weak beat of his heart and it spurred her on. Three more vampires, then Vincent.

The last three kept back. They were wary of her; it was the first time she'd seen that. She had them worried. She watched as they decided what they were going to do, fight or flight, the most basic animal instinct. She was going to fight, flight was not an option she wanted or needed. She could almost hear the synapses in their brains firing as they decided. There was three of them, one of her; she had no bullets, what could she do against them?

All three of them flew at her at once; Elsa stood still and let them come. They got closer; she slowed down everything that was happening with her mind. Two females and a male were left, all of them coming at her in a flash of teeth, arms reaching for her, intent on tearing her limb from limb. She planned her movements as they approached. She would dart to the side and grab the one on the right, twisting off its head as she dropped to the floor and kicked the feet of the other two out from under them. As they fell she would jump up and bring her foot down hard on the neck of one, hard enough to separate bones and flesh. Finally, as the third was getting back to it's feet she would deliver an upper cut blow to it's chest, tear out it's heart and dust the ash off her clothes before turning her attention to Vincent.

This decided, Elsa waited the last, smallest part of a second that it took the vampires to reach her. Still within the same second she executed her plan and by the time the second was over and the next about to start, she was brushing ash off her sleeve and turning towards the doorway where Vincent had stood and mocked her only moments before.

Unsurprisingly, he wasn't there. She walked through the doorway, listening intently for any movement. She could smell blood, Sebastian's blood. Ahead of her was another doorway, the door open and inviting, the room beyond dark with none of the harsh lighting every other room in Vincent's lair had. A flickering glow told her it was lit by candles instead and the sound of a heartbeat, slow and weak, along with the smell of blood told her Sebastian was there. It took every ounce of strength she had not to rush to his side. Instead she crept quietly to the doorway and scanned the room. Sebastian was alone. On the back wall he was chained by the wrists, his arms outstretched above his head, his shoulders clearly dislocated. His body hung limp, the chains around his ankles were hardly needed and his head lolled down against his chest. Now that she could see Vincent was not in the room, she flew to Sebastian.

"Oh God Sebastian, what have they done to you?" she whispered, lifting his head to look at his face. His torso was bare and he was covered with bite marks all over his body in various stages of healing. Knowing how quickly his body could heal, Elsa knew that these bites were no more than minutes old and took small comfort in knowing that almost all of those bite marks belonged to a vampire that was now dead or dying of werewolf blood poisoning in the other room. Sebastian's cheeks were hollow and covered in coarse stubble. He was clammy with sweat and had lost weight; his eyes were closed, his lips dry and cracked. His skin was dry and tight and clung to each one of his muscles as if every last drop of moisture had been sucked from his body.

"Sebastian, it's me Elsa," tears flowed down her cheeks as she tried to rouse him but got no response, "Please."

She placed a hand on his chest, she could hear his heart beating but she needed to feel it, to know that he was really alive. There was a gentle thud beneath her palm that gave her renewed strength. Gritting her teeth she pulled each of his chains from the wall and caught him as he slumped to the floor. She knelt down, cradling him in her lap just as she had when she'd found him on the warehouse floor that night before she'd gone to Canada but this time she wasn't going anywhere.

"Come on," she pleaded, "Wake up, come back to me." Her tears dropped onto his face as she leant down to kiss him softly. She felt the slightest of movements of his lips against hers and a whisper of his voice reached her ears, the sweetest sound she thought she'd ever heard.

"Elsa," he whispered hoarsely.

"It's me, Sebastian, it's going to be all right, I'm getting you out of here," She shifted her weight, preparing to lift him up.

"No," he croaked, "Elsa, he's-"

"Behind you." Vincent finished the sentence for him.

*Thanks for reading and to those of you that have said you will recommend me to be a featured writer. Feel free to join in and recommend me to the Wattpad team if you think the story deserves it :) *

# Black Heart

✱ AN – The track for this chapter is Feuer Frei by Rammstein :) *

"I'll admit," Vincent continued to speak as Elsa tenderly placed Sebastian back on the floor and stood to face him, "I underestimated you, it seems your boyfriend has quite an effect on you."

"I'm going to kill you now," Elsa said calmly, without moving as he approached.

Vincent laughed, "You really believe that don't you?" he said, "You really think you can kill me. ME!" The last word was delivered with terrifying venom and with that he had Elsa by the throat, pinned against the wall, his long fingernails digging into her pale skin, sending tiny rivulets of blood running down her neck.

She wasn't afraid. She pictured her mother in her mind, the clearest picture she'd ever been able to conjure. Alongside her, Elsa placed Sebastian, Kate, her father, Katherine … all the people she was going to do this for.

She reached up and snapped Vincent's arm as if it were a twig. He grimaced and released her, his arm hanging by his side for a split second before he stretched it out and Elsa heard the bones knit back together almost instantly.

"Is that the best you've got?" He laughed and came back at her, baring his fangs. They circled each other for a few seconds, each sizing the other up. Vincent had age on his side and Sebastian's blood in his system. Elsa had Hesper's formula and Sebastian's blood with the heightened effect it seemed to have on her alone. She felt she could match Vincent; it was just a case of who would make the first move.

"You think his blood is going to help you?" Vincent asked as if he was reading her mind, "Only if you can keep it inside you!" He lunged forward, producing two daggers from his belt. He crossed them in front of him and then drew his arms out sharply to his sides, slicing across Elsa's abdomen. She fell to her knees, blood gushing out onto the floor, her hands grasping at the deep slashes across her stomach, unable to stem the flow.

"I'll bleed his strength straight out of you girl," Vincent hissed, "You can't win, I've told you before, I'm older and stronger than you."

The wounds were already beginning to close but Elsa had lost a fair amount of blood. She could feel the effects of Sebastian's blood had eased slightly but she was still strong. She allowed Vincent to get close to her and then jumped up, grabbing at one of the daggers. This caught Vincent slightly by surprise and she managed to release the dagger from his right hand, the blade cutting deep into her palm as she did so, spilling yet more blood onto the floor. She span the dagger in her hand to take hold of the hilt and flew around Vincent like a whirlwind making two deep cuts, one to his neck, one to his inner thigh. He gasped, her first cut had been slightly off target but still bled profusely, the second cut, to his leg, caught the main artery and blood began to spurt from the wound instantly. He recovered quickly, grabbed her arm and pulled hard, wrenching her shoulder from its socket. She barely registered the pain this time, her adrenaline was pumping hard but she knew that she would have to put it back in the socket herself to give it chance to heal and give her full use of the arm. She used her good arm to thrust a fist into the deep cut in Vincent's leg, grasping at the flesh and tearing to open the wound further, increasing the steady, pulsing flow of blood. This time Vincent howled and threw her to the side, his injured leg failing him as he stumbled on the blood drenched floor.

Elsa jumped to her feet, her arm still out of joint. She was unable to stop Vincent pulling her into a headlock; his cuts were beginning to heal and the blood pumping from them slowed gradually. He squeezed hard, intent on tearing off Elsa's head. She dropped to the floor heavily and twisted, releasing his lock then ran as hard as she could away from him and towards the wall, hitting it at an angle to knock her shoulder back into place before pushing back of the wall with her feet to back flip and land on Vincent, bringing the dagger down hard and straight into his right eye.

He screamed with rage, clawing at his face to pull the dagger out, blood pouring from his eye socket. He swung wildly, temporarily blinded and his remaining dagger found it's way to Elsa's neck where it lodged in just above her collarbone; he twisted it and brought it down sharply, imbedding it deep in the bone. Both of them were badly wounded and bleeding, the effects of Sebastian's blood oozing out onto the floor around them. Vincent recovered first; throwing the dagger Elsa stabbed him with to the floor. His fury gave his black eyes an incandescent glow as he bore down on Elsa and she struggled to her feet to meet him. She could feel that she was weakening and for the first time, fear began to creep in. Sebastian remained motionless, now lying in a pool of blood created by Vincent and herself. Vincent seized her before she had chance to properly defend herself, he had drunk more blood and more recently than her, he was an older vampire and he was stronger than her now. He lifted her up above his head and threw her hard against the wall.

Elsa felt her skull and cheekbone crack as she hit the hard concrete and then fell to the floor face first; she placed her hands down to push herself up but she had slowed and Vincent was faster. He was already standing over her, his foot raised and a manic expression on his face. He brought his foot down with such force that Elsa heard and felt her spine snap before her whole body went numb. Vincent bent down and rolled her over, taking hold of her roughly under the arms and lifting her to sit against the wall. Her body was trying to heal but it wasn't working fast enough anymore, her back was broken and for the moment at least, she couldn't move.

Vincent crouched in front of her, his head to one side, studying her and smiling triumphantly. The eye she'd stabbed him in had not yet healed so only one ice blue eye glared at her broken form as he absently wiped blood from his face.

"Well," he said, "You put up quite a fight Elsa." He stood up and grabbed her by the ankles, pulling her roughly away from the wall until her head hit the floor hard. She felt the slowly healing vertebrae in her back dislodge again and wondered what it was going to be like to die. Vincent began dragging her across the floor, "It's almost a shame to finish you off, if I had any human's to hand I might have considered feeding them to you, seeing if I could still persuade you to join me." He had dragged her over to Sebastian's motionless form and stood between them, looking down at her, "But I think we're past that now, don't you? Your boyfriend here is very useful to me, I think I'll keep him. You however, I can do without. I think I'll just wake him up enough to watch me –"

Elsa watched as Vincent's face froze mid sentence. He looked down at his chest with a look of mild confusion and placed both his hands over his heart, his mouth opening and closing silently as his knees buckled. He stumbled to the ground and Sebastian was revealed behind him, his breath sharp and ragged, his arm embedded in Vincent's back, his hand holding the vampires black heart and threatening to tear it straight out. His face was smeared with blood, his eyes glowed amber and his features protruded sharply as he looked at Elsa.

"Do you want to do it?" he asked in a low, hoarse growl.

Elsa was beginning to find some feeling in her limbs, she started to test out her movements and slowly, gradually pushed herself up to sitting. She could see it was taking every last bit of strength Sebastian had to hold Vincent who could do nothing as he hung between life and death. Finally, Elsa was able to get to her knees and she faced Vincent who looked back at her with pure, unadulterated hatred from his one good eye.

Elsa placed the tips of her fingers on his chest and pushed slowly, feeling the fabric of his top tear and his flesh give way. As his ribs cracked and her hand continued into his chest, Vincent's eyes became wide and Elsa saw fear on his face for the first time. She found his heart, tight in Sebastian's grip and she took it as Sebastian let go and sat back heavily on the floor, exhausted with the effort in his weakened state.

"You can't," Vincent whispered, "You can't kill me."

"Can't I?" Elsa asked, "After everything you've done?" she prepared to pull his heart straight out of his chest, her eyes never leaving his.

"You don't understand," Vincent gasped as her grip tightening and his heart began to tear. Elsa had had enough, she wasn't going to listen to him anymore, she was more than done with Vincent.

She pulled hard and felt Vincent's heart detach from his body as he tried to speak his final words.

"You don't know what really happened – " and with that Elsa held Vincent's heart up for him to see as his skin turned grey, cracked began to crumble. He remained there for a moment, frozen in time, his last words lost on shrunken lips. Elsa dropped his heart to the floor and swiped a hand across the face she hated, watching as it finally crumbled to dust.

She fell forward onto her hands, her fingers clenched in the pile of ash that had been Vincent and she felt a hand on her back. Sebastian's hand, warm and comforting. She looked up into his burning amber eyes, the fire was dimming and he was returning to his usual self, her Sebastian. She wrapped her arms around his neck as his eyes slowly faded to their familiar grey and wept into his shoulder, feeling his heartbeat, still weak but getting stronger. It was over. She had him back. Vincent was gone.

* AN - See how dedicated I am to you all? I'm off sick an what am I doing? Updating Devil Inside for you lovely people. It's almost finished - there's going to be a twist in the tail! *

# Everything.

--------------------------------------------------

✱ AN - the track for this chapter is Breathe Me by Sia, I just love this song*

Elsa watched Sebastian sleep as they flew home. She couldn't take her eyes off him. They had both been covered in blood and ash when Marcus, Gray and Logan had found them, still wrapped in each other's arms in the middle of the room where they had just killed Vincent. Now they were cleaned up and going home and Elsa was beginning to feel, for want of a better word, human again.

Sebastian looked calm and all his wounds had healed but he was still undernourished. She knew the time would come for him soon when he would need to satisfy the urges he hated so much, it was the only way he would properly get his strength back, get back to his old self. At least it used to be the only way. She had not told him about Hesper's serum, about the possibility of a release from the prison of flesh and blood he had loathed for so long. She didn't want to get his hopes up right now, he just needed to rest.

He was holding her hand softly; his muscles relaxed in sleep and his head leant against the window of the jet. She envied him his peace slightly, she had almost forgotten what it felt like to surrender to sleep and let all the horrors of the day drift away. There were images she couldn't shift from her mind; she'd done such violent things, things she'd have never thought herself capable of. Some time ago, Hesper had offered to teach her to meditate as a way of overcoming the respite that sleep gave to humans. Elsa had felt she didn't need it then, maybe now would be a good time to take Hesper up on her offer.

Her father appeared at her side and crouched next to her seat, "You ok?" he whispered.

Elsa smiled and nodded, glancing for a moment to Marcus before taking her eyes back to Sebastian, who had not stirred, "I will be," she replied and Marcus place a hand over hers.

"What happened to the others," he said, "There was nothing any of us could have done to predict that."

How did he know what she was thinking? Was her guilt that obvious? She had wiped Sebastian's blood from the floor with her fingers to give her an edge when she confronted Vincent. She couldn't help reliving that moment over and over again in her head. Could she have shared it? She tried to remember exactly how much there'd been; if they'd all dipped a fingertip in, if there had been enough, the others would still be alive. Part of her knew that it wasn't the case, there had been two tiny drops, almost congealed, barely a taste. But she knew that there would always be a part of her brain that would conspire against her, the human part that she held on to so tightly, that couldn't always remember things exactly as they were and that told her she could have saved them.

"It wasn't your fault," Marcus insisted quietly and Elsa looked back at him to see the sincerity in his eyes. He truly believed what he was saying, he wasn't just saying it to make her feel better and she took some comfort in that. It didn't remove the fact that two people that had left England with them, were not coming back.

Marcus stood, lightly kissed her forehead and went back to his seat next to Katherine who was also sleeping, as were Gray and Logan. They were all exhausted. Elsa found her mind going over Vincent's last words as he'd been trying to talk himself out of the inevitable. He'd told her she didn't understand, that she didn't know what had happened and she wondered what he'd been talking about, what excuses he had been about to make, what reason he was going to try and give her not to kill him. She closed her eyes against the memory but that just made it clearer, something in his tone bothered her now. She shook her head; she couldn't decide if it was her human brain playing tricks on her or her vampire one giving her the facts. Vincent was dead; there was no going back now. It was what he'd deserved and she'd prevented him from having the last word, another comforting thought.

Sebastian stirred; his grip on her hand tightened slightly as he moved his head and opened his eyes. A moment's confusion passed over his face then his eyes fell on Elsa and he became calm again, "Hey," he said sleepily.

"Hey," Elsa replied, "How are you feeling?"

"Hungry," he said, his face clouding once more. Elsa knew what he meant. His body could only last so long before his demon's hunger took over and he'd been weakened by his time as Vincent's captive. She leaned over and kissed his lips softly, taking her hand to his face to stroke the stubble that was still there.

"Don't worry about that now," she said, "Everything is going to be fine."

"Thank you," Sebastian said sincerely, placing a hand over the one that caressed his face and looking deep into Elsa's eyes. The intensity that always drew her in was back, his eyes clear and grey, his emotions raw and open for her to feel, "I don't think I've said that yet."

"You don't need to," she said.

"I do. I need to thank your father too. No-one had to come after me, my life wasn't in danger."

Elsa shook her head, "Yes it was," she said, "Just because you can't die doesn't mean you should have to live like that. I hate to think what that must have been like for you, I just wish we could have-"

Sebastian placed a finger over her lips, "It's over," he said simply and all she could feel from him was his gratitude, his pain at his hunger and something else, something she felt too and something they would have to come back to later.

"How did you find the strength to stop Vincent?" Elsa asked, trying to distract her thoughts from where they'd been heading, "If you hadn't …"

"I was barely aware of what was happening at first," Sebastian said, looking down at his hands, "Then there was so much blood, on the floor and all over me. I could taste it in my mouth and I started to come round. You know it's what my body needs, instinct took over and I was drinking it up off the floor," he looked disgusted with himself, "Nice right?"

"If I hadn't of scraped a couple of drops of your blood off the floor we wouldn't be having this conversation," Elsa said, "We both did what we had to do."

They sat in silence for a few moments, Sebastian put his arm around Elsa and she leant into his shoulder, enjoying the warmth of his body and the now steady beat of his heart.

"So," Sebastian said after a few minutes where Elsa could virtually hear the cogs turning in his brain, "Your dad knows about us now."

"Yup," Elsa replied and she lifted her head, turning to look around the seat at her father. He was asleep now too and Katherine's head was resting on his shoulder in a way that gave Elsa a feeling she couldn't quite put her finger on. She shrugged it off and turned back to Sebastian.

"He's asleep," she said smiling, "You won't be getting the fatherly inquisition just yet."

Sebastian grinned back. Oh how she'd missed seeing that smile on his face, a smile that only she seemed to be able to put there, "Then I guess he won't notice this," he said, leaning towards her and wrapping her in his arms. Elsa melted instantly and all the images that had been flashing through her mind, all the blood and the violence just dissolved. It was just Sebastian and her and she knew in that moment she had everything she would ever need.

*It's not over yet, just a few more chapters :) *

# A Positive Initial Outcome.

Back at Haven, Elsa and Sebastian had to tear themselves away from each other for a short time. Elsa needed to be fully debriefed and Hesper was anxious to give Sebastian a full check up and begin to test the serum she had developed for him. His eyes had lit up when he heard about it, Elsa could feel the hope surge inside him and she prayed it wouldn't be unfounded. So whilst Sebastian went with Hesper, Elsa went with Marcus to tell him every single thing that had happened the previous evening; it was not something she was looking forward to.

They had collected as much as they could from Vincent's refuge. There was a lab where there were vast stores of Sebastian's blood and all the computers, lab equipment and stores had been brought back with them. Marcus showed Elsa and she shuddered to see the sheer volume of blood that had been harvested from Sebastian.

"My God Dad, they must have bled him dry every hour."

Marcus nodded grimly, "It's clear that Vincent was planning something big," he said, "We need to find out who else might have been involved. Some of the blood was already packed up and ready to be shipped out."

"Do you know where?"

"Not yet," Marcus gestured to Elsa to sit down, "I'm sorry you have to go over all this again," he said, "but the more we know the more we can do with the information."

"I understand," Elsa said and she recounted her experience of the night from the moment they had seen the beginnings of Layla's attack until Marcus had burst into the room where Sebastian and she had been found, alone amongst the carnage.

"So it was the gas that killed them?"

Elsa nodded, the memory of it would haunt her for a long time to come, "They started to choke at first, coughing up blood. Then it started to leak from everywhere. Their eyes, their ears, it was horrific. Rueben managed to speak, he said it was attacking their hearts."

"The blood was very thin," Marcus said, rubbing the bridge of his nose, he was clearly still exhausted and listening to Elsa explain how people he'd known well and considered friends had died in such a terrible way was proving wearing, "Hesper's team will analyse it and I think we may have found some canisters of the gas too. We need to find out how it works so something like that can't happen again. I've never come across it before."

"Dad, you really need to rest," said Elsa, concerned, "You'd been working too hard before all this happened and I don't think you've really slept for days."

"I slept on the plane," Marcus argued.

"For a maximum of half an hour," Elsa countered, "We can go over the rest later, it's not like I'm going to forget it."

Marcus' shoulders sagged, she could see he was giving in, "You're right," he said, "My mind needs to be clear and right now it isn't." He looked at her, his eyes full of tears suddenly, "I nearly lost you didn't I?" he said and his vulnerability stabbed at Elsa's heart.

"No," she said softly, "You didn't, Sebastian saved me."

Marcus looked down at his hands, which Elsa was now holding, "You've grown up so much," he said, "You really love him don't you?"

Elsa just nodded.

"I can see, by the way he looks at you – I mean, well – he did save your life in there." Marcus was obviously trying to say something he was finding difficult, "It seems like he deserves a chance," he said finally with a sigh and Elsa smiled.

"So you're not going to give him the mildly threatening fatherly chat?" she asked.

"Oh no, I'm going to very him the very threatening fatherly chat," Marcus said, "You're still my baby even if you can dispatch fifteen plus vampires single handedly."

Elsa jumped up and gave Marcus a hug; "Go to bed dad," she said, "You look like hell."

Sebastian was still in the clinic with Hesper when Elsa found him.

"How are things going?" she asked.

Hesper smiled, "Very well," she said, "I think we are ready to trial the serum on Sebastian if you're agreeable?" The question was directed at Sebastian who nodded.

"What's the worst that can happen?" he joked and Elsa placed a hand on his arm.

"You don't have to," she said earnestly, "It might not work and I don't want you to be disappointed. You know I love you no matter what."

"I want to," he said, "I've coped with disappointment before, I can do it again. I've got an open mind Elsa, of course I'm excited that it might work but Hesper has explained everything to me, I'm prepared for the fact that it might not," he gave a grin, "Besides it will be nice to have something being put into me instead of taken out."

Elsa cringed at the memory of vial upon vial of Sebastian's blood that had been recovered after they had killed Vincent, "At least Hesper didn't need to take any more blood from you," she said, forcing a smile as Hesper hooked Sebastian up to an IV drip which would begin the first part of his trial. Sebastian was sat in a chair, bare-chested with various wires attached to him. He leant his head back as the first few drops of serum entered his system. His eyes closed and Elsa watched how his body began to react. She could smell the change in his blood and hear as his heart rate quickened slightly. She watched the muscles in his arms tense and his fingers slowly close into a fist as his jaw tightened and she heard his teeth grind together.

"It's hurting him," she said, worried.

"Wait," Hesper said softly.

Gradually Sebastian's skin began to change, becoming darker, the veins more prominent. His cheeks bones and brow began to protrude, his fingernails thickened and lengthened.

"He's changing!" Elsa cried, "It's supposed to help him!" She reached towards the IV bag but Hesper grabbed her arm, "Wait," she repeated.

Sebastian's eyes snapped open, they were glowing fiery amber and Elsa could feel that he was scared he was going to lose control. She stepped closer, crouched down beside him and held his hand.

"It's ok," she said, "You're in control Sebastian, it's ok." She didn't know if what she was saying was true but Hesper seemed confident and Elsa trusted her. She'd not known her to be wrong yet, she just hope this wouldn't be the first time.

Suddenly Sebastian let out a roar and bent forward, his wings breaking through his skin and unfolding around him, causing black feathers to fly into the air and float gently to the floor in contrast to the tension of every muscle in his body. Elsa continued to hold his hand tightly, Hesper watching intently, her eyes darting from Sebastian to the computer screen where the wires attached to him were obviously transmitting their data. Gradually, Sebastian's breathing began to calm. His wings receded, his heart rate slowed, his muscles softened and, as he finally sat back up, leaning back against the chair with his eyes closed once more, his face began to return to normal.

He sat there like that for a minute or two; neither Elsa nor Hesper said a word. When he eventually opened his eyes, they were clear and grey and they focused immediately on Elsa.

"Are you ok?" she asked.

Sebastian nodded.

"How do you feel?"

Sebastian rubbed his face with both hands, pushing his sweat soaked hair from his forehead, "I feel," he searched for the words, "I feel different."

"How?" This time it was Hesper asking as she studied the data that was streaming on the computer screen beside her.

"I feel like I do when I've ... "

"When you've fed?" Hesper finished the statement for him and he looked grateful.

"Yes," he said, "Whereas before I felt like I was getting close to needing to... feed"

"That's good then isn't it?" said Elsa, excited, "It worked?"

"It's a good sign," said Hesper, "Let us not assume that is all there will be to it, but it is certainly a positive initial outcome."

"Thank you," said Sebastian earnestly, "Whatever happens, thank you for trying."

"You're welcome," said Hesper graciously, "There is more work to be done but I believe the effects should last at least a short while. I will need to continue with regular tests to check the effect the serum has had on you physiologically and I'm afraid I will need to take some more blood to test."

"Of course," Sebastian offered his arm, "I'm sure you'll be a lot more gentle than Vincent was."

Elsa frowned, every time she heard Vincent's name it reminded her of his final words and as much as she tried to put them to the back of her mind they kept bubbling back up to the surface.

"All done," Hesper said and Sebastian stood up, "I'll need to see you again in eight hours."

Sebastian nodded, pulled on his t-shirt and took Elsa's hand, "Come on," he said, "You need to drink and you can tell me what's up."

"What do you mean?" Elsa asked.

"I can see it in your face," he said, guiding her out the door, "You're worried about something and you're going to tell me what it is."

Ten minutes later, they were sat in the staff room, Sebastian with a steaming mug of tea, Elsa with a warm mug of blood.

"He was just trying to buy himself some time," Sebastian said, "Don't let it play on your mind Elsa, it will drive you mad."

"I know, I know," she said, "I really need to find a way to clear my head. Everything that's happened lately just keeps playing through again and again. I keep wondering if I could have prevented any of it in any way. If I could have stopped Kate getting hurt and you being taken and Rueben and Layla …" her voice trailed off as tears threatened and she gripped the mug so tightly it cracked and the blood spilled out over her hands.

Elsa swore and was at the sink in a second, holding her hands under the tap to wash the blood away.

She gave an ironic laugh, "Look," she said, "I've got blood on my hands."

The tears came then and she brought her hands down in fists on the edge of the stainless steel sink, which buckled and came away from the wall. Sebastian appeared in front of her, taking her arms by the wrists.

"No," he said firmly, "Not on your hands. You are not responsible."

"It started because of me," Elsa cried, "He wanted to take me to get back at my dad."

"Then it started before you were even born," Sebastian insisted, "You just had to deal with the repercussions of events that you had no control over and you did deal with them Elsa, you dealt with Vincent." He wrapped Elsa in his arms, "Nothing that has happened is your fault."

"Kate hates me," Elsa mumbled into his chest.

"Kate doesn't hate you," Sebastian said, stroking Elsa's hair and kissing the top of her head, "Kate just doesn't understand yet, she's scared and confused, give her time."

Elsa became quiet. Sebastian continued to hold her until she stopped crying and pulled back from him, looking up into his eyes. There was a time when that amount of crying would have left her skin red and blotchy, her eyes puffy and her head aching. But she was a vampire now and she looked as flawless as she ever did, a single tear left trickling down her cheek the only evidence of her emotional outburst.

"I love you," she said quietly.

Sebastian wiped the final tear from her ivory cheek with his thumb and then kissed softly where it had been.

"I love you too," he replied, "Things are going to get back to normal, you'll see."

Elsa gave a small laugh despite herself, "Normal?" she questioned, raising an eyebrow.

Sebastian held up his hands in mock defence, "It all depends on your definition," he said, "Now what can we do to get that head of yours clear?"

"I think I know where to start," Elsa said.

"Let's go then, lead the way!" Sebastian stood to the side and held out an arm, inviting Elsa to go first.

"Thank you," said Elsa sincerely, "And I will need you soon but right now, this thing I need to do, I need to do it by myself."

\*

# Death Thou Shalt Die

It had begun to get dark, Elsa had lost track of how long she had been sat on the gravel path in front of a rose bush that had a small plaque resting beneath it. It was not in flower now, but she knew that when it was, the flowers were long and elegant with deep crimson, velvety petals, rich and luxurious. She knew that the name of the rose was 'Thinking of You' and she remembered her father telling her that they would always remember her mother, Sarah, as they'd patted down the damp earth around the base of the tiny, young rose bush fifteen years ago. She'd been two.

She shouldn't have such a clear memory of planting that bush but she did. She could select memories from the deepest recesses of her mind and recall them with perfect clarity, as if they had happened only moments before; one of the many new abilities she was discovering all the time. She remembered too, going back to the bush many times with her father, sometimes when it bloomed with it's luscious red flowers, sometimes in winter when it was bare and sprinkled with frosty dew. It almost looked more beautiful then, with tiny jewels of ice and water glittering in harsh November light.

What Elsa couldn't recall, what she could never remember, was her mother. She knew what she looked like, she'd seen pictures of course. But she had never known her. She had always felt detached somehow when visiting the rose bush, even as a small child she knew that she didn't understand the true meaning of those visits, she didn't feel what her father felt, an aching sense of loss, a painful pull towards a person that was no longer there. As she got older, she'd stopped joining Marcus on his visits. She thought about her mother but she never felt her presence, not at the bush, not anywhere.

After all that had happened though, after finding out how her mother had really died and how that had affected her own life now in ways she could have never imagined, Elsa had begun to feel something she hadn't felt before. A connection to her mother. She'd come to visit this memorial to see if it felt any different now. It didn't.

Elsa had stayed all the same, it was quiet, and peaceful and she hadn't had that for some time. The connection she now felt to her mother didn't need a special place or a special 'thing' to make it stronger but Elsa knew she wanted to know more. More about the kind of woman her mother had really been, more about what she and Marcus had done working at Haven together, and more about why she had been targeted. Everything that had happened to Elsa recently, to the people she cared about, had started before she was born, Sebastian was right about that. If she ever hoped to get her head around her life now and come to terms with what she had seen and what she had had to do, she needed to understand where it had all truly begun.

Elsa smiled to herself, wondering for a moment what she had really hoped to achieve by coming here. Had she thought her mothers ghost would visit her and explain it all? That would have made it far too easy. Elsa was pretty sure she was not destined for an easy life any more.

A sudden, barely perceptible sound made her jump. It was an exhale, the sound of air passing slowly and gently over smooth, perfect lips, accompanied by the acrid scent of cigarette smoke. Elsa knew she was in the company of a vampire, no other creature could have snuck up so quickly and quietly. She tensed, waiting to see if the stranger was friend or foe. Her companion made no movement other than to bring the cigarette back to their lips and begin to inhale once more; Elsa could hear the faintest crunch of the cigarette being gently compressed between the strangers lips and she stood and turned quickly to face the visitor.

They stood in shadow, Elsa could make out a female form, petite and slight. Slender fingertips glowed faintly in the dim light of the cigarette end as the woman took a long, lazy drag and then exhaled once more, pale smoke curling sensuously out of the darkness. Elsa said nothing, waiting for the woman to explain her presence.

"Hello Elsa," came the voice finally, rich and flowing from the woman's throat like warm honey.

Still, Elsa said nothing. The woman stepped forward from the shadows that concealed her and walked slowly past Elsa towards the rose bush where she crouched and traced a long finger across the words on the plaque beneath it.

She had the typically pale skin of a vampire, ivory smooth with not a single imperfection. Her eyes were cast low and Elsa couldn't make out their colour, her long hair was jet black, poker straight and lay about her shoulders like liquid night. She was wearing a long, dark coat that clung to her tiny frame but Elsa knew that she should not be fooled by the vampire woman's slight build. She could tell she was old, older than any vampire Elsa had come across before, and stronger.

"Aren't you going to ask me why I'm here, who I am?" The vampire sounded amused.

"My asking won't make a difference will it?" Elsa countered, "If you planned to tell me, you will; if you didn't, you won't."

The vampire stood, a smile curled on her lips. Not a cruel one as Elsa had become accustomed to seeing on the faces of unwelcome vampire visitors, but a smile that suggested amusement with a child. The woman drew on her cigarette once more and Elsa could see now her eyes were a startlingly bright, ice cold blue, in deep contrast to her dark hair.

"I knew her, your mother." the voice flowed smoothly, intertwined with ribbons of smoke before dispersing into the night air. Elsa tried her hardest not to react, "I've been watching you closely, you are very like her."

"What do you want?" Elsa asked, unable to stop herself.

"Want? I don't 'want' anything Elsa – but you do, you want answers to so many questions."

"And you have these answers I suppose?"

"I have many answers," the vampire said, "To many questions; some of them to the questions you would ask, some to questions you do not know yet to ask."

Elsa was getting irritated, the vampire was clearly toying with her and she had no idea why, "Well thanks for the chat," she said, turning to leave.

The vampire's tiny hand gripped her arm tightly to stop her, "What was Vincent going to tell you Elsa?"

Elsa froze and snapped her head back to lock eyes with the vampire, "Who are you?" she asked angrily.

"I am Florence," the woman said, "And I could answer all of your questions."

"But you won't?" Elsa knew what the answer would be.

"I won't," Florence said with a smile, "Because I am interested in you Elsa, I am interested in what you do and how you live and who you spend your time with. That is what I do, I observe, I study, I never intervene."

"So why are you here?"

"Because I like you," the vampire said simply, "And because you are different. You intrigue me." Elsa stared back at her, her mind burning with questions.

"Don't brush off Vincent's words Elsa, they will lead you to the truths you are looking for."

"He didn't finish what he was going to say," Elsa said, frustration coursing through her like an electrical current.

"Which is why you have tried to push it to the back of your mind, to convince yourself you didn't make a mistake."

"Did I? Make a mistake?"

"Not in killing him no, he was an – annoyance," Florence's nose curled slightly with distaste, "but I am here to tell you that maybe you should have listened for just a little while longer."

"And what am I supposed to do about that now?" Elsa asked.

"That is for you to decide," Elsa felt the grip on her arm release, "Everything is linked Elsa."

"I don't understand."

"And that is the beauty of it Elsa." Florence smiled again, almost warmly and dropped her cigarette to the floor, stubbing it out with the toe of a black, pointed boot, "Now you must seek out answers, it will give you purpose."

"Who are you to decide I need purpose?" Elsa asked, "You don't know me."

"I do know you," Florence said, "I know you very well. Vampires need purpose, they live for so many lives that without purpose they would go quite mad."

"And what's your purpose?"

"My purpose is my own to keep Elsa, I just wanted to make sure you didn't miss yours."

"Because you like me?"

"And because I liked your mother."

They both stood in silence for a moment, Florence gazed at the plaque under the rose bush once more and Elsa followed her eyes to read the words upon it. It was a pretty standard epitaph: Sarah Shaw, loving wife and mother, never forgotten.

"It is not fitting," Florence said, pressing a small, folded piece of paper into Elsa's hand. Elsa looked down at it and felt suddenly alone. Florence was gone as silently and suddenly as she had appeared. Elsa unfolded the paper and read the words. Another epitaph, which she assumed Florence felt more fitting for her mother:

One short sleep past, we wake eternally. And death shall be no more; Death, thou shalt die.